Catherine Robertson hails from Hawke's Bay (New Zealand wine country). She is the proud co-owner of a bookstore in Wellington, and is the author of romantic comedies and contemporary fiction, many of which have been #1 bestsellers for Penguin Random House NZ.

www.catherinejrobertson.com

instagram.com/catherinerobertson11
facebook.com/catherinejrobertson.author

Also by Catherine Robertson

Corkscrew You

To Barbara Greenberg and Sue Copsey.
Thanks for reading and fixing my first drafts.

Playlist

Wildest Dreams - Taylor Swift ♥
Nonsense - Sabrina Carpenter ♥
i'm yours - Isabel LaRosa ♥
Sunflower, Vol. 6 - Harry Styles ♥
stupid - Tate McRae ♥
Cruel Summer - G Flip ♥
Golden Hour - Kacey Musgraves ♥
All My Love - Noah Kahan ♥
Daylight - Taylor Swift ♥
Dandelions - Ruth B. ♥
Belong Together - Mark Ambor ♥
Loving You - Wet Leg ♥
Out of My League - Fitz and The Tantrums ♥
Slow Burn - Kacey Musgraves ♥
Quit - Cashmere Cat, Ariana Grande ♥
Someday We'll Know - New Radicals ♥
July - Noah Cyrus, Leon Bridges ♥
What If I Love You - Gatlin ♥
Missing Piece - Vance Joy ♥
I'll Call You Mine - girl in red ♥
You're Gonna Go Far - Noah Kahan ♥
West Coast - Lana Del Rey ♥
Till Forever Falls Apart - Ashe, FINNEAS ♥

YOU'RE SO VINE
Flora Valley

CATHERINE ROBERTSON

One More Chapter
a division of HarperCollins*Publishers* Ltd
1 London Bridge Street
London SE1 9GF
www.harpercollins.co.uk
HarperCollins*Publishers*
Macken House, 39/40 Mayor Street Upper,
Dublin 1, D01 C9W8, Ireland

This paperback edition 2024

1

First published in Great Britain in ebook format
by HarperCollins*Publishers* 2024
Copyright © Catherine Robertson 2024
Catherine Robertson asserts the moral right to be identified
as the author of this work

A catalogue record of this book is available from the British Library

ISBN: 978-0-00-865793-2

This novel is entirely a work of fiction. The names, characters and incidents portrayed in it are the work of the author's imagination. Any resemblance to actual persons, living or dead, events or localities is entirely coincidental.

Printed and bound in the UK using 100% Renewable Electricity
by CPI Group (UK) Ltd

All rights reserved. No part of this publication may be reproduced, stored in a retrieval system, or transmitted, in any form or by any means, electronic, mechanical, photocopying, recording or otherwise, without the prior permission of the publishers.

Chapter One

AVA

Weddings give me hives. For a start, it's bad form to wear black and black is all I wear. Okay, I had a purple phase in my teens, by which I mean I still wore black, but I dyed my hair purple and cut it mohawk style. My dad said I should have gone the whole hog and shaved it off—better airflow for track. Then I won all my race meets and he stopped complaining.

At fourteen, I painted my bedroom black. Thirteen years later, it's primrose yellow because Mom finds black depressing. Can't see that myself. Black is smart, simple, and efficient. Every item comes pre-coordinated: no fuss, just grab and go.

Except when you're at a wedding. Your big brother's wedding at that. In the vineyard he now partially owns with his new bride. The ceremony was under an arbor built for the occasion from old, woven vines, the backdrop red-gold—the last of the fall leaves hanging in there so as to be as picturesque as possible for the happy couple. There's a chill in the air but the sky is blue and there's not a breath of wind. It's beautiful. Perfect. I want to take a flamethrower to the whole scene.

Okay, no … no I don't. I'm super happy for my big bro, Nate. His last attempt at getting married ended with him being jilted the week before, so us Durants breathed a sigh of relief that this time he got to say "I do"—and to a girl who we all love almost as much as Nate does.

Shelby's cute and funny and *way* more relaxed than Nate. Which isn't hard. When God was handing out the sweet treats of inner calm, Nate was loading up on a double helping of gristly determination with a side order of dried duty. As our family doctor says, "If there's a type above Type A, Nate's it." Actually, he says that about our whole family, but this is Nate's big day, so he gets singled out.

Yep, it's Nate and Shelby's big ol' wedding day and I'm wearing a dress that I bought in a hurry because—I may have mentioned this—everything I own is black. The dress is dark green and makes me look like I've been poisoned. I also did not follow Mom's advice to take a shawl and now I'm blue with cold as well as poisoned-looking.

We're being ushered toward the barn for the reception, which means this wedding is not even halfway through. Shelby and Nate own pigs that Nate swears would eat a human if you let them. Has anyone ever committed suicide by pig? Asking for a friend.

"You're looking a little peaky, sis. One too many caramel apple martinis?"

Danny. Durant sibling number three. Up from LA for the weekend. Makes the perfect usher because he comes across as charming. Don't be deceived.

"If you tell me we're sitting together, I'll brain you with an ornamental pumpkin."

"Nope," says Danny, way too cheerfully. "Durant clan's being split up. Tables are all a random mix and match. Idea being that we get to mingle, meet the other guests, make new friends."

Where did Nate say the pigsty was again?

Danny runs his finger along the seating plan.

"You're on table three. Straight down, hang a left."

A brief lurch in my gut. What if *he's* on the same table—?

"You're with Chiara," says Dan, "Shelby's brother Jackson, Ted, Ted's girlfriend du jour, and a guy named Doug."

"The famous Toothless Doug?"

"I didn't ask him to open his mouth."

"Oh, Doug has a full set of teeth. Shelby told me."

"Huh," says Danny. "Shelby and Nate's kids are going to be pretty weird, aren't they?"

I don't stay to answer because a queue is forming behind me. Everyone is eager to get into the warmth and start drinking in earnest. Or maybe that's just me: the only person at this whole wedding who's cold and morose.

Ava, snap out of it. It's the happiest day of your brother's life. Just because your life is in the crapper doesn't mean you can skulk about all green and pinch-faced like a vengeful enchantress. Do better.

I make an effort to admire the barn. It's cute. If you're into décor based on an advertisement for pumpkin spice lattes. Loads of fairy lights strung from the rafters. Trestle tables covered in simple white cloths, tea lights, and flowers in jelly jars. Wine barrels with more jelly jars, surrounded by pinecones and the aforementioned ornamental pumpkins, a vegetable I don't mind looking at as long as I don't have to eat it.

Shelby's mom, Lee, did the décor. She's an artist and moved up the coast when Shelby's dad died from cancer, leaving Shelby to run Flora Valley Wines on her own. That's how Shelby met Nate. He was brought in to manage the place when McRae Capital took a stake in it. That's J.P. McRae, who's two tables away, sitting with his wife. J.P.'s an old friend and former business partner of my dad's.

Yes, it's a small world. But not small enough, apparently, for me to spot the one guy whose presence *somewhere* in this barn is partly responsible for my antsy mood. Last time he and I were in proximity, I asked him on a date. He turned me down—in a kindly manner, but as you know, a refusal no matter how polite often humiliates. I took the hint and backed off, kept my distance. That was two months ago, and I haven't stopped thinking about him since.

Damn it, I *wish* we were seated together so I could get that uncomfortable first-meeting-after-a-knock-back over with. I don't know how I'll feel about seeing him, and not knowing is one of the things I hate most in the world. After being rejected, of course.

"Ava, how lovely to see you."

I know two people at table three, and this is one of them. Ted. Blond, foppishly handsome in that upper-class British way. Current owner of Bartons, a boutique hotel that would fit perfectly in cosmopolitan London but because it's in the main street of small-town Verity, looks like it's been beamed down from an alien planet. Its patrons are like aliens, too: rich, shiny, and mostly English with hee-haw accents. Ted doesn't hee-haw. He's much too smooth.

Ted gestures to the woman sitting next to him.

"Ava, may I introduce"—there's an infinitesimal pause—"Imogen."

Imogen (because surely she would have protested if that hadn't been her name, no?) twiddles her fingers in a wave. She's anywhere between twenty-three and a Botoxed thirty-five. Glossy blonde hair. Slender, polished, extremely beautiful: an exact clone of every other woman Ted's dated. We call them the Ted-ford Wives. Not that Ted's about to marry any of them. I'm amazed he didn't skip this wedding for fear of catching marital cooties.

I see Chiara give me an eyeroll. She works for Ted at Bartons hotel and knows his ways. Chiara is one of Shelby's two best girlfriends. She was born and brought up in Verity but isn't destined to spend her life here. Chiara has ambitions, and the brains and looks to achieve them.

"Ava, this is Jackson," she says, "Shelby's oldest brother. Jackson, this is Ava—"

"Nate's sister." He reaches out a hand, smiling. "Yeah, I can spot the resemblance."

It's true. Nate and I have basically the same face, plus

Dad's dark hair and cool blue eyes. Jackson Armstrong is big and burly, with pale blond hair and a beard. Looks nothing like his petite, strawberry blonde sister.

"Whereas I'm the spitting image of my dad," he says, then looks rueful. "He'd have loved today. He always thought this barn would make a great wedding venue. Isn't that right, Doug?"

"Sure," says Doug.

Doug's a lean weather-beaten guy in his late fifties with a mustache that gives him a Sam Elliot vibe. All I know about him is that he does the mowing at the vineyard and occasionally helps out Flora Valley Wines' cooper (that's a barrel maker) and main handyman, otherwise known as the guy whose apparent invisibility is currently frying my brain.

To distract myself, I say, "Okay, seriously, why do they call you Toothless Doug? You look like you've got a pretty good set of choppers there."

Doug grins, proving my point.

"When I was a kid, I started a tooth collection—"

"Not at all creepy," remarks Chiara.

"Animal teeth," he explains, "from animals we hunted or found dead in the woods. Other kids used to bring 'em to me, too. Cleaned 'em up, made a box to put 'em all in. Thought I might make a necklace—"

"Ugh." Chiara shudders delicately.

"We got a new dog, a Labrador called Maisie. She found my box of teeth and ate the lot."

"How can a dog eat teeth, Doug?" is Ted's question. "They're much harder than bones."

"Maisie kind of swallowed them whole, like kibble. I guess I hadn't cleaned them all *that* well."

"Trip to the vet?" I ask.

"Nope, she just—"

"Don't say it, Doug," Chiara insists. "Ted's very sensitive."

"My dear," Ted protests. "I have done my fair share of mucking out."

"Is that what you call it in England?" says Chiara, with a lift of an eyebrow.

"You still a hunter, Doug?" says Jackson. "I remember you taking me on a…"

I tune out. Ted's mention of mucking out reminded me too much of the *other* reason I'm not in a party mood. You see, until a couple of months ago, I used to work for a racing stable in Kentucky. I've been a horse lover since I was a kid—nothing but running and riding when I was growing up. Given I'm small, I thought I might be a jockey, but I found that world too cut-throat, so I became an exercise rider. My job was taking the racehorses for their morning workouts and teaching them the skills they'd need to win. I quit because my dad, Mitchell, developed a life-threatening heart condition, and all five of us Durant siblings rushed home to be with him and Mom. At least, that's the reason I gave. In reality, it was a useful cover story. I didn't choose to quit; I *had* to. I'd been finding the job more and more exhausting—crawling into bed at the end of every day and dragging myself out again in the morning. I quit because I couldn't do the job and my bosses knew it. They knew I was worn out, like an old nag.

Another reason why the last two months have sucked. I'm unemployed, I'm living back at my parents', and I'm still exhausted. The tiredness just won't go away. And I can't tell anyone because that would be admitting weakness and defeat. A Durant would be voluntarily impaled inside an iron maiden before they let slip an iota of vulnerability. And I am a Durant through and through.

Shit. Of course. Now that I'm at my absolute lowest ebb is the moment I finally spot him. Who's he talking to? Oh. Right. Shelby's mom, Lee. The artist. The very beautiful red-headed artist who's in her late fifties but doesn't look it. The very beautiful red-headed artist whose head is bending super close to his … and now he's said something that's made her laugh, and…

"There'll be dancing later. You can make your move then."

It seems Chiara is more interested in spying on me than discussing hunting. But then, as Nate's pointed out, Chiara's name doesn't include the letters CIA for no reason: she's got skills that make their top agents look like the Goonies.

Thing is, being a Durant means you've spent your whole life honing your poker face. Don't let anything show and you'll always have the advantage.

"My move?" I ask.

"Don't even *try* to out-bluff me," says Chiara. "You've

been looking around for him all evening because you're still conflicted over how you feel about him. My advice is to stop wasting time and emotional energy and find out."

She makes a valid point. I hate her for it.

"Have you ever seen Cam Hollander dance?" I ask.

"Never," says Chiara. "But you're hardly one to fall at the first hurdle. If he doesn't want to, invite him to join you at the mulled wine station."

"What if he says no? Again."

I've no doubt that Chiara knows about the knock-back. It happened at the Crush, the big community event when the Flora Valley grapes are pressed. And though I was convinced Cam and I were alone when I asked him out, I wouldn't be surprised if Chiara somehow made a secret video recording.

"He might," says Chiara. "Then again, he might not. You'll never know unless you try."

Another valid-yet-hateful point. I used to think of myself as brave, but lately, I've been a giant weenie. One little "no" and I retreated into my shell like a snail. I can blame my physical state but that's not what's holding me back. It's fear that his rejection signals some greater deficiency in me than simply being tired and worn out. What if my life has peaked, and at only twenty-seven, I'm on the downhill slide?

I wanted to know how I'd feel seeing him again, but to be honest, I don't know. He's over there with Shelby's mother. Lee's laughing and Cam looks like he's won a prize. I don't know what emotion I'm experiencing. Is it possible to simultaneously feel red-hot attraction *and* white-hot rage?

"He looks pretty busy right now." My poker face is set to rigid, but unfortunately so is my jaw, and the words come out with full giveaway grit.

"Shelby says Cam and her mom have a special kind of friendship," Chiara tells me.

"*How* special?" I'm not even trying now.

Chiara shrugs. "Well, if Cam used more words a day, we might have found out by now." She gives me a small and only partially evil smile. "Guess we'll have to rely on *you* to solve that little puzzle for us."

She picks up her empty champagne glass and emits some kind of telepathic signal because in an instant, a young server is at her elbow. It's also possible no signal was required because Chiara is the most striking woman in the place by some margin. She's wearing a pale gold camisole top and matching wide pants under a cream silk blazer. On her feet are stiletto pumps. If you broke off the heels, you could use them as knitting needles. Beside her, I feel small, green, and crumpled. Like a leprechaun who's had a hard night.

I look over at Cam again because I'm a glutton for punishment. He's dressed in a shirt and tie, which he never is. His normal look is what my brother Nate calls "Survivalist Ken", but that's only because he's jealous. Nate is six-feet easy, fit, and lean, but Cam Hollander is six-five and muscled like guys who do physical labor all day, every day. He has shaggy blond-brown hair and brown eyes.

Shelby told me he'd been a soldier but said he doesn't talk about that part of his life. Or any part of his life. He might have grown up in Wyoming, might not have, and I should really stop staring at him because he's going to notice...

He's noticed. Shit.

Okay, the *worst* thing that could happen now is that he nudges Shelby's mom and they both have a good old chuckle at the cross, crumpled green chick.

He doesn't. He nods, once, and the corner of his mouth lifts ever so slightly. So slightly, I could be imagining it.

"Move slowly," says Chiara. "Softly-softly catchy big guy."

I hate her for knowing me better than I know myself. But the only outlet for my irritation is a stack of breadsticks, so I reach for one and give it a good hard snap.

"Ladies and gentlemen."

Best man Danny is dinging a wine glass with a spoon.

"The moment you've all been waiting for... The speeches!"

I need another drink, but only Chiara seems to have the mindpower to summon servers.

"Traditionally," says Danny, "the father of the bride would give the first speech. At this time, we'd like you all to raise your glasses and toast the memory of Shelby's dad and founder of Flora Valley Wines, the late Billy Armstrong."

"To Billy," we all say.

"And seeing as Billy couldn't be with us today, we're going to throw tradition to the wind and open instead with the mother of the bride," says Danny. "Will you welcome to the mic, Lee Armstrong!"

Applause and a few wolf whistles. The very beautiful red-haired artist who does not look her age gets up from the table and because I'm watching like a hawk, I see her rest her hand on Cam's shoulder as she passes by him. Could be nothing. She could have been caught a little off balance and needed to steady herself. To me, though, the gesture looked affectionate, purposeful. *Don't worry*, it said. *I'll be back soon.*

Without a word, Chiara hands me another breadstick.

Chapter Two

CAM

I don't mind speeches at weddings because they give me a break from small talk. Not that I've been to many weddings. Went to my older sister Blair's ... seventeen years ago now. I was about to turn eighteen. Still a kid. Enlisted in the U.S. Army the day after my birthday. No idea what I was in for.

Blair's had three kids since then. I've made barrels. Blair and her family live on a small homestead in Oregon, in a rustic cabin, surrounded by bees and chickens, and goats that they milk. I live in a shed. My second-best friend is a goose. My best friend is getting up on stage to make the first speech. She pats me on the shoulder as she passes. Her way of saying, "hang in there". Lee knows I don't do well in crowds.

If I had my choice, I wouldn't be here. Wouldn't be wearing a shirt and tie that Shelby bought me. Goodwill can have them. Can't think of when I'd wear them again.

Shelby warned me that she and Nate had decided to mix up the guests, but she also promised not to sit me with strangers. Promised to sit me with Lee, the person I owe everything to.

Lee's up there talking about her late husband, Billy, Shelby's dad. Shelby's listening with a big smile and tears running down her cheeks. Nate's got his arm around her. It's only a handful of months since they met, and now they're married. Guess that's what happens when it's true love. Some folks thought they should have waited, but what for? If you can't see into someone's soul right away, then when will you be able to?

I saw into someone's soul once, but it wasn't love. It was … well, today's not the day to think about it. Today's all about happiness.

Lee finishes her speech to a round of applause. She goes to hug the new bride and groom.

"Shelby's mom looks more like us than our own mom."

This is Izzy, Nate's youngest sister. Twin to Max, sitting next to her. I've met them before, so not complete strangers. But I don't know much about them except that they're twenty-two, both at college, one studying science, one music. And they've got red hair, which prompted the comment about Lee. Izzy and Max have dark red hair, though, like a wet Irish setter. Lee's is brighter. Like a maple leaf in fall.

"You know genes are weird, Iz," says Max. "You study them."

"I study nanotechnology, doofus. There's *some* crossover

if you're into DNA nanotech," says Izzy, "but I'm into environmental applications."

"Whatever," says Max. "It's all science."

"Sure," says his twin. "Bob Marley, Black Sabbath, Beethoven—what's the difference? It's all music."

Max winces. "Point taken."

"But you're right about genetics being weird," says Izzy. "I mean, look at us Durants. Mom's blonde and so's Danny. You and I are red-haired like who knows who back down the ancestral line. Dad's dark, like Nate and Ava. The gene pool works in mysterious ways."

Ava. Her name gives me a jolt. I saw her looking this way earlier. She seemed ... unhappy, I guess. I don't know her well enough to say. She gave me the opportunity to get to know her better and I turned her down. Tried to be kind about it, but...

I hated that I hurt her, but it would have been dishonest to get her hopes up. I'll never be anyone's partner, and I'm okay with that. That's just how some lives are meant to turn out. And geese are great company. Won't hear a word against them.

"Shame Billy isn't here to see this, don't you think, Cam?"

This is Javi, short for Javier, who musters the vineyard workforce. Javi's full-time job is actually concierge at Bartons hotel, but Ted, the owner, believes in giving back to the community so he gives Javi time off to rope in workers for those peak times. Flora Valley Wines is an organic, low-tech winery. We hand pick, and we crush by foot stomping.

It was Billy's idea to do it this way—the hard way, some might say. Probably why he and I got on so well.

"Billy would be a blubbering mess," I reply.

"Any father would, seeing their daughter married."

Valentina, Javi's wife, is the last person at our table for six.

"Javi will cry like a baby when our girls are wed," she adds. "All the way up the aisle, sobbing."

"Our girls are six and eight," Javi protests. "You don't even know if they'll *want* to get married."

"I know you'll cry *como un bebé* if they do," says Valentina. "So that's that."

"*I'm* not getting married," says Izzy. "Stupid, outdated institution."

"Are you saying your older brother's stupid?" says Max. "And everyone here who's ever exchanged vows?"

"Don't try to pick a fight," says Izzy. "If you're bored, you can go play outside with the dogs."

"Shh," says Valentina. "Your brother's about to make his speech."

Nate's up at the mic now. I look for Lee but she's still at the top table, her arm around Shelby. Fair enough, I guess. It's an emotional time for them and a big reminder of the hole Billy's death left in their lives. I miss Billy, too, but sometimes I wonder what would have happened to me if it'd been Lee who got sick. Sometimes I feel like she's the one person who's kept me tethered to this Earth.

Everyone's laughing at a joke Nate's made. When I first met Nate Durant, I didn't take to him much. Found him high-handed. Thought he was the kind of guy that had to boss people around to puff up his own ego. Turned out he was having a hard time personally and was fighting his feelings for Shelby. Made him more than a little tense. He apologized to me for it. We get on fine now. Though he can still be kind of uptight.

Nate passes the mic to his brother Danny. Handsome like all the Durants. Makes a killing repairing and dealing in classic cars down in LA. Has a touch of the showman to him.

"He's in his element," Izzy confirms. "Dan loves an audience."

"Did you see the car he came up in?" asks Max. "It's a Porsche 550 Spyder. Super rare. I googled it. They're worth, like, three million bucks."

"*What?* Bullshit," says Izzy. "It'll be a replica."

"Shh!" hisses Valentina.

Izzy shoots me an "oops" grin. Can't help grinning back.

Danny's finished his speech. Offers the mic to Shelby, but she shakes her head, smiling, still tearful. Nate's the one with his arm around her now. Lee's chatting to Nate's mom —another fine-looking woman in her fifties.

Time to cut the cake. Everyone cheers. Looks like Shelby's never going to stop crying. Nate wipes her tears with a napkin. Danny directs us all to the buffet lined up against one wall. I'll just sit here and wait until everyone's had theirs. Everyone's mingling now, swapping seats, talking around the buffet. I'm on my own at the table. Might loosen this tie…

Oh, shit, the band's started up. Music's not the problem: they're a local indie group, heavy on beards and banjos, but they know how to get a crowd on its feet. It's the getting on the feet that's the problem. I don't dance. Never have, never will. Better find a dark corner to hide in.

Shelby and Nate are out on the floor, looking as happy as any two people could possibly be. Wonder what sort of kids their mix of genes will create. Got to say, I quite like the idea of being an honorary uncle. If I can babysit a cantankerous goose, then a toddler will be no—

"Hey."

Shouldn't have been daydreaming. Should have found that dark corner.

It's Ava. Wearing a green dress that I sense she feels as comfortable in as I do in this shirt and now sloppy tie. She's smiling but she's got dark circles under her eyes. Unhappy is still my best guess as to her true mood.

"Hey," I say back.

"I've been told you don't dance," she says in her straightforward way. "Do you want to get a mulled wine with me instead?"

She sees me hesitate. I see her shoulders stiffen.

"I'm not coming on to you," she says, brisk and brittle. "Just thought we could spare each other having to talk to anyone else."

Thought Lee might have come back by now, but I guess she's got family priorities. She is the mother of the bride, after all. And I like Ava. I like her directness, her determination. But, as I said, I'm not cut out for relationships for a whole stack of reasons I won't go into here. Happy to be her friend. Just don't want to be anything more.

"Sure," I say. "But I'm not much of a mulled wine drinker, either."

"Neither am I," says a marginally happier-looking Ava. "Let's hit the hard stuff."

I get to my feet. I'm six-five, Ava's five-four. Good thing we're not going to dance. We'd be the comedy floor show.

The bar has been set up by some of Ted's people from Bartons hotel. There's the usual wine and beer, and a menu of fall-themed cocktails.

"Got anything with bourbon?" I ask.

"Yes, sir," says a young man who looks like he's modeling himself on Ted. "There's the Wood Fire: reserve bourbon, Tentura, maple syrup, ground peanuts, grapefruit juice, and a hint of refined rowan berry. Or, if you prefer, there's the Wild Boar: rye whiskey, amaro di angostura, cacao agrodolce, mandarin juice, and chartreuse."

Ava's laughing.

"He lost you at 'yes, sir,' didn't he?" she says to me.

"Help," I say.

"Two bourbons on the rocks," she tells the young man. "Double shots."

"Right away, ma'am."

"Ma'am," Ava mutters to me. "Way to make me feel like my mother."

We get our bourbons. There's a twist of orange peel hanging off the side of each glass because I guess standards must be maintained. Ava takes her peel and mine and flicks them onto a nearby empty plate.

"Let's find somewhere no one else is," she says.

That proves to be behind an artful pile of barrels and pumpkins. Lee got the pumpkins for free from a local farmer. Lot of people round here love Lee and wish she hadn't moved up the coast. But she loves her artist studio. It's what she'd always wanted.

"You know, I come from a biggish family," says Ava. "Five kids. Five *competitive* kids. We were always full-on and always in each other's faces, so you'd think I'd be used to being surrounded by people and noise. But I'm not."

"People and noise aren't my thing, either."

"Do you have brothers and sisters?" she asks. "Don't answer if it's too personal."

"It's not," I say. "One sister. Blair. Five years older. She lives in Oregon with her family and a bunch of goats."

"Goats?"

"For the milk. One of the earliest-known superfoods, according to Blair."

"You should mention that to Ted," she says. "He can put it in a cocktail. Along with fifteen hundred other startling and incomprehensible ingredients."

The band hooks into a line dance number. Most of the folks here are locals, born and bred close by. They've been good to me, but even after almost ten years, I still feel like I'm only here temporarily. Like tomorrow I could pack up and head out.

Ava's staring up at me. Guess she doesn't have a lot of choice, being a foot shorter.

"I'm sorry," she said. "About hitting on you at the wine pressing. Took you by surprise and that's never a good thing. Sorry I made you uncomfortable."

I feel a weird flinch in my gut, like I've been pecked hard by an invisible goose. That apology took a whole lot of courage. Her asking me out at the crush also took a whole lot of courage, and even though it's true and she did take me by surprise, I'm not sure she's the one who should be apologizing. I rejected her without giving her a chance. And that's not something to be proud of.

In this dim light, her blue eyes look indigo, like the sky settling into night. Hard to read but it doesn't matter—the way she shows expression is all around the mouth. When she's happy, her mouth's all smiles, mobile, generous. When she's unhappy, it tightens up into a kind of wavy line. Right now, it's in between. She's curious but not tense.

Two things suddenly occur to me. One is that I *should* have given her a chance. First moment I met her, there was a spark between us. If I'd said "yes" a couple of months back, we might have kindled that spark into something hotter. But I'll never know because I reacted in my usual way, otherwise known as the three Rs: Resist, Refuse, Retreat. I hurt her for no reason except my own fear.

And that's the second thing that occurs to me: that she can apologize because she's *not* hurt anymore. She's moved on. And put me in the friend zone.

Okay, so a third thing has suddenly occurred to me. You

know what I said about wanting to only be her friend? Now that I'm there, I realize without a doubt that I lied. *Great sense of timing, Hollander. I think it's commonly known as "way too late".*

"Cam, there you are."

It's Lee, all smiles and beauty. Her hand on my arm.

"Ava, I'm sorry," she says. "I need some help putting out some more lights. Didn't think it would get so dark in here. People start dancing with one partner and end up with someone they don't even know. Is it okay if I steal Cam away?"

"Of course," says Ava. "I'd better go talk to Nate and Shelby, anyway. Don't want them thinking I don't love them."

She's gone, into the crowd, her pace quick and athletic. Too late for me to say anything.

Lee's hand is still on my arm. So I follow her. Because that's what I always do.

Chapter Three

AVA

My heart's racing, and I'm afraid I'm going to throw up right in one of these frigging jelly jars. Which, let's be frank, couldn't make me feel any worse than I do right now.

You've got to admit, though—it's got that Lady Bracknell comedy vibe to it: one humiliating knockback can be regarded as misfortune, but two looks like carelessness. I should have just stuck to non-personal stuff, talked about the music or whatever. But I didn't. I went straight to the subject I should have avoided *and I goddamned apologized*! May as well have ripped out my beating heart and handed it to him. Here! Take it! Oh, you don't want it? Okay, I'll just throw it on this pile of pumpkins then, shall I? Cool, cool, cool…

Did she split us up on purpose? Was that all BS about the lights? I mean, who cares if it's dark? Who wants to see everyone all red-faced and sweaty? Dim lighting is a partygoer's best friend.

I know, I know. Lee's not to blame for how I feel. If she wants more frigging fairy lights, then rock on. Cam's a grown-ass man who makes his own decisions. Lee may have arrived before he had a chance to respond verbally to my apology but that didn't matter. I saw his physical response. I saw him flinch. He hated that I brought the subject up. Probably thought I was using the apology as a way into asking him out a second time. I wasn't and I ended up as humiliated as if I had, though. Good job, Ava. Just proved to yourself how dangerous it is to be vulnerable. What's the Durant family motto? Never show weakness! Make the other guy blink first! Know when to hold 'em! No, wait, that's Kenny Rogers. Still, he has a point. I showed my whole hand to Cam and came out a loser.

I said I was going to find Nate and Shelby, but what I need to do is regain control. It feels like someone accidentally dropped a lit match into my box of emotional fireworks and they're blasting everywhere in random directions. Some aimed at me, some aimed at Cam. One, at least, is aimed at Lee.

I head outside, where the cold night air is like a slap on the cheek. I'm shivering but the temperature's not the cause. Breathe, Ava. Breathe and take in the smell of the night. Smoke from the braziers, some kind of sweet wood. Hint of fermented grape. More than a hint of farmyard. Maybe if I follow that I'll find the pigsty?

What the hell is *that* over there? Is it ... a ghost child?

Oh-*kay*. It's Dylan. The Flora Valley Wines white goose. Waddling off to do … whatever geese do at night. Shelby told me there used to be a Mrs Dylan, but she died and because geese mate for life, he's been on his own ever since. Could explain why he's so loud and belligerent: he's pissed at being short-changed by life.

God, it's cold. Now I'm shivering for purely physical reasons. All the adrenaline from the emotion explosion has died down now, and all I want to do is sit down here on the ground and hug my knees while I slowly die of hypothermia.

I lean against the outside corner of the barn. Someone comes round from the other side and walks right into me.

"Holy shit!"

It's Jackson, Shelby's older brother. Big blond burly Jackson Armstrong.

"You okay? I did not see you at all."

"That's because it's really dark," I reply.

I can see a gleam of teeth. Smile, I hope. Or else it's close to midnight and he's about to turn into a werewolf. The beard is always the giveaway.

"What are you doing skulking around in the really dark night?" he asks.

"I could ask you the same question."

"You could. But I asked you first."

Guy's sharp. I like him.

"I'm berating myself," I reply. "What are you doing?"

"Ditto. Also illicitly smoking because I'm sad."

Now that my eyes have adjusted, I can see that he does indeed have a pack of cigarettes in one hand.

"What are you sad about? Your dad?"

"Yeah," Jackson says slowly. "And Shelby. Actually, that's more guilt."

"Guilt?"

He taps a cigarette out of the pack and sticks it in his mouth. Pulls a lighter from his pocket and a small glow of red appears in the dark. Jackson inhales and blows smoke away from me.

"All of us cut and run," he says. "Me, my brother, and youngest sister. Couldn't wait to leave Flora Valley behind. Shelby was the only one who wanted to stay. But when Dad died and Mom hightailed it for the coast, we should have come back to help her. One of us, at least, probably me, because I'm the oldest. But we didn't. Left her all on her own in charge of an almost-bankrupt business."

"Her decision wasn't your responsibility."

"She's family," he says. "We should have helped her more."

"She's got the winery. She's part owner and it's doing well. And I've never heard her say a bad word about *any* of you. She thinks the sun shines out of your rear ends."

"Only at the equinox," says Jackson. "Besides, could you just let a guy wallow in self-pity for a moment? What are weddings for if not to get stupidly overemotional?"

I shiver again. It's cold. And I'm ... overemotional.

I hear a rustle of cloth and feel a jacket being placed

around my shoulders. It's huge, like wearing a gabardine marquee.

"What are you berating yourself for, Ava?" he says gently.

I haven't the energy to lie.

"Being attracted to someone who's not attracted to me."

"Oh, shit," says Jackson. "You're positive it's one way?"

"Yup. They let me know that loud and clear."

"Oh, man."

A big arm wraps round the big jacket and gives my shoulders a squeeze. Cigarette smoke wafts around us. I don't mind it.

"I haven't spoken to Nate and Shelby once tonight," I admit. "Don't want to ruin their evening with my buzzkill vibes."

"They haven't been short of attention," he says. "And there's still time. Night's not over yet."

Jackson drops his cigarette on the ground and stubs it with his shoe. Then he squeezes my shoulders again. His hands are *big*. Like catcher's mitts.

"Come on," he says. "Before I have to chip you off the ground and carry you in like an ice sculpture."

I do not want to go inside. Can't face the prospect of catching even a glimpse of Cam. But if I stay out here, I will die, and Dylan the goose will peck on my frozen remains.

Plus, I'm not feeling quite so awful now. Amazing what a friendly word can do.

"Do I look like shit?" I ask Jackson.

"Can't tell. It's really dark. You looked great before."

Amazing.

"Everyone's blitzed, anyway," he adds. "Can't feel their own faces. Those cocktails. Woo-ee."

After the crackling cold of outside, the warmth in the barn feels clammy. It could be the sweaty fug of a couple hundred people dancing, shouting, and drinking, but that's repulsive, so I won't think about it.

I let Jackson steer me toward the happy couple. Shelby, in her cute white lacy dress, looks pink-cheeked and dazed. Nate looks like he's got to the drunk stage where you love everyone and insist on telling them so—many, many times. Or he could just be high on being newly married. I'll soon find out.

"Ava!" Shelby reaches her arms out wide. "Where have you been?"

Jackson saves me from having to answer. "Keeping me company outside while I indulge my filthy habit."

"You told Mom you quit!" says Shelby.

"I did. I've quit a whole bunch of times."

Grinning unrepentantly, Jackson envelops his little sister in a hug. I notice my own brother doesn't offer to hug me. Then again, we're the worst huggers in our family. The others say it's like embracing robots that need oil.

But Nate does move closer and says, "You okay?"

Instantly I'm on the defensive. Never show weakness! The other guy blinks first, even when he's your brother! *Especially* when he's your brother!

"Why shouldn't I be?"

Shelby and Jackson are nattering away. Nate moves

closer still and backs me almost into a corner. He's stone-cold sober, it seems. The glow was all happiness.

"Because you've been home for two months now, and you're still living in your old bedroom at Mom and Dad's," he says. "You haven't got a job. And every day you look less and less happy."

"Why are you saying this *now*?" I demand. "Don't you have better things to do at your own wedding?"

"I've been meaning to for a while," Nate says. "Life's been full-on. I'm sorry."

I wish he was drunk. I'd have an excuse not to listen to him.

"Let's not do this now." Without thinking, I add, "It's been a long night."

Nate gives me a good hard stare. I block it with my best poker face. All of us Durant siblings have mastered the art, though some are better than others. Nate has a tell: a small twitch of his left eyebrow. He denies it. He's deluded.

"I love you, you know," he says. "I want you to be happy."

Goddammit. Can't hold the poker face. Shit, now I can feel tears. I am losing it. Best I can hope for is not to bawl out loud like a baby.

Fortunately, Nate spots my dilemma and does give me a hug—our usual rigid fiasco but very welcome. Despite the added fairy lights, it's still dingy enough for me to cry briefly against his wedding suit. Nate fishes a handkerchief out of his pocket.

"Came with the suit," he says. "Along with a pair of silk socks."

"Fancy." I blow my nose. "Want it back?"

"Amazingly, no."

Nate squeezes my shoulders.

"Let's talk next week. I'll take you out for coffee. Or tequila. Whatever."

He and Shelby aren't honeymooning right away. They're taking a couple weeks off after Christmas when the vineyard is at its quietest.

"Okay." I give him a quick kiss on the cheek. "Thanks."

"Do you think you might be able to have a *little* fun tonight?" he asks.

I'm about to lie when Jackson slots himself into the convo.

"Shelby's told me I've got to dance at least once," he says. "I suck at dancing. I'm like a circus bear on a bicycle. Do you want to risk being my partner?"

The band's playing a peppy number, heavy on banjo and "hey heys". God knows what kind of moves you're supposed to make to that.

"What the hell," I say to Jackson. "Let's go and cut a rug."

"You want to lead?" says Jackson. "I mean, one of us should look like they know what they're doing."

He's funny. I'm actually smiling.

"Let's make it up as we go along," I say. "Just don't tread on my feet."

We're in the crowd now, the sweaty crowd. Jackson's

dancing is as promised: terrible. Less bear on bicycle and more big, hairy dog on ice. I know I look like shit: tear-stained, red-eyed and now sweaty, but I don't care. For the first time in weeks, I'm having a good time.

I spot Chiara dancing with Ted. Wonder where Imogen's got to? Maybe she dissolved at midnight. Or turned into an ornamental pumpkin. I spot my parents, too. Dad still has a dodgy heart, so he'd better not overdo it.

Best of all, I don't spot Cam. He might not even be here, might have headed home. I'd like to say I don't care, but that would be a lie. Right now, though, I can choose not to think about him, and focus on Jackson, who appears to be doing some kind of Scottish dance that involves kicking out your legs. It's ridiculously amusing. Also dangerous for anyone nearby.

The band segues into "Happy" from the Minion movie.

"Beat's too fast," puffs Jackson. "Or I'm unfit. My ego locks in answer number one."

"You can sit it out if you want," I tell him. "But if you stay, I'm warning you. I've got my second wind now. Going to dance all night."

Chapter Four

CAM

I had a girlfriend in high school. She wanted to stay my girlfriend when I enlisted but I told her it wasn't fair to her. What I meant was I didn't love her enough to want her to wait. She knew that. We were talking in my pick-up, and she got out and walked home. Never spoke to me again.

Army took seven years of my life. Been in Flora Valley almost ten. I'm not going to lie and say I've been a monk, but sex is one thing, a relationship is another. I've not had a girlfriend since the last one quite rightly dumped my ass and left me sitting alone in my '71 Chevy pick-up. I'd bought it cheap with the aim of fixing it up but never did because I was a teenager and an idiot. When I drove home that evening and slammed the driver's side door shut, it fell off. Hinges had rusted through, and I hadn't noticed. Still drove it, doorless, for the whole month before I left for Fort Benning. See previous point about being an idiot.

Not paying attention to the signs—to anything, period—

means that when the reckoning comes, it comes hard. People with experience had told me what the army would be like. I ignored them. People told me I shouldn't try to fix myself, that I should get professional help. I ignored them. Lee Armstrong told me I needed to find something to do that made me feel like my life had value. I ignored her. But she persisted until, finally, I listened. Until I saw exactly how much my idiot stubbornness had cost me.

That was a tough moment, seeing how much pain had been down to me and my choices, my actions. I was bitter at Lee for forcing me to shine the spotlight on myself. So much easier to blame others or circumstance, black cats or loaded dice, anything that isn't you. But I came through it, stayed on this Earth. Realized how much I had to be grateful for. Lee Armstrong being top of that list.

Thought then that I'd learned some important lessons about personal responsibility. Now it seems I still have a way to go. Because even though I know it's entirely my fault that I was too slow to recognize how I feel about Ava, I'm focusing all my resentment on Jackson Armstrong.

Jackson. Lee and Billy's oldest. First met him almost ten years ago when he came back from college. He was twenty-two and your typical frat boy, into beer, sport, and goofing around. Kind of guy who gets laughs by crushing beer cans on his forehead. More genial than asshole, but sometimes out of control. Thinking it's a hoot to hang out the window of a speeding car. Or to bellyflop drunk into the local swimming hole.

Sure, I'm hardly one to judge. I was an idiot, too. I'm just bringing this up because, right now, I don't want to think good thoughts about Jackson Armstrong. I want to run him down, mash his face into the ground, and drag him along in the dust for a spell.

He and Ava are dancing. Well, she's dancing. He's … I don't know, imitating a seal flapping on a beach? Demonstrating how hard it would be for a gorilla to walk in heels?

Again, not one to judge. I don't dance at all. Did once, long time ago. Last time was at my sister's wedding.

Weddings have a lot to answer for. If Shelby and Nate hadn't got married, Jackson and Ava would never have met.

And with that thought, I have officially scraped the bottom of the barrel.

"It's your fault."

For a second, I think it's the voice of my subconscious. Lucky for me—or maybe not—it's a real person. Shelby's one-of-two best friends of all time, Chiara. Her stiletto heels make us the two tallest people in the room.

"My fault?"

Chiara nods at Ava and Jackson. "You had your chance. You blew it."

Does she mean at the crush when I turned Ava down? Or has she got some secret intel about tonight? I totally did miss my chance, owing to being painfully slow to work out how I felt. But no one knows that except me. Do they?

"Ava asked you to get mulled wine with her because she wanted to bridge the gap between you two," says Chiara. "Not in a I-want-to-bone-you-at-the-earliest-opportunity way. More in a I-was-too-hasty-before-so-how-about-we-get-to-know-each-other-and-see-how-it-goes way."

She gestures to the couple on the dance floor.

"Now you're here and she's there with another guy. I don't know what you did, and I don't really care. What matters is that it was not the right thing. You blew it."

Shelby thinks Chiara has witchy superpowers. I'm beginning to see what she means. I also ignore her criticism and single out the one spark of hope in her little speech.

"You're saying Ava still likes me?"

"Of course. Unless what you did was so wrong it cannot be forgiven."

Again, I ignore that last part. "How come you're so sure?"

"Pfft, please." Chiara turns scorn into a high art. "When it comes to the human psyche, I know everything."

She looks me in the eye. Only person in the room who can do it near enough straight on.

"I know you're lurking in the darkest corner of the barn for the sole reason that you don't want Ava to see you. You want to leave but you've become rooted to the spot with jealousy watching Jackson and Ava dance. Bet you're dredging up all the times Jackson was thoughtless and stupid just to make yourself feel better. Next step is to get irrationally annoyed that Shelby married Nate and gave Jackson and Ava an opportunity to meet."

How does she do that?

"So ... why exactly are you scolding me?" I ask.

"For your own good, of course," says Chiara. "You're

not a go-getter. You need encouragement."

"This is you being encouraging?"

"No, *this* is me being encouraging."

Chiara points her finger right between my eyes and makes sure my attention remains on it as it moves to indicate the intended target.

"What I need you to do," she says, "is go over to Jackson and Ava and cut in. He's about to collapse anyway, so he won't protest. Ava's first reaction will be to resist because she's hurt about whatever it is you did—not the right thing, remember? Keep at it but not to the point where you're being a caveman jerk. Do not under any circumstances grab her arm. If she continues to refuse, yield with dignity. Try again another time, several other times if necessary, but don't be a stalker. Got all that?"

"Don't be a caveman. Don't be a stalker."

Chiara raises an eyebrow. "Impressed. Most guys completely fail to hear those instructions. I'm thinking of printing flashcards."

"What if I don't do it?"

I feel a pressure on the top of my shoe. Chiara's stiletto. The heel style that's named after a particularly thin and lethal dagger. Usually, I wear boots, but Shelby got me some fancier shoes along with the shirt and tie. Thin leather. Chiara's dagger heel will pass through it without even trying.

"I've been in combat," I say. "I've been shot, stabbed, and blown up."

"You're still more scared of me, though."

"Okay, fine," I say gracelessly. "I'll do it."

But even with the stiletto heel danger removed, I hesitate. Feel like I'm on display.

Chiara shoos me with her fingers. "Now's good, Cam."

"Are you going to watch?"

"Of course not," she says, as if I've insulted her. "It's none of my business."

And off she stalks, in search, I guess, of someone else who needs encouragement.

Shit. If Chiara's gone, do I really need to go through with this? My three R's are shouting at me in my head, and I've been listening to them for so long, it's hard to hear anything else.

One of the waiters appears beside me.

"Sir, I'm to tell you that Chiara has eyes everywhere," he informs me. "And if you don't act now, she will pay people to graffiti your personal phone number on every spare wall in town."

"She'd do it, wouldn't she?"

"Without hesitating, sir."

I hand him the empty glass I've been hanging on to all night. Crick my neck in preparation, loosen my shoulders. Breathe deep and start walking.

Jackson sees me first. He looks like he's been trying to outrun zombies, all wild-haired and sweating. He lifts a hand in greeting but is too puffed to speak.

Then Ava sees me. Stops dancing, stiffens her whole body, and shoots back her head, like I'm about to go for her jugular.

"Mind if I cut in?" I say, because I've been told to.

Jackson's bent over now, resting his hands on his knees, wheezing.

"You don't dance," says Ava, who's still looking at me like I'm a lizard person.

Knew there was a flaw in Chiara's plan.

Then, right on cue, the band starts playing a slow number. The kind you can just shuffle to, no skill required. Want to bet who organized that?

Apart from no caveman/no stalker, Chiara's instructions were pretty non-specific. So, I reach out my hand in the hope that Ava will take it.

With some effort, her former dance partner stands upright, notices my outstretched hand, flaps his own hand in a "go for it" gesture and hobbles off. I take back everything I said about Jackson Armstrong. He's okay.

Trouble is, this'll only work if Ava thinks I'm okay, too.

"Finished hanging fairy lights?" she says.

"Hour ago."

"No other duties to fulfill?"

I shake my head. My hand's still out there in mid-air, waiting.

"I'm sorry," I say. "I fucked up. Can we start over?"

For a second, her face kind of crumples. Then she pulls it together and her expression's wary again. I can't tell which way this will go.

"Watch out for my feet," she says. "Jackson stood on them one too many times."

And she takes my hand and moves in closer. Rests her

other hand lightly on my waist, so I follow suit on hers. Her head comes barely up to my sternum, but it doesn't matter. Having her in my arms, even this tentatively, is the most amazing thing. Got no idea where to go from here but that's a problem for later. Right now, I'm focusing every sense on Ava: how her hair smells like woodsmoke, how she feels, fine-boned, almost fragile, but strong, too.

Also focusing a whole lot of effort on keeping my feet from crushing hers. Even shuffle-dancing requires skill I don't have.

Making conversation's another skill I lack. But we can't shuffle forever. I'll need to communicate soon and in a way that doesn't undo all the progress I've only just made. The waiter's warning about Chiara having eyes everywhere is still sounding. No pressure now.

Because my head's in another space, I don't immediately register that Ava suddenly feels ... heavier. She's leaning against me, head drooping, her hand's slipped from my waist. It's like she's—

"Shit!"

I make a grab for her as she starts to slide. To anyone watching it might look like we're doing some kind of dance dip but she's completely out cold and if I hadn't been holding her, she'd have crashed to the floor.

Got to get her away from the crowd. Bend my knees and lift her into my arms. To anyone watching now, it looks like Fay Wray passed out in the arms of King Kong.

"Ava!"

Nate's right here. Shelby, too. Instinct tells me they've

been spying on us, probably tipped off by Chiara. I'm glad to see them nonetheless.

"What happened?"

Nate touches Ava's unresponsive face, then reaches for her wrist and takes her pulse.

"Dunno," I say. "She just ... passed out."

"Doc Wilson," says Nate to Shelby. "He's still here. I saw him talking to Dad."

"I'll fetch him."

Shelby picks up the bottom of her wedding dress and runs off like a prairie homesteader cutting through a field of wheat.

"Come on," says Nate. "Let's find somewhere to lay her down."

By now, a bunch of people have seen what's going on. There are a few chuckles from those who probably think she's had one too many Wild Boar cocktails. She didn't have a single drink in the hour I spent watching her and Jackson dance, so I know it's not that. What it is, I don't want to think about.

Nate, helped by a couple of the ever-alert wait staff, clears a trestle table. It's a hard surface but it's all we've got. I lay Ava down gently as I can...

... And I'm shoved aside by a short old dude. Doc Wilson, I presume.

He does a brisk triage assessment of the still unconscious Ava. Pulls out his phone.

"I'm calling 911," he announces.

A big crowd has gathered around us. No chuckling now. This is serious.

"What's up, Doc?" An ashen Nate makes the unintentional Bugs Bunny joke.

"Pulse is low and she's still out for the count. Not taking any chances."

Doc shakes his head at Nate and the rest of the family gathered around: Danny and the twins, who are all looking as pale and worried as Nate.

"You Durants are keeping me from my retirement."

"Ray, is it her heart?"

This from a handsome, older man, who's obviously Nate and Ava's father, Mitchell Durant. Shelby told me all about his own heart condition. Hence his concern.

"Can't say, Mitch. But don't fret until you know there's something to fret about."

Mitchell Durant looks like he's about to demand a better answer. A man used to getting his own way, Shelby says, though he's apparently mellowed a lot in the past few months.

His wife, Ginny, takes his arm, and Mitch Durant settles for glaring.

And then Ava starts to stir.

"Can we get some room here?"

The crowd obeys and pulls back. Doc Wilson has a natural command.

Ava blinks, trying to get her bearings. Confusion becomes panic. She starts to sit up way too quickly, but Doc Wilson gently prevents her.

"Woah there," he says. "Easy now."

I know Ava's a horsewoman, but she's not actually a horse. Still, I'm not in charge here.

Sound of a siren coming closer. Ava registers it and clutches Doc's arm, eyes wide with alarm.

"Precautionary," he says. "You know me. I like to do it by the book."

The crowd parts as the paramedic crew comes in.

"Hey, Ray," says the first one, a woman. "What've we got?"

They confer, and I wish I could get closer. Izzy, I notice, has snuck behind the trestle table and is holding Ava's hand. Doc then moves off to have a hushed conversation with Ava's dad, who nods once, curtly. Doc gives the thumbs up to the paramedic.

"Okay, ma'am," she says to Ava. "Doc says you're coming with us. Your folks will pick up the bill."

And suddenly, Ava's looking directly at me. Eyes big, pleading. I hate hospitals, like, *really* hate them, and my instinct is to draw back, wait.

But I can hear Chiara in my mind. "Now's good, Cam."

"Can I go with her, Doc?" I say.

He glances up at me in surprise, and back to Ava. Makes a swift assessment.

"You fit to drive?" Doc says, and when I nod, adds, "What's your name, son?"

"Cam."

"Okay, then, Cam. Let's take our leave of these good people and follow on behind to the hospital."

Chapter Five

AVA

This is ridiculous. Why the hell is Doc Wilson making all this fuss? Calling the paramedics, for Pete's sake. I fainted – that's it, that's all. Always had low blood pressure and a low pulse. Comes from being athletic. Okay, I don't always faint, for sure, but I haven't eaten a lot today and I had a couple of drinks, and I was giving it my all on the dance floor, so…

I'm fine. There's nothing wrong with me. That's my story and I'm sticking to it.

"Is this all absolutely necessary?" I ask the male paramedic.

The female paramedic is driving, so my guy here has been assigned to check my vitals and then interrogate me with a million questions. Did I have any unusual sensations prior to the event? Was my heart rate erratic? Any pain? Any bleeding? Am I on medication? Am I diabetic? What did I eat? What did I drink? If a train leaves a station…

"I just fainted," I say. "Really."

He gives me a tolerant smile. He's used to patients being stubborn.

"Doc Wilson seems to think it's worth checking you out more thoroughly. You sure you don't have any underlying conditions that might have caused you to pass out?"

You mean, like the fact I've been exhausted for months? But who needs to know that? Not this guy, for sure. I'll use the time-honored Durant deflection tactic and throw the question back to him.

"Do you think I have any underlying conditions?"

"That's way above my pay grade," he says.

I hate it when people use the deflection tactic on me.

The ambulance turns a corner and slows right down. Guess we've arrived.

Suddenly, I'm panicking. I do not like hospitals. Dad was in and out last year with his heart condition, but that's not the main reason I don't want to be here. I don't want people poking and prodding me and maybe finding things that are bad. I don't want to know why I'm exhausted, and I don't want anyone else to know, either. I want to be back at the wedding, dancing with Cam.

Cam. Thank God. He's on his way. At least, I hope he is.

I'm out of the ambulance, into a wheelchair and into the hospital ER – this team is as efficient as a NASCAR pit crew. I hear the words "syncope" and "Doc Wilson," and now a nurse is in charge of my wheels, and in two minutes I'm on a bed in a cubicle, curtains whisked shut around me, my vitals being checked yet again. This is the worst combination of tedious and terrifying. Where is Doc Wilson? Where is Cam?

"Okay, then, Little Missy, let's see what's up."

Doc bustles in and behind him is Cam. I'm so relieved to see them both but also instantly anxious. Why was Doc so worried he had to send me here? And Cam – he said he wanted to start over, but we only got to dance for, like, five minutes before I collapsed on him. Pretty sure his idea of starting over wouldn't have included a medical emergency, *if* this is an emergency, which I refuse to believe.

Cam looks anxious, too, but there's also a small smile on his face.

"Little Missy?" he says.

I glare at Doc. "My dad's nickname for me. Which I hate."

Doc ignores me. He's reading the chart, his face serious. I'm anxious again.

Cam draws up the one chair in the cubicle. In this compact space, he takes up a chunk of room. And he looks about as happy to be here as I feel.

"This sucks," I say. "I'm sorry."

Small smile again.

"I usually have to make up some excuse to get out of socializing," he says. "Shelby can't give me shit this time."

"Oh, God – I've ruined Shelby and Nate's wedding!"

I want to put a pillow over my face.

"Not at all," says Doc, slotting the chart back. "Bar'd been drunk pretty much dry anyhow. Party was coming to its natural end."

"You always know the right thing to say," I tell him. "Even when it's a big fat lie."

I feel those stupid tears rising again. Combination of gratitude and anxiety, I suppose. I want this to be over. Cam puts his hand over mine and I clutch onto it. But I can't look at him. I'm too worried about what Doc Wilson's about to tell me.

"Ava, I'm sorry to put you through this," Doc says. "But your mother's already told me she's been worried about your health."

Goddammit, Mom, why didn't you tell me first? Forewarned is forearmed. I would have been better prepared for this.

"Mom?!" I protest. Deflect! Deflect! "But she's worried about all of us. Ever since Dad got sick, she—"

"She's become a little hypervigilant, that's true," says Doc. "But she's got good instincts for what's normal and what's not. She says you quit your job because of exhaustion. Is that right?"

I feel Cam's hand tense. Deflect!

"It wasn't just that," I lie. "I … fell out of love with it. Lots of hard work for not that much reward. Rather work as a stable hand, truth be told."

"But you were exhausted?" Doc presses me.

"It's grueling!"

Doc's expression suggests I might want to give up on being defensive, as it's only prolonging things.

"Okay, I got tired." If I admit this much, he might be more inclined to believe me. "To the point where I was getting clumsy, which is not good when you're trying to control a highly strung racehorse. I figured this was my body's way of confirming that I was over the job, and what I needed was a break, a rest. So, I quit."

That's it. That's all. No more questions.

Doc has more questions.

"You have any numbness?" he asks. "Pins and needles?"

"No." I can be honest about that, at least.

"Light-headedness? Dizziness?"

Cam's hand twitches again. I resist glancing at him.

"Not apart from tonight."

That's mostly honest, but it doesn't seem to cut much ice with Doc.

"I want to do some more tests," he announces.

I hear Cam give a small grunt and I realize I'm crushing his hand. But I can't seem to loosen my grip. This is my worst nightmare.

"Why?" I demand. "What do you think this is?"

"Ava, it could be nothing," he says. "Or it could be one of a whole range of conditions. I won't know until I test."

"Doc, please give me a clue! What kind of conditions?"

He sighs, but I know him well enough to know it's not because I'm being difficult. It's because there is no easy answer.

"I want to check for mineral and vitamin deficiencies," he says. "Nerve damage, brain lesions. Any possible viral or parasitic causes. So that's blood tests, EP tests and an MRI for starters. Possibly a lumbar puncture."

That's it. I'm all out of self-control. I burst into tears.

Cam pulls me to him and wraps his big arms around me. He smells like sweat and woodsmoke. I probably do, too.

"I'm sorry, Ava," says Doc, and I know he means it. "Wouldn't put you through this if I had any choice. But not to do it would be negligent. I'm too fond of you and your family to cut corners."

Cam speaks over my head. "Does she have to stay here? Can I take her home?"

Doc nods. "If she can walk out of here under her own steam, she can go home. There's nothing more we can do today."

Oh, I can walk out of here. Even if it kills me.

Cam hands me a cup of water. I'd prefer bourbon but I'll take what I can get.

I slide off the bed and bat Cam's hand away. Have to do this myself.

I'm on my feet and my head is fuzzy but not swirling. Deep breaths, Ava. Slow movements.

Cam is hovering, but I'm feeling good. The rush of relief that I can leave is giving me a much-needed boost. The three of us make it all the way to the hospital entrance without incident.

"I'll check in with you tomorrow, Ava." Doc makes it sound almost like a threat. "You take good care of her, son."

He heads back inside, and soon as he can no longer see us, I grab Cam's arm.

"You okay?" Anxiety makes his voice go squeaky.

"I'm wiped out," I tell him. "Take me home."

There's a slight pause.

"Uh, your home?" he says. "Or—?"

Up till now, I hadn't considered this to be an option. But, oh boy, I need to be away from prying eyes. Away from people asking questions because they "care". I need a distraction, and preferably one that might involve some sexy action with Cam. Nothing like multiple orgasms to take your mind off your problems.

My conscience starts nagging. *Don't use the guy, it's not fair to him.* Every other part of me shouts it down. *He made the offer! He might* want *to be used! Why are you hesitating for even a second?*

"Your home, definitely," I say. "Mine will be full of worried people. Don't need that stress."

"Might be more worried if you don't come home."

"I'll text them."

And then I'll switch off my phone.

We've arrived at the Flora Valley Wines truck, an ancient Dodge.

"Shelby let me borrow it," Cam explains.

"Don't you have a car?"

"Nope," he says. "Usually walk."

He helps me up into the passenger seat where I take a moment to rest my head and close my eyes. I open them before Cam gets in. Don't want to freak him out.

He gets in, looks across at me. Dodge's interior lighting is non existent, so all I can see is a big dark shape. But I can sense the nerves. Sense his inner struggle.

Slowly-slowly, I hear Chiara say.

"Honestly, this is for the best," I only part-lie. "I need

peace and quiet. The Durant family don't do peace and quiet."

"Okay," he says. "If you're sure?"

Oh, I'm sure.

"Drive on, Hollander," I say. "I'll text my folks. And then I'll lie back and have a little nap."

Chapter Six

CAM

Ava's still sleeping. It's almost noon, and I've fielded more calls in the last few hours than I have in the last decade. Only a slight exaggeration.

Doc Wilson called first. Said to let Ava sleep and he'd come round mid-afternoon. Then I spoke to Nate and Shelby; Ava's other siblings; Ava's mom, nice lady; Ava's dad, less nice but given his own recent health scare, I can forgive him for being a bit short; Chiara, genuine in her concern but also using the opportunity to snoop; and Jackson, worried he'd contributed to Ava's collapse. I told him he hadn't, partly to reassure him but mostly to prevent him from coming around.

Fact is, I put everyone off coming round. Told them Ava needed rest, and that we'd send an update later today after Doc Wilson's visit. Everyone accepted this without question except Chiara, who seemed to think this was all part of her successful plot to bring Ava and me closer together and that we were going to spend the day "getting to know each other." Practically saw her make the air quotes. I was too weary to put Chiara straight and tell her that it's kind of hard to get to know someone when they're dead to the world. All you can tell is that they're a side sleeper and that they snore lightly and occasionally mutter. And to be honest, it's been a relief to have this time to myself. Ava and I have been thrown together way earlier and more intensely than I'd anticipated. Last night, when I realized I had feelings for her, I figured the next step would be a casual date, where we'd talk and decide whether we should keep seeing each other. We'd take time to work out whether we were a good match.

Lee tried to set me up more than once, and none of those first dates went on to become a second. Okay, so part of that was down to me and my inclination toward resistance and retreat, but I don't regret it because I knew those women weren't right for me. I didn't have feelings for them the way I do for Ava. There was never that spark. But I've spent a lot of years taking things slow, and old habits are hard to break. I have no idea how to act when Ava wakes up. No idea what she's going to expect from me. Is this the start of something between us? Or should we put everything on hold until we figure out what's wrong with her? That seems like the most responsible approach, and the slowest and steadiest, but there's just one hitch: I can't stop thinking about holding Ava in my arms last night and I definitely can't stop thinking about her being upstairs in my bed. My conscience says, be responsible, and my body says, fuck that. I'm glad she's still asleep, so I don't have to put my internal struggle to the test.

Ava's in my bed because one bed is all I have. I lent her a T-shirt to sleep in, sat up for an hour or so to make sure she was peaceful, then crashed in one of the downstairs armchairs. Army's good for teaching you to sleep anywhere, on any surface. Good for training you to be neat, too. Didn't have to worry about the place being a dump because it never is. I keep my few possessions in good order, everything clean and tidy. Dishes washed, bed made, floor swept. Even though it's only me here.

In case you're wondering, the shed I call home is a big workshop space with living quarters tacked on the side. Two levels, bedroom upstairs, galley kitchen and two old armchairs downstairs, bathroom out the back. I added extra insulation in the dividing wall for the wood dust, but it still creeps in. My industrial strength vacuum cleaner that's the size of R2D2 gets a regular workout.

Sunday morning, I'd normally be at my regular volunteer gig, helping out at the local Therapeutic Riding Society. It's a pretty terrible name for a great organization that uses horses to help kids with disabilities. As my boss, Therese, points out, when you can't walk, the freedom of being on horseback is like suddenly being able to fly. I do barn chores and am what is known as a side walker: I walk alongside the instructor, give physical support, talk to the kids, say stuff like "Good job" and "You got this." I can manage that.

I'd already told Therese I'd be taking this morning off. I

was expecting to help out with the post-wedding barn clean-up but I've got other duties now. They come under the general heading of "waiting until Ava wakes up".

Past noon now. I could go check on her, make sure the room's not too hot, not too cold, she's still breathing, that sort of thing. What I really want to do is look at her, watch her sleep, see if I can work out what words she's muttering. But my conscience is so far winning the internal struggle, and I suspect that's for the best at this stage in our relationship. You know. The stage when there is no relationship, just a bunch of primitive physical impulses and jumbled emotions. The stage that I'm not cut out to deal with at all.

Okay, shit. I hear movement above. Creak of feet on the floorboards. I built the living quarters from reclaimed timber: a mixture of oak, pine, and some hickory. I like being surrounded by natural material; I like the way wood looks and feels warmer than any other.

"It's frigging freezing in here!"

Ava appears on the stairs, wrapped in a blanket, scowling down at me.

"How do you survive in winter?" she demands. "Do you hibernate?"

She stomps down and drops into the armchair I've just vacated.

"Want me to put the stove on?"

I've got a small wood burner, with two hotplates and an oven. Heating and cooking. Works for me.

"I want to know why it isn't on already." Ava hunches

up her knees and pulls the blanket tight around her whole body, forming a cocoon where only her nose is showing.

"Guess I don't feel the cold like you do," I say. "Coffee?"

"Are you boiling it in a camping pot?"

"Nope. Got a Breville in the workshop. Present from—"

Shit.

"From?"

"Shelby's mom," I have to confess. "Lee."

From the blanket cocoon comes a small grunting sound. Can't tell what it means.

"Cream and sugar?"

"Black," she says. "Strong."

"I'll get it. Then I'll go get some wood."

Stove emitting heat, coffee drunk, Ava starts to emerge from the blanket. For someone who collapsed, got carted off to the hospital and has now slept around eleven hours, she looks in good shape. Cute. Dark short hair is a little mussed, but then mine's always messy, even when I comb it.

"Hey," I say. "How are you?"

She screws up her face. "Embarrassed. Also a little freaked out."

I get a buzz that she's comfortable enough to be honest with me. I try to prevent the buzz from moving south. Responsible Cam needs to be in charge.

"Doc Wilson's coming around in a couple of hours," I say. "I told everyone else to stay away. Hope that's okay?"

"More than," she says, and adds, "thanks."

Her coffee cup is empty. Technically, it's lunch time, but I'm suddenly self-conscious. Would she want any of the food I could fix her? Haven't cooked for another person in ... can't recall.

"Uh, if you're hungry, I could make you a sandwich? Or some eggs?"

Ava's blue eyes light up. "What kind of eggs?"

"What do you like?"

"My mom makes a mean huevos rancheros with black beans and avocado, with a fresh tomato salsa and hot sauce."

We lock eyes for a beat. I think she's messing with me but can't be sure.

"Scrambled on whole wheat?" I suggest.

She grins. Totally messing with me.

"Coming right up," I say.

"Do you have a shower?" she asks. "Or do you tip a bucket over yourself?"

"Out back." I point to the door at the rear of the kitchen. "Clean towels are in the closet."

Keeping the blanket wrapped around her, she gets up. At the door, she pauses.

"Don't suppose you own a bathrobe? I mean, this old T-shirt of yours is effectively a dress on me, but my legs and arms are a little chilly. And I can't wear this blanket all day."

Dilemma. No bathrobe. And nothing I do own will fit her. Shelby lives nearest but it's the day after her wedding. She and Nate will be ... busy.

"Could ring your sister, Izzy?"

"Hell, no," says Ava. "I mean, I love her, but open the

door a crack to one Durant and the whole lot will be in here before you can say 'mass invasion'."

"Long socks and a sweater?" I suggest.

"Or…" she says, slowly, staring right at me, "I could go back to bed?"

Holy shit. Carton of eggs in my hand almost hits the floor. Not a hundred percent sure she's implying that I join her, but—

She drops the blanket. Stands there, wearing my old T-shirt that comes down to mid-thigh. And, judging by the lack of visible underwear lines, nothing else.

Okay. A hundred percent sure.

And unable to move or speak.

I'm so not used to things moving this fast, my whole system is locked into freeze mode. But if I don't react, she'll be hurt. Again.

"Uh…" My hand's going to crush these eggs, so I put the box on the counter.

Ava's watching me. She doesn't look pissed. Yet.

"Is that a 'startled-but-hell-yeah' uh?" she says. "Or a 'no-idea-how-the-hell-to-respond' uh?"

Get it together, Cam. "Both?"

She laughs. I'm relieved. I am also so out of my depth, I might as well be at the bottom of the Mariana Trench.

Ava moves toward me, her body relaxed, pace unhurried. I'm reminded of Therese at the Riding Society instructing us volunteers on how to approach a nervous horse. My own nervous system has shifted from freeze mode into full anticipation. Responsible Cam has been caught in a chokehold by Primal Cam and his warnings are now feeble squawking sounds.

She's right here, and Primal Cam gives Responsible Cam one last neck twist and drops him unconscious to the floor. I bend to meet her mouth, pull her into me, my hands under the T-shirt, on her skin, cupping her naked rear and lifting her up. She's so small and light, I can hold her up no problem. Her legs wrap around me, her own hands move under my shirt, over my chest and abs ... and I am about as in control of this situation as a pine needle in a brush fire. So much for slow and steady. My primal instinct is all hare, racing ahead and giving the tortoise the finger.

"Counter," breathes Ava in my ear.

"What?" Okay, so my brain is still in low gear.

"Shift around."

Got it. I turn, so she can perch her rear on the kitchen counter. It's wooden, not too cold. Mind you, we could both be in the midst of a swarm of hornets for all we care. Counter is exactly the right height. My hands are freed up now, and I begin to slide them up her thighs, but am forestalled by the fact that she's trying to undo my jeans. Fact we're kissing makes communicating a little tricky, so I break off, and whisper, "Hang on."

Luckily, my jeans are old and the buttons aren't tight. Don't stop to think about the age of my jockeys, just yank them down, free my straining hard cock and take it in hand, ready to—

"Shit."

"What?" demands Ava.

"No condom."

Wasn't expecting to need one.

"I'm on the pill," she says, and wraps her legs tighter, her heels clamping my ass into position.

"Yeah, but—" I can sense Responsible Cam starting to come round.

"Cam," she says, "I don't have any STDs. Do you?"

"Well, no, but—"

"No buts," she says. "Only fuck. Right now."

She's so close. The musky scent of her signals how ready she is. All I have to do is slide right into that slick tightness, right in up to the hilt and—

Car wheels crunching on the gravel. Ava's so intent on getting me inside her that she doesn't hear. I should perhaps mention it, but she's got my cock in her hand now and I'm kind of having to go with the flow here.

Rat tat tat on the door. Jaunty. Friendly. Incredibly unwelcome.

"Do not answer it," hisses Ava.

Unmistakable voice of Doc Wilson calls, "Hello in there?"

"You said he'd be here in a couple of *hours*!" is Ava's accusing whisper.

"That's what he told me!" I whisper back.

The doorknob rattles. This is not a big room. Front door opens right into it. And when I'm here, I never lock it. If Doc decides to come on in, he's going to get an eyeful. Me with my pants around my ankles, cock still raring to go. Ava half naked, hand on aforementioned cock, legs clinched around me tight as a possum on a branch.

"Cam? Ava?"

He is not going away.

Ava curses, releases her hold on me.

"This isn't over!" she says, like a threat. "Minute he leaves, I'm jumping you."

Her fierce expression, combined with the farce of rushing to pull up my pants and button them over a resistant hard-on, suddenly makes me laugh.

Ava glares at me.

"Come on." I toss the blanket to her. "This is funny."

"Hilarious," she says and abruptly re-cocoons.

I open the door just as Doc Wilson's fist's about to land for another knock.

"Sorry," I say. "Was showing Ava how the shower works."

Dumb, but first thing I could think of.

Doc looks past me. Sees Ava, grouchy in her blanket, still sitting, I realize, on the kitchen counter. Looks back to me, and my shirt hanging outside my jeans.

"All righty then," he says cheerfully. Bustles on in, doctor's bag in hand. "Let's take a look at the patient."

Ava hops off the counter and drops into the armchair.

"I haven't showered, and I have nothing on but this T-shirt," she announces.

"Wouldn't be the first time."

Doc opens his bag and pulls out a blood pressure cuff.

All righty then, as I didn't think anyone in the real world actually said.

"Uh, I'll—" I hook a thumb toward outside.

No one's looking at me. I grab my jacket off the hook by the front door and head out.

Door closed behind me, I lean against the side of the barn, and breathe in and out, long and slow. Getting a grip.

Primal Cam has a lot to answer for. Now that the horny adrenaline is fading, he's skulking off like he's leaving the scene of a crime. Responsible Cam is sitting up, rubbing his neck, and giving me a full-on accusatory stare. Jesus, Ava was in the hospital only last night, and here I was about to pound her on a kitchen counter. Without protection, too. What the almighty fuck was I thinking?

I wasn't thinking. I was acting on my worst impulse. Last time I did that, I almost ruined my entire life.

The adrenaline clears out, taking with it any last impression that this was funny. I'm left with a guilt and shame double combo that's warming me on this chilly day, only not in a good way. I just did everything I've spent years regretting. Lost control. Gave into hasty dumb urges without stopping to think about the consequences.

And now what? When Doc Wilson leaves, Ava made it crystal clear that she expects to carry on where we left off. The thought of it starts to summon back Primal Cam, so I shake my head, stomp my feet on the ground, and try and get the blood back to my brain where it should have been in the first place.

The door creaks open. Doc Wilson peers out, looking

way more cheerful than I feel, but I suspect that's his factory setting.

"She's in the shower, son," he tells me. "No problem operating it. Guess you gave good instructions."

He sees right through me.

"What's the verdict, Doc? She really going to need all those tests?"

Doc wags his head side to side.

"If her mother hadn't come to me, I'd say this wasn't out of the ordinary," he says. "Those Durant kids are hard drivers, and Ava and Nate are the worst of the bunch. They exercise way too much and don't eat properly. No idea how to spell 'relaxation', let alone do it."

He looks a lot less cheerful now. Worried, even.

"But from what Ginny's told me about Ava over the last few weeks … as I said last night, I'd be remiss not to be thorough."

"So … what next?"

"I'll set up a series of appointments – my office and the hospital. Take it step by step." Doc's suddenly cheerful again. "But for now, son, look after her. Make sure she eats. Don't overtire her."

He knows what we were up to. He knows I know he knows. But that was earlier, when Primal Cam was in charge. Rest of today, I'll be on my best, most Responsible Cam behavior. Rock solid self-control.

I shake Doc's hand and watch him leave in his dusty old Camry. Walk inside again.

Find Ava waiting for me. Stark naked.

Chapter Seven

AVA

Soon as I see Cam's face, I know we're not getting back on that counter. Curse Doc Wilson and his promptitude. Don't care if that's not even a word, I curse it anyway. Or "cuss" as Doc would say. I won't stay pissed at Doc, I'm too fond of him. But if he'd been even just fifteen minutes later, Cam and I would have been in a post-quickie coma, and I would have been a lot more relaxed about the medical check-up.

But would a quickie have been a good thing? Just because I'm desperate for a distraction and, let's face it, very focused on achieving my goals, it doesn't mean it would have been the right choice. Sure, Cam responded, but any straight guy who isn't dead generally does respond when a woman has her hand down his pants. Judging by the fact that he now looks as if he wants to clap both hands over his eyes, I'd guess he's had second thoughts about us being hasty.

Slowly-slowly. Words of advice I ignored. Because I wanted to feel something other than terrified.

So, what now? Given the circumstances, and the fact that Doc Wilson's visit hasn't exactly boosted my libido, I think the best thing is for me to help us both escape with dignity. I'll start by folding my arms to cover my bazooms.

"I'm standing here naked", I tell Cam, "because the towel is damp, the blanket scratchy, I slept in the T-shirt, and we've already discussed that I don't have any other clothes. Got another of those flannel numbers you're wearing?"

Cam looks like someone dropped a brick on his skull. If he says "uh" again, I'll smack him.

"Sure," he says. Must have read my mind.

He makes a dash for the stairs. Thump of boots up. Rummaging. Thump back down.

Cam holds a flannel shirt out in front of him so it blocks his vision. I grab it, throw it on. It comes to just above my knees, but it's clean, soft, and comforting.

"Thanks," I say, and mean it.

He smiles. Relief, mainly, but who cares. When he smiles, his brown eyes get a glow, like burnished chestnut in firelight, and they crinkle around the edges. Cam's smile makes you feel warm and safe. If he were a horse, I'd be confident to put anyone on his back. But let's not have riding and Cam in the same thought. Not right now, anyway.

"Don't suppose eggs are still on offer?" I ask.

"Sure. Yeah. Coming right up," he says, and leaps into the kitchen space in a single bound.

Honestly, it's like I'm a judge giving him a stay of execution. I could feel offended, but I haven't the energy. The medical check-up not only snuffed out my sex drive, it also brought back all the fear and panic of last night. But I won't tell Cam that I'm feeling scared because I don't want him to take pity on me. I hate being pitied more than I hate feeling out of my depth. I want to know what's wrong with me, so I can start doing something about it. But Doc won't commit to any diagnosis until he's run fifteen million tests! Stubborn old coot.

It suddenly occurs to me that the reason Cam's being cautious might be because Doc Wilson gave him the same lecture he gave me. Doc knows patience has never been my strong suit, so he basically forced me to agree to rest up. Emotional blackmail is probably against some medical code of ethics, but I swore on the family grave of the Durants I'd take it easy. Maybe Doc bailed Cam up against the wall outside and forced him to promise, too? Doc may be half Cam's height, but he's got sharp instruments in that bag of his.

And, really, it could be worse. Cam told me no one else is coming to visit, so I can spend the rest of the afternoon just with him. And then, maybe later, we can… It's not like I have any plans for today. Or plans for any day after, for that matter.

I take a seat at the small kitchen table, which I realize folds up when not in use. The stool I'm sitting on looks like it folds up, too. Cam's whole home is a marvel of space-saving smarts. If Cam designed this as well as built it, he should start a business. The tiny house movement is taking off, and this is the best example I've seen. Along with the compact woodburning stove, there's a dinky pull-out pantry and a tiny fridge. There's storage everywhere; even the staircase has cupboards and shelves slotted into it. The bed upstairs is elevated on top of a sort of wardrobe. I say "sort of" because it's made to fit only guy stuff: shirts, jeans, underwear, socks. No hanging space for dresses. It's a one-dude pad, no doubt.

I watch Cam cook the eggs and make toast. Bread looks homemade, and I wouldn't be surprised if Cam was the baker. There are so many questions I want to ask him.

Patience, Ava. Eat your eggs. Then interrogate.

"Here you go. Hope they're okay."

Cam slides a plate in front of me. The scrambled eggs are perfect, buttery and soft but not sloppy. And they're topped with—

"Are these chives?"

"Yeah." Cam looks up from his own plate, uncertain. "Don't you like them?"

"I do," I say. "But where'd you get them?"

He points to the wall space beside the window, on which, now that his head's out of the way, I can see a pegboard. Kitchen utensils hang from rods and pots of herbs sit on small shelves, all stuck into the holes.

"Is this place all your design?" I have to ask, though the

smell of eggs and toast is urgently reminding me how hungry I am.

"Yup, though most was less design, more trial and error." He points his fork at my plate. "Eat."

Don't need to be told twice. I'd devour this table if it had enough butter on it.

I look up from shoveling food into my mouth to find Cam watching me.

"Doc Wilson said you and Nate don't eat enough," he says.

I cuss Doc yet again. I hate it when people know stuff about me before I'm ready to tell them. And even Doc doesn't know the whole truth. When I was exercise riding, the hours were long, and I got in the habit of living off protein bars because I could stuff them in a pocket and eat them on the fly. Management also expected me to stay small and light to replicate the feel of the jockey as much as possible. The combination of those pressures wasn't great, and I became seriously underweight for a time. The stables vet was the one who suggested I might want to boost my calorie intake. Said if she saw a horse that skinny, she'd sue the owner for neglect. Said no wonder I was tired all the time. So, I started making better choices around food. But the tiredness didn't go away.

I'm not ready to tell Cam the whole truth yet. As I said, I detest being pitied. "Nate's worse than I am," is what I say. "And it's not that I don't want to eat. I just get busy and forget."

"Have no clue how that works," says Cam. "If I were a

car, my gas gauge would be beeping at me before the tank was half empty."

Suddenly, I spot my chance to steer the conversation away from me and my stuff.

"You know, Shelby told me early on that you didn't talk much," I say. "And when we first met, you didn't. But now here you are, speaking in full sentences. What gives?"

Cam lifts his shoulders briefly, won't meet my eye. "Small talk's not my thing."

"Unsatisfactory answer, Hollander."

Seems I can eat my eggs *and* interrogate.

Cam pauses, which is usual. But then he comes out with another full sentence that freezes me in place.

"I wasn't in good shape when I came out of the army. Physically or … mentally. I kept my distance from people. Got out of practice. Some habits are hard to break."

Oh, God. That's deeply personal territory, and I had no right to push him into it. Especially when all I wanted was for us to stop talking about my personal stuff.

"Sorry," I say, and mean it. "That's more answer than I deserved. Let's change the subject. What would you normally be doing this morning if you didn't have to babysit me?"

I can't tell if he's glad of the segue or not. It occurs to me that my own habits have robbed me of a chance to get closer to him, and I almost backtrack. But then he gives me a crooked grin.

"Not sure babysitting is the best choice of word," he says. "Given … you know."

He brought it up. Not me.

I give him a flirty look. "You never had fantasies about your babysitters?"

Get a steady look in return. "Only one I ever had was my sister."

"*Okay.*"

I load the last of my eggs onto a square of toast and shove it in my mouth.

"That was delicious," I tell him. "Thank you."

"More coffee?"

"I shouldn't," I say. "Don't need any more nervous energy."

Aaand right on cue, I nose-dive into a crash. This is what it's been like for me for months. I used to be able to go and go all day, survive on little food and less sleep, and now it's as if my fuel tank's getting secretly siphoned off, leaving me with nothing but fumes. For a control-freak action-bunny like me, it's the worst punishment possible. And I've no idea what's causing it.

"Ava? You okay?"

As I said before, we Durants are masters of the poker face. When we're fully focused. Now that I've been caught in a weak moment, I could admit all my fears, let them tumble out and pile up for all to see. But Cam's right. Some habits die hard.

"Two things I'm not good at," I say. "Not the complete list, but it'll do for now. I hate not knowing if something's good or bad, and I hate having to wait to find out."

"Yeah," Cam says slowly. "That sucks."

I sense he's holding back, and my need to know overrides my need for caution.

"Doc say anything to you?" I ask.

Cam shrugs. "Tests. No more than that."

Uh-uh. No shrugging on my watch. "Did he seem worried?"

He goes super still.

Fuck. The last fume of energy evaporates and takes my self-control with it. I drop my face into my hands and try to breathe.

"Fuck," I mumble though my fingers.

Cam's hand lightly touches my shoulder.

"He's worried because he cares about you," he says. "Only natural."

Nice try, but his unease is palpable.

"Fuck!"

I jump up from the table, grab my plate and Cam's and take them to the sink. Run the water too hard and get a jet right in the face.

"FUCK!"

I start rubbing my eyes furiously until a calloused hand takes mine and gently pulls them down.

"Here."

Cam has a dishtowel, and he wipes my face like I'm a little kid. I half expect him to get a tissue and say, "Blow."

That's it. I'm officially a wrung-out wreck. Cam's chest is conveniently at head height, so I wrap my arms around him and rest my cheek on the soft flannel of his shirt and breathe deep the woody smell that probably never leaves him. His arms circle me in return and under his shirt, I can hear his heart's steady beat and feel his amazing muscles. A tiny spark of energy zings through me, but I don't want sex right now, I want comfort. Okay, sex would be good, too, but right now, I'm loving this hug.

"I can come with you," he says. "If you want. To the tests."

And I'm loving this offer. But I feel like I've already asked way too much of him.

"That would be boring for you," I say. "And I would be cranky. Want to re-think?"

"No."

Wow. I'm glad he doesn't seem in a hurry to break the hug, because I may want to rest against his chest forever.

"Are we getting off to a good start?" I ask him. "Or is this a complete shit show?"

Cam's ribs move up and down with silent laughter.

"My whole life's been a shit show," he says. "This is the best thing that's happened to me in … forever."

Wow, again.

I lift my head and look up at him, checking his expression for … what? Sincerity? He's frown-smiling, like you do when you're worried you've said too much. I have a sudden urge to be more honest with him than comes natural to me.

"Last night, before you asked me to dance," I tell him, "I was so unhappy, I wanted to feed myself to Nate and Shelby's pigs."

Now he's guilt-frowning. "Didn't mean to hurt you. It's just… I'm out of practice. Like I said."

His apology is sweet. He's a good guy. Maybe better than I deserve.

"Don't sweat it, Hollander." I mean it, and I hope he knows that. "It's done. Behind us."

Then I think about what's in front of us. Medical tests. Maybe results that will turn my life upside down…

This time, I'm focused, and the poker face is firmly in place. There's no way I'm ruining this moment by spewing my fears out like lava. But they're there, churning inside me. My urgent need now is more comfort. Lots more. I want to hide away here in Cam's flannel comfort house forever.

"Can I stay here tonight as well?" I ask him. "You can say no. I'll be cool about it."

He's hesitating. He's going to say no. I was totally lying about being cool.

"Doc said I wasn't to overtire you," he says.

Well, that was unexpected. It's usually me who brings sex back into the conversation. I mean, that *is* what he's referring to. Isn't it—?

As always, I opt for being direct.

"We can take breaks. And avoid – you know – positions that require serious cardio."

He goes super still again. I may have miscalculated…

"Might also be a good idea," he says, "if we locked the front door."

Chapter Eight

CAM

"Also, we need condoms," I say to Ava. "Which means I'll have to go to Martinburg."

All Verity has to offer on Sundays are alcohol, pizza, and ice cream. In no particular order.

"Could swing by your folks' place and pick you up a change of clothes?" I add.

Ava makes a face. "I can think of better ways to spend the afternoon," she says.

"So can I. And condoms are a non-negotiable part of that. Pill or no."

"But it's a forty-minute round trip to Martinburg," she protests.

Forty!? The Flora Valley Wines Dodge is slow, but it's not that slow. Round trip for me is an hour.

"How the hell fast do you drive?" I ask her.

She gives a guilty little grimace. "Maybe just a teensy bit over the speed limit…?"

Teensy. Right.

"You want me to get clothes?" I prompt.

She looks cute in my shirt, but even with sleeves rolled up about five times, she's swimming in it. Plus, she's going commando and it's not the weather for that at all.

"Is there anyone else you could borrow from?" she asks. "If you go to my parents' place, you'll get subjected to the full family inquisition. Believe me, it's destroyed stronger men than you."

I know she's being flippant, but the "stronger" gut-punches harder than it should. Once upon a time, I thought of myself as strong. Came to realize I had no idea what the word even meant. Spent the last few years trying to achieve some semblance of real strength, but most days, it feels like it's a goal I have no way of reaching. And I worry that Ava sees me as something I'm not.

She misreads my expression.

"Don't worry, my family will love you," she says. "That's another reason why you won't escape; they'll probably want you to move in."

One thing I've learned about Ava is that she's honest. What she says she means. I owe it to her to pull myself out of this funk and step up.

"Okay. I'll text Shelby," I say. "She and Nate have to come up for air some time."

"Tell him to eat," says Ava with a grin. "Food, I mean."

And then she gets up on tiptoe and kisses me lightly on the mouth.

You'd think that after the lecture I gave myself about

being responsible and showing self-control, that I'd kiss her lightly back and be on my way. Yeah. You'd think.

But she tastes so good, and it's been so goddamn long since I kissed someone I've truly wanted to kiss that I skip the lightly part and move right on through to heavily, my hands moving up under her shirt, my shirt, so there's a lot of room to maneuver. I'm relishing the feel of her skin. Commando might be a little chilly for her but it's legendary for me. I have free access to her glorious taut ass, and I cup it with both hands and lift her up and against me, my hard-on making it known that it wouldn't mind me going commando also.

Ava's arms are wrapped around my neck, and her tongue starts exploring mine in a way that sets off a worryingly intense reaction. Got to slow down, or self-control might not be an option. But I can hardly dump her on the floor. That's just rude.

Luckily the decision's made for me. Ava breaks the kiss.

"Go," she says against my mouth. "Oral sex is great, but I want you inside me."

My cock physically bucks, and it's all I can do not to forget everything I said about control and condoms. *Good work, Hollander. You talk big about resolve but put it to the test and you're as unyielding as a scrap of sawdust in a high wind.*

Turns out shame is a pretty good motivator, so I gently lower Ava down. She gives me an amused knowing smile. This time she's the one who can see the funny side, and I'm the one out of sorts.

Ava shoos me with a wave of her hand.

"Go!" she says. "Clock is ticking."

"Roger," I say, from habit. "I'm gone."

I start the Dodge, and let it warm up while I text Shelby about borrowing clothes for Ava. Pretty sure she won't answer, but—

Instant response.

Sure! Come over!!"

Shelby likes her exclamation marks. She is one of life's naturally positive people, and I'm grateful for all the slack she's ever cut me. Hope I repay her well enough by doing good work around the vineyard.

It's a three-minute drive to Shelby and Nate's door. I'm relying on the noise of the truck to prevent any surprise at my arrival. I know from recent experience how easy it is to get carried away.

Worked. Shelby opens the door before I knock. She's dressed. A little flushed but fully covered. I try not to think about Ava naked. Not good for your long-term employment prospects to give your boss an eyeful of crotch bulge.

"Cam!"

Shelby throws her arms round my waist and gives me a hug. Grabs my hand and pulls me inside, into the kitchen. Nate gets up from the table and gives me a look of inquiry.

"How's Ava?"

"She's doing fine," I say. "Doc Wilson checked her over again."

We both know what I'm not saying. But as the Doc said last night, what's the point in fretting until you have something to fret about? This is the day after Nate and Shelby's wedding. Fretting can wait.

"Coffee, Cam?" says Shelby.

"No thanks," I say. "Just came to see if Ava could borrow a change of clothes."

"Of course! I'll go grab some."

Off she runs upstairs.

I notice Nate's half-smile.

"Did Ava tell you to avoid the Durant household?" he asks.

"Pretty much."

"Good advice."

Nate drinks his coffee and makes no further comment.

Shelby races back in. Don't know where she gets her energy from. No wonder Nate's mainlining caffeine.

"Jeans, shirt, sweater, socks." She hands them to me. "No undergarments. Figured that would be weird."

Commando under jeans is a recipe for chafing. I'd better pick her up some briefs in Martinburg. Prophylactics and women's underwear. Could be a more embarrassing shopping list but I'm not sure how.

"Thanks."

Shelby beams at me.

"It's so great that you and Ava are a thing," she says.

Can't even look at Nate. I remember how I used to feel about my sister's boyfriends. And I'm not sure if Ava and I are a thing yet. It's not like we've really, you know, talked.

"Early days," I say, hoping that will put an end to it.

No such luck.

"Of course, Chiara thinks it's totally all her doing," Shelby says. "I reminded her that it was me who was there when you two first met. Not that I did anything about it, but I still call dibs."

So everyone in the county thinks we're a thing now. Great.

"Mom said it's about time," Shelby adds. "You're lucky she had to head back up the coast early, or she would have come around to celebrate with some kind of organic wine that smells like feet."

The mention of Lee gives me a jolt of guilt. Would have liked to be the one to tell her myself. She was always honest with me. Even when I hated her for it.

Not that there'd be much to tell yet. It is early days. Not even one day, and that's ticking by faster than I'd like. Everything's moving faster than I'd like.

"Gotta go," I say. "Thanks again."

"You two have dinner plans for tonight?"

"Shel, please," says Nate. "Have mercy."

I suspect he's speaking as much for himself as for me and Ava.

Shelby's uncrushable. "Okay. But come around soon."

Another quick hug and I'm free. Martinburg and the world's most embarrassing purchases, here I come.

On the road, I start wondering about Lee. Why did she have to head back to the coast so early? She's a self-employed artist, so her time's her own. It's not like she feels out of place here: Flora Valley Wines was her and her late husband's business; the house I just came from was their family home, and the whole town knows and loves her. I also know she'd been getting on well with Nate's mom, Ginny, so she'd have been welcome at the Durants. Seems odd that she didn't hang around to spend even a little time with her newly married daughter.

Maybe I should call her? Lee looked out for me. More than she should have, considering how ungrateful I was. She insisted on giving me what I needed, not what I wanted. Or what, on one occasion, I demanded. But I'll put that uncomfortable thought aside for now.

The Dodge barely has brakes let alone a hands-free phone system. I pull over and dial Lee's number. Straight to voicemail.

"Hi, it's me," I say, like an idiot. She knows who it is. "Just checking in. Seeing if you're okay."

I sit there in the Dodge for a few more minutes – like an idiot. No response. I check my mirrors and pull out. Phone stays silent all the way to Martinburg.

At the RiteAid, I get a box of Durex and a three-pack of cotton briefs. It occurs to me that I could come across as some kind of sex pervert, holding a woman hostage. But the guy at the checkout barely glances at me. Which is good because by now I'm so wound up, I look shifty as hell.

Doesn't help that I keep checking my phone, like I'm awaiting confirmation of a ransom drop. No call or text from Lee. I shouldn't be worried; she could be working on a new painting. Could have got all inspired at the wedding and rushed back to her studio to get started. Could be out in her garden.

Or could be she's been abducted by aliens or whirled to Oz in a tornado. Pointless to try and guess. Lee will get back to me when she's ready. My job's to start up the truck and drive.

Almost home. Pass the turnoff to Flora Valley Wines. Shelby would have said if there was anything wrong with Lee. Unless Lee didn't want to spoil her big day...

Give it a rest, Cam. Time to focus. Ava is only three minutes away. And as I'm the one currently in possession of the Hanes three-pack, she'll still be wearing no underwear.

I half expect Ava to hear the truck and open the front door. But it's me who opens it. No sign of her in the kitchen, either. Must be upstairs.

I have a moment of hesitation. Like I said, everything's moving way faster than I'm used to. Responsible Cam is muttering about letting Ava rest properly and reminding me that a good talk can be way more intimate than sex. But Primal Cam can't forget the feel of his hands on Ava's bare taut rear. And he takes the stairs two at a time.

There she is, lying on the bed. Room's warm now from the risen stove heat, and she's decided to ditch my shirt and, once again, greet me naked.

"Hey," she says, with a smile.

"Hey yourself," I reply, and dump my phone and purchases on the bedside shelf.

"Want to join me?"

Primal Cam knows a rhetorical question when he hears one. My boots and jacket got taken off downstairs, only shirt, jeans, and jocks to go. Forty seconds, tops.

Ava kneels on the bed. It's elevated, so she's at the perfect height to undo buttons and belts. I let her. The touch of her hands on my skin raises goosebumps. Raises something else, too.

Done. I am naked as a jaybird, as Doc Wilson almost certainly says. Ava reaches out to pull me onto the bed with her. Her eyes have that lust darkness to them, and she shivers all over when I run my thumb over one nipple, put my mouth to the other. We are both *very* ready for this and there's nothing – no Doc Wilsons, no lack of condoms – stopping us now.

My phone rings.

Chapter Nine

AVA

I do not frigging believe it. Not the phone ringing – given our luck so far, *that* I can believe. What I don't believe is that Cam stops to check who it is. He doesn't even hesitate. Sits right up like he hasn't been trailing slow kisses from my breasts downwards, like I haven't been arching in pleasure, begging him to get a move on because foreplay-schmoreplay – I'm ready!

The phone rings, and he freezes, and then it's like he forgets I even exist. He's off me and sitting on the side of the bed reaching for his phone in half a second. I'm so astonished, I don't even know how to react.

At least he doesn't answer it. But he does tap out a quick text. And he waits for a response. Blip. It arrives. Cam nods, slowly sets down his phone. And only then seems to realize what he's done. He turns around, face all guilty alarm. His mouth opens and shuts, as he obviously tries to figure out what to say to me. Guess I'll have to kickstart things myself.

"Must have been important."

"Fuck, I'm sorry, Ava," he says. "Just … I was worried and…"

He shakes his head, like he can't believe what just happened. Join the club.

"Who were you worried about?"

Cam swallows hard. He'd rather not tell me, but he's going to. Small point in his favor. Not that I would have let it go until he did.

"Shelby told me her mom left early this morning," he says. "And that's not like her. Lee's sociable. She wouldn't skip out and miss the day after her daughter's wedding. So, I got—"

"Worried. Yeah, I know."

I nod slowly. I don't want to fight. I want to get back to the sexy action. But my sexy hot feelings got instantly quashed when all the ones I hate most got roused. Vulnerability, weakness, ignorance – I see them all as a threat. And when I feel threatened, I tend to get pissy. I'm pretty frigging pissy right now.

"And were you right to worry?" I won't ease up. "What did she say?"

He forces himself to look at me. "Said she's fine. Thanked me for checking in."

His shoulders hunch up as he adds, "I'm sorry. Ava. Lee's an old friend and we look out for each other. But that doesn't excuse my shitty timing. Can we start again?"

Jesus. Now, I don't know if I'm pissy or amused. He looks so hangdog, so guilty. And it's nice that he cares about people so much. I just wish it was other people, and not beautiful, single Lee frigging Armstrong.

We'll have to have a conversation about why she has such a hold on him, but it can wait. I could let Cam stew for longer, but one of the upsides of being impatient is that you don't waste time on pointless activity. Okay, so I'm absolutely begrudging Lee Armstrong for coming between us but, frankly, I don't want to give her another thought. Right now, right here, it's only me and Cam. Who'd frigging better have switched off his phone.

"I'm sorry, Ava," he says again.

His shoulders are still all guilt-hunched. I tend to be wary before I trust, but Cam has only ever seemed sincere. Right now, that's good enough for me.

"Phone's off, right?" I say. "Not just on silent but completely dead?"

Cam looks like he doesn't dare be hopeful.

"Door's locked, too," he says. "Bolted and chained."

"Condoms within reach? Good brand, not some cheap, flimsy crud?"

"One hundred percent electronically tested."

Flicker of a smile with that. He's sitting straighter, too. Half-turned to me like he is, his abs are wondrously taut. I've dated gym-obsessives before, but Cam's muscle definition isn't like that. Gym guys look artificial, like they've been designed to fit the latest trend, which is currently that absurd combo of big muscle and super low-fat, aka "ripped". Cam's definitely got big muscles, but they look natural, like they've developed over time through physical work, not through pumping iron and chugging down creatine and whey.

Sexy hot feelings are starting to kick in again. I can feel my nipples tightening and my nether parts loosening. I lie back, propped on my elbows, back slightly arched so my perky breasts are on full display. Stretch my legs in a centerfold come hither pose.

Cam's got on his stunned-by-a-brick expression. If he goes all "I can't do this. You deserve better," I really will smack him one. There's only thing he needs to do now, and that's roll on one of those electronically tested bad boys and slide inside me pronto.

Luckily for him, Cam reads the room. There's a momentary lag as he breaks into the box (why so much annoying plastic?) But then I hear the beautiful sound of tearing foil, and here's Cam, his amazing, tantalizing cock fully sheathed, poised over me, his eyes staring into mine.

"You're sure?" he has to say because he's Cam.

In reply, I draw his hand downwards so he can discover how sure I am. On contact, he gives a small groan and screws his eyes shut. He'd better last the distance, or we'll be having words.

"Fuck," he breathes.

Then he opens his eyes and smiles at me, I could swear almost wickedly. Starts moving his finger and thumb, slow and steady, stimulating every erogenous part down there – including a couple I didn't know I had. Seems like a small hiatus was beneficial, even if I didn't appreciate it at the time. I'm so close to coming it's excruciating, the tension stiffening my whole body until I'm desperate for release.

But even though I know he knows I'm close, he won't pick up the pace. I get an inkling that this is our sexual destiny: me impatient, Cam refusing to be rushed. My orgasm is building and building, inexorable but oh, so goddamn slow. My breathing's ragged and I hate him for torturing me.

God, it's here, finally, the last big wave that will push me over the edge. And right then, Cam enters me. The sensation of his cock filling me, connecting with every nerve, triggers an orgasm that feels like it lifts me off the bed. It keeps coming – *I* keep coming – pulsing through me like I'm super-charged with electricity, my lady parts gripping Cam's cock, which is still moving inside me, slowing as my orgasm ebbs and my body goes limp as a rag.

I've been in la-la land, unaware of anything but orgasm. So selfish, but, I feel, earned. Now my breathing has returned to almost normal, I open my eyes. There he is, looking a little smug.

"Well, that's one," I say, to knock him off his perch.

He's smiling again.

"How many do you want?" he asks.

Touché.

"Limits only exist in your mind," I say. "I read that somewhere. Probably a locker room wall."

"Okay, then. We'll leave it open."

Cam's keeping his weight off me, resulting in a pleasing

view of his remarkable biceps. His cock is hard as ever, but parked up inside me, stationary. He's being true to his nature, no rush, taking his time. I know from our kitchen counter episode that Cam is quite capable of being crazed by lust, even though it was mostly me urging him on. The memory of him wanting me that badly brings out my inner imp. He thinks he's in control of this situation. He hasn't bargained with the determination of Ava Durant.

"Let's change it up," I say. "Position-wise."

Cam's expression shifts between interested and wary.

"Me on top," I add. "With a twist."

He seems reluctant to move. Fair enough; guess his cock's pretty happy where it is.

I slap him lightly on the shoulder. "Up and over, my guy."

A more pleasing flex of arm muscles as Cam cups my ass and pulls me over with him with minimum interruption of sexual connection. I settle myself on top, lay my palms flat on his abs, and relish the flinch of desire that instinctively drives his cock deeper into me. But he can only go so far because I am in charge of the rhythm, and I can lift myself up and, cruelly, off him. Or I can just let the tip of his cock in, which is both cruel and maddening. I'll do that for a short time, shall I?

Cam's glute muscles are fully engaged as he strives to get all the way in. His jaw is tight with frustration, and I know he's a nanosecond away from clamping my hips so he can take back control. Time for phase two: the twist.

I lift off him. He curses under his breath.

"Dammit, Ava."

"Stay cool," I tell him. "It'll be worth it."

I do a swift one-eighty turn, so I'm now facing away, and Cam has a view of my back and ass. Slowly, I lower myself down onto him again, and he groans and gives in to grabbing my hips. Thing is, in this position, I've got even greater control, especially as he's raised his knees a little, giving me more leverage. I also have easy access to his balls and his sensitive rear zone, along with my own front-facing erogenous go-tos, my breasts and clit. He is absolutely at my mercy and I'm going to drive him insane.

I love this position, and I let myself sink into the pleasure of it, moving slowly up and down the length of his shaft, letting my hands wander over my body and his. Setting my pace, despite Cam's clear wish to make more of a contribution.

Not seeing your partner's face means you lose a little something, but what you can't see, you can totally feel. And hear in their breathing and involuntary noises, including the odd expletive that lets you know you're on the right track. I reach down to cup Cam's balls and he swears quietly but with feeling. I lick a finger and run it from his balls southwards, and he bucks underneath me like I've plugged him straight into a power socket. Take that, Mr Slow and Steady.

His hands are so tight on my hips now, they'll probably leave marks. His own hips are driving upwards, all restraint gone now, and I hear a muttered stream of "Fuckfuckfuck." He's close and he's desperate. I won't let him suffer too much longer. But first, a little attention to my own needs.

I prize one of his hands off my hip and place it on my breast. My other hand gets busy with my own pleasure, and with every gasp I make, I feel Cam get more and more worked up. He's caught between wanting to do right by me but worrying that his balls will literally explode if he doesn't come soon.

I don't know if it's on purpose or an accidental reflex, but he tweaks my nipple hard, and it's enough to send me over the edge. The instant I start, he drives his cock into me in strong hard thrusts until I feel the surge of heat as he comes with a shout of relief and release.

My finger is still on my clit, which starts protesting at the pressure. So, I give it a break and let myself sink onto Cam's knees, drawn all the way up now, and rest my head on folded arms. I wouldn't be able to do this if he wasn't so goddamn tall, and I'm making the most of it.

Under my ass, I can feel Cam's diaphragm heaving up and down, as he gets his breath back. His cock is jumping lightly inside me, still hard but not for too much longer.

Cam's hands slide off my hips and start to fondle my ass.

"So," he says. "What do you call this position?"

"No idea," I tell him over my shoulder. "But I like to think of it as the position where I got you to lose control."

"That important to you?"

I shrug, which isn't an answer. "It's fun."

"You know, I'm four times your size," he says. "I could

pin you to the bed, no problem."

"Sounds like a plan." I grin.

His cock is slipping now, and he carefully extracts himself. I dismount, so to speak, and lie back on the bed to enjoy the sleepy post-orgasm glow, and the fact that it's Cam who has to trot all the way downstairs to the bathroom to deal with the condom.

The ceiling of Cam's bedroom is simply but beautifully constructed. I stare up at it, listening to the quiet noises from downstairs. All of a sudden, like it's emitting a subsonic message, I become acutely aware of Cam's phone. I trust that he turned it off, I really do. But what if he only thought he did, and I can see what Lee Armstrong actually texted him?

I trust that he told me the truth about what she said, too. But it's those little touches, the emojis, the xx's, that change a standard message into one that's more … intimate.

What I should do is ask Cam straight out. Ask him about Lee, and their shared past. What I shouldn't do is snoop.

But it's calling to me, like some possessed object. And all I have to do is roll over and quickly tap the screen. Work of a moment.

Cam must have been already halfway up the stairs. His bare feet don't make the noise of his boots. He comes through the door, glass of water in each hand, to find me lying on the edge of the bed, arm outstretched, one hand on his phone.

He looks appalled, and I don't blame him.

Shit. What now?

Chapter Ten

CAM

The rational part of me understands why Ava would want to check my phone. I mean, I quit in the middle of foreplay to read Lee's text, which Ava took amazingly well, considering. And no doubt I sounded pretty cagy when I explained why I was worried. Someone as smart as Ava would know immediately that there was a whole lot more behind that story. She didn't press me, which, again, was generous of her, but I can understand why she might have unanswered questions. And why she might want to look for some of those answers on my phone.

But the rest of me feels gut punched. By checking on me, she's highlighted that I fucked up. I acted in the moment without thinking, and like all the other times I've done that, it's turned everything to shit. We were in a good place, and I ruined it by being a knucklehead. Sometimes, I wonder if I'm capable of being anything else. No matter how hard I try.

Ava's sitting up now, her face a mixture of guilt and defensiveness. I'm standing here holding the water glasses. We're in a silent stand-off, me trying to ride my wave of emotions, Ava trying to work out how to explain. The pause is weighing heavy on both of us.

"She took you from me last night," says Ava, who was, let's face it, most likely to break the silence first. "And you went with her without hesitating. You answered her text without hesitating. I feel like I'm being kept out of a loop. The Cam and Lee loop. And I hate that."

I admire her honesty. Wish I was brave enough to say what I feel straight out, and not be choked by the worry that it'll be the wrong thing.

"I wanted to see if she'd put love heart emojis or kisses on the text," Ava goes on. "Or I *didn't* want to see them, if you know what I mean…"

Time I said something. Ava's doing all the heavy lifting here. Be good if I also stopped holding these water glasses in a death grip.

"Do you want me to show you?" I say.

"Do you want me to see?" she counters.

There you have it. A question I don't quite know how to answer. My friendship with Lee has always been private. No one but us knows what we've talked about and what we've revealed to each other or confessed. If her late husband, Billy, ever had a problem with Lee and I spending time together, he never let on. I doubt he did, because Billy was like Shelby, a hundred percent open and honest to the point of oversharing. He trusted everyone and because of that, no one ever took advantage of him. The community here could see he was something special, and so they decided to repay his trust by looking out for him.

Shelby, like a mini-Billy, has never once questioned her mom's friendship with me. Never once asked me about it. Ava's the first to put me on the spot, and I'm not sure what response would be the right one.

Ava interprets my hesitation in her own way.

"All right, it's none of my business how you talk to each other," she says. "I don't need to see your texts. I just want to know… Is she going to be a constant third wheel in our relationship?"

This question I can answer.

"Like I said, Lee's an old friend and we look out for each other," I say, "but she's only a friend."

"So, if she texted right now with a problem and asked you to drive on up the coast to help her, would you?"

"No, I wouldn't," I assure her. "Might make a couple of calls to rope in someone else to help, but I wouldn't abandon you."

Ava looks like she wants to be convinced but hasn't quite got there yet.

The damn water glasses are freezing my hands into blocks of ice. Doesn't help that I'm completely naked and have been standing stock still for the last few minutes. I walk over to the bed, hand Ava a glass, and set the other down beside my phone.

"Okay if I get back in bed?" I ask.

"It's your bed," she says, with a wry little smile.

I get in beside her, and we sit upright, sipping on water, not talking.

"I'm sorry," Ava says, in a quiet voice. "Shouldn't have snooped."

"I should've left my phone downstairs," I say. "Left it alone period."

Lesson learned. Hard way, as usual.

Ava's silent. I risk a glance at her, and she's staring straight ahead, not smiling. I realize how much I've come to appreciate—and rely on—her openness and honesty. Helps orient me, helps me know which direction I need to head. But I can't keep relying on other people to take the lead—Billy, Lee, Shelby and now Ava. I have to start setting my own course before I forget how it's done.

"I can tell you about me and Lee," I offer before I can have second thoughts. "Just warning you, though, I don't come out of it looking good."

That startles her, and I'm suddenly caught in the spotlight of her frank, blue gaze. Her eyes are quite something, bright and clear like a cut gemstone. I recall cringing when my mom gushed over Paul Newman's blue eyes, but now I see she had a point.

"You said she helped you at a bad time," Ava says. "That's enough for me, for now."

She reaches across me to place her empty water glass on the one bedside shelf. Her arm brushes across my stomach and I feel my abs contract and my cock start to stir. But Ava and I need to get back to a better place emotionally before we start getting physical again.

She's back to staring at me, a small frown creasing her forehead. Ava has amazing skin as well, pale but perfect, like a Renaissance Madonna. Only without the gold halo. Or the holy infant.

"I've never had a really close friend," she tells me. "When I was growing up, us Durant kids were so busy with sports and studying and, you know, generally striving to be the most high-achieving humans on the face of the planet, that none of us had time for friends."

She scoots around on the bed so she can sit cross-legged, facing me. It's hard not to be distracted by her nakedness but Ava is completely unselfconscious. I guess if you've been an athlete all your life, you become so in tune with your body that you stop noticing it.

"I mean, sure," she adds, "we hung out with our schoolmates, but after that we all scattered to the four winds, pursuing our different goals: me to Notre Dame then Kentucky and horses; Nate to Harvard, France, and wine; Danny straight to classic cars in LA; Izzy to MIT and Max to Juilliard. Did I mention we were high achievers? Danny's probably the most social of all of us, and Izzy and Max have each other, like twins do. Nate and I, though … we were always loners. If we don't have any close friends, I guess we have no one to blame but ourselves."

She screws up her mouth.

"I envy you, is what I'm trying to say," she tells me. "Envy you for having Lee. Envy you and Nate for having Shelby. *I* want to be your best friend as well as your lover, but I guess that position is filled."

There's the hint of a question at the end of that sentence. Close as proud Ava will ever get to pleading.

I'm considering how best to answer … too slow, as usual. Ava shivers all over, like a dog shaking off water, and fixes on a smile.

"Besides, you never did answer my earlier question about what you'd normally be doing today," she says.

My brain cycles backward. "Didn't I?"

"No, we got distracted by talk of babysitters," she says with a grin.

"Oh … yeah."

Water glass is empty. I set it down. Feeling slightly embarrassed about what I'm about to say. Ava's a skilled and experienced horsewoman, whereas I—

"I volunteer at a riding school for kids with disabilities."

"Right." Ava nods. "Shelby mentioned that."

Of course she did. And people wonder why I keep myself to myself.

"I needed something to take me out of myself, force me to focus on other people," I say. "Something that gives back to the community."

"Lee's idea?"

Ava's tone is light, but I know what I say next matters.

"Kind of a joint plan. I like kids."

"And you're a good rider?"

I knew she'd go there. People assume that because you work with horses, you're basically a horse whisperer. I know Shelby's made that assumption. I also know I've been too embarrassed to set her right.

"My sister, Blair, is a fine horsewoman," I tell her. "Me, not so much."

"How many times have you fallen off?" Ava is grinning.

This is humiliating.

"Think the worst was when Blair gave me a leg up and I tumbled right over the other side."

"Your sister sounds strong."

"Can carry a hay bale in each hand."

Ava folds back so she's lying on the bed again and gives into laughter. Me and my fragile male ego try to maintain our dignity.

"Then why horses?" she says, still smiling. "Why not —I don't know—rescue dogs?"

Shit. The answer to that lies in a very dark place. But Ava has been so open with me…

She picks up on my sudden stillness, and sits up again, smile gone.

"You don't have to tell me," she says. "About your reasons. About Lee."

My turn for a smile, a rueful one.

"You've got to stop giving me an out," I say. "If we're to do this, you have to know stuff about me. Stuff that's … not pretty."

I see her acknowledge the truth of that. See her hesitate, too. I'd do the same in her place. Sometimes secrets are better left unsaid. Trouble is, you don't always know which until it's too late.

"Can you tell me about the riding school first?" she says. "Maybe I could help out there, too?"

"Sure. We always need volunteers. How about you come out with me next Sunday?"

"What would I do? Teach the kids to ride?"

"It's not so much about learning to ride, more about how the experience of being on a horse gives them confidence. Some of these kids have intellectual as well as physical disabilities, and the team who work directly with them are all trained-up health professionals. The volunteers … we're just there to walk alongside, give extra support. And to do the stable work," I add.

"Done plenty of that in my life," says Ava. "What other skills are they looking for?"

"You need patience, and you need to be calm," I say. "And you need to like kids."

Ava stares at me for a beat. "Is zero-point-five out of three acceptable?"

"Where'd you score the half point?" I ask, amused.

"I quite like kids," she says. "I've met a couple who were pretty cool."

Guess everyone has these critical moments when you're starting out in a relationship. When you realize what the deal-breakers are. Like how much you trust each other. And what paths you both want to go down in life.

But I'm leaping ahead. I've promised to tell Ava about my past and when I do there'll be no taking it back. We might be over before we've even got started.

Chapter Eleven

AVA

Cam's going to spill about him and Lee, and part of me wants to shove a pillow over his face and hold it down until he stops twitching. Setting aside the fact that he could lift me and the pillow off him with one hand, I know that won't solve my problem. Because the problem is me. If Cam shares his secrets, then I should share mine. And I'm not even sure I've admitted them fully to myself yet.

Feeling vulnerable sucks. Jealousy sucks. Waiting, not knowing and being anxious suck big time.

"Do we need alcohol for this?" Asking for a friend.

"I'm all out of mandarin juice and refined rowan berry," he replies.

"Nate said he saw a cocktail on the menu at Bartons with octopus' milk in it."

Cam goes quiet.

"How do you—?"

"Very carefully."

"O-kay." Cam swings his legs over the side of the bed. "I was going to say alcohol was a bad idea. But now I have that picture in my mind, two beers it is."

I'm ashamed to say I look to see if he grabs his phone on the way out. He doesn't. Which is good. But the stupid thing is packed full of his conversations with Lee, to the point where I still feel like she's partly in the room. Which is bad.

I could really use that beer.

Cam's back. I admire his full naked glory framed in the doorway before he slides under the blankets and gives a quick all-over shiver.

"Damn, it's cold out there," he says.

"Out there?" I frown. "You were naked and went outside?"

"Just behind the workshop. It's where I keep the beer," he replies. "Fridge is too small."

He has a bottle of said beer in each hand. A local IPA. He hands me mine. It's certainly chilled, he's right about that.

I have questions. "Doesn't it freeze solid?"

"Made a box for it. Cedar because it's rot resistant. Insulated with wood shavings. Lined with an old copper washtub so I can fill it with ice in summer."

The weirdest feeling shoots through me, radiates from my gut right out to the tip of every nerve. It's like I want to cry, but with joy or sadness, I can't tell. Both, I guess. I feel safe but scared, excited but wary, open-hearted but desperate to run and hide. All because of a stupid handmade beer cooler. What the actual?

Oh, shit. I think I have it. Cam makes things by hand. He is a handy man, a craftsman. Growing up a Durant, the only thing we were expected to build was a track record of success. Mitch, our dad, didn't even care about money that much. Well, not as much as what it signified: that you'd made it to the top of your field. That's why he was okay with us kids following whatever path we chose—Nate into wine, Danny into cars, Izzy into science, Max into music, and me into horses. Didn't matter *what* we did, so long as we were super successful at it. So long as we never settled for second best. And never quit.

The rest of my family thinks Mitch has mellowed since his recent health scare, citing the fact that he's begun hugging people—even his own family—as evidence. But even if old Mitch's view of the world has a rosier tint thanks to narrowly averting a date with death, there's nothing happening to provoke him. Nate's happily married and turning Flora Valley Wines around. Danny's car business grows exponentially every year. Max and Izzy are top of their respective classes. What's not to like?

Me. That's what. Ava Durant. The quitter. Now that's guaranteed to snap Mitch out of his mellow trance. I've been on the receiving end of our father's scorn, and it can peel skin. I escaped it most of the time by becoming prickly—the time-honored porcupine defense—and by focusing only on what I could excel at, namely athletics and horses. Now I don't have either of those. I'm twenty-seven, and I'm already washed up and broken down.

And that's why I went all weird when Cam described

his beer cooler. Cam fixes things. He fixes them thoughtfully, intuitively and with a real affinity for his materials. He's patient and calm and takes his time to ensure his work is both functional and beautiful.

My subconscious hopes he might be able to fix me. There. Nailed it. So to speak.

Goddammit, Freud. If you were alive, I'd brain you with an upcycled copper washtub.

Cam fixes things. But for him to fix me, I'd have to admit to him that I'm broken. I'd have to let that secret out into the world, along with all the judgment and pity it will no doubt unleash. Okay, I don't believe Cam will judge or pity me, but he might draw away from me. If I really am ill, then I could be a burden to him. And I refuse to be a burden to anyone.

"You don't like IPA?"

Cam's smiling but there's a shade of concern in his brown eyes. He's about to share secrets and I've just decided to hold mine close ... until I know exactly what I'm dealing with, and how to handle it. Until I feel more in control.

"I love IPA," I say. "Just waiting until it doesn't feel like it could be used for cryogenics."

"Bartons hotel has a special warm beer on tap for Ted's British friends."

"A man who makes a cocktail with octopus' milk is capable of anything."

Cam slumps into the pillows behind him and sighs. Is he having second thoughts about telling me about him and

Lee? That would solve a few of my problems. Not the least being the stab of jealousy I feel every time I think about her.

"Lee," he says, because of course. "Do you want the whole story, or do you want me to cut straight to the worst bits?"

"Do the worst bits make sense without the background?" I ask.

He upends his beer and finishes it. Sets it on the floor. Sighs. "Whole story it is."

Suddenly, I need to pee. Stupid body, always letting me down. I can hold it. No way I'm leaving this room now.

Cam's gone super still and quiet. Our arms are touching, and I can smell his musky, woody scent with a top note of IPA. All I want to do right now is press my whole body against his and breathe him in. But if I move even an inch, I'll spook him. And though I am deeply conflicted about what's coming, I've no right to let my own fears get in the way. And maybe—just maybe—a little of his courage might transfer across to me.

"Okay…" Cam exhales, and then rolls his shoulders, like he's preparing to step in and break up a bar fight.

"Okay," he says, again, and then the next words come out in a rush. "So, you know I was in Afghanistan and … shit happened, and I got invalided out and came home in a bad way, not just physically but, you know, in the head. I mean, not like that makes me special. Everyone there who wasn't a complete psychopath got scarred, so … shit…"

He's hit a wall. Should I help him over?

"Thing is, when you're back home, you can't talk about it."

He's made it. Only just, though. His breathing is really rapid and shallow.

"You can't talk about it because you freak people out. People want to believe that if their country ever has to enter another major war, that their army will know what to do. Their soldiers will be highly trained and organized, and the leaders will have a plan. They don't want to hear about chaotic skirmishes and collateral damage and kids who…"

His chest stops moving, like he can't breathe. This is hard enough for me to sit and watch. What must it be like for him, reliving that time?

"People only want to hear about success and heroics because anything else is too terrifying for them," he says quietly. "So, you never talk about what really happened. And that … has a cost."

Wow. And here I am believing I know what it's like to not feel safe to tell the truth. This puts my petty little fears in the shade. But now's not the time. This moment, I'm focused on Cam.

"When I got my discharge," he goes on, "I went home to see my parents in Wyoming. But I only lasted a couple of days there. Don't get me wrong, my parents are great, but I couldn't handle how worried they were about me and how they tiptoed around me, not wanting to upset me. So I went to Oregon, to my sister, Blair. That was better. Blair's the nurturing kind but she also doesn't take any shit. She made me get out and do farm chores, look after the goats. Tried to teach me to ride…"

For the first time, I see the hint of a smile. I realize I've not been breathing properly either and I quietly let out the air I've been holding.

"Does she have any video footage?" I ask.

"Pretty sure I deleted it all."

He pauses again because we both know what comes next. Or, rather, who.

"Blair and her husband, Jake, were happy for me to stay as long as I wanted," he says. "But I couldn't. Their life wasn't perfect by any means, but it still highlighted for me everything I didn't have … everything I thought I didn't deserve to have."

This time, the small smile is rueful.

"I have Lee to thank for that last part."

Here we go. I could legitimately ask for a toilet break but the sooner this is over, the better.

"I left Blair's with no plan. It was getting into winter, so I decided to go west. Started off hitchhiking but, amazingly, not too many people want to stop for a big, scruffy guy with a thousand-yard stare. So, I caught buses, the odd train. Slept rough most nights. Ended up in Santa Rosa. Saw that it was only twenty miles to the beach, and I hadn't seen the sea in years. So I stuck out my thumb. And Billy Armstrong picked me up."

"Shelby's dad."

"Lee's husband."

Got to admit, I don't like the way he emphasized that.

"Billy was a special kind of man," Cam tells me. "He believed that everyone wanted to do good. Just that some had never learned how … or had forgotten. Billy wasn't a rescuer, though. He was a connector. He wanted to connect—or re-connect—people with the good inside them, so they could do good."

Cam shakes his head, smiling. "He was a *terrible* driver, but a really great man."

"I feel sad I didn't get to meet him," I say.

Cam turns his head and plants a kiss on my temple. "He'd have loved you."

"Sounds like he loved everyone," I say, then regret it as petulant. And needy, let's not forget that.

"True. But Billy still saw *you*, if you know what I mean. He saw me that day he picked me up. He saw the damage and he saw the need. Said he had a place for me to stay, and some work if I wanted it. Brought me here."

Cam gestures around. His place. His home now.

"Back in the day, it'd been used as a woodshop for carpentry and joinery, and there were still some ancient woodworking tools hanging on the walls. Billy had equipped it with some basic power tools—electric saw, planer—but most times he found it quicker to go to the hardware store. Don't know why Billy thought I might be interested in working with wood—it was his superpower, I guess, seeing what you can't. But I wasn't ready for that. Billy gave me a camp bed and blankets, and directions to their house and said I was welcome to join them for dinner. Said he and his wife, Lee, had four kids but only two were still living at home. That was Shelby and her little sister, Frankie."

Moving this along. "So ... you went to dinner and met Lee?"

"Nope." Cam shook his head. "Stayed put. The place had power, an old outdoor toilet and running water. Had some food that I ate cold. Sat out in the woods for hours. Slept. Did that for eight days."

"They left you alone for eight whole days?" I'm amazed. "Not even a tuna casserole left on the doorstep?"

Cam screws up his face. "Like I said, Billy wasn't a rescuer. He wasn't going to force me to do anything. Had to be my choice."

"What finally got you up to their house?"

"Ran out of food," says Cam. "Considered nuts and berries, but I wouldn't know an edible berry from one that would kill me soon as it passed my lips. Briefly wondered how long I could last on water alone, but I'm not like you—I *have* to eat. Followed Billy's directions, knocked on the door. It opened, and there she was—"

His very good friend. His text pal. Lee Armstrong.

"—the most beautiful woman I'd ever seen in my life."

I think I'm going to throw up.

Chapter Twelve

CAM

I'm about to add, "until I met you" but I don't get a chance.

"Gotta pee," declares Ava, and she dumps her beer bottle on the floor, scrambles out of bed and hightails it down the stairs, like she's being chased by the demon of incontinence.

Or by some other demon. She said before that she was afraid Lee would be a third wheel in our relationship, and I haven't exactly helped ease that concern. I should have just said, "And that's when I first met Lee", but like an idiot, I plunged into the "most beautiful woman" quicksand. Communication has never been my strength. I've talked more to Ava in the last day than I've talked to anyone in the past eighteen years. Except Lee, of course.

Shit.

It's quiet downstairs, and I have a sudden fear that Ava

might have left. Grabbed a jacket of mine and ran off into the cold. Because I'm an idiot.

I'm half out of bed when I hear her feet on the stairs. She's walking slowly and leans on the doorway looking kind of pale.

"You okay?"

I sound worried. I am worried. What with one thing and another, I'd almost forgotten that Ava isn't well. That she's about to undergo a battery of medical tests because the doctor doesn't know what's wrong with her. And here am I using up all the oxygen and tiring her out with my lame-ass story.

"I hate Lee Armstrong," she says.

"O—"

"I mean, I really fucking hate her."

"Got it."

Ava schleps over and falls on top of the bed face first. Lets out a muffled, "Gah!"

Can't help it. I laugh.

"Not funny," she says into the crumpled-up blanket.

Then she slowly rolls over onto her back and gives me the side-eye.

"The most beautiful woman you've ever seen in your life?"

"I was about to add 'until I met you'."

Ava snorts. Which is all that deserves.

I'm propped up on one elbow, looking down on her. She's still pale, but she's smiling. And she *is* the most beautiful woman I've ever seen. Her beauty is outside and inside, too—in her spirit, and in her courage. Not many people would openly admit to feeling jealous like she just has. I'm finding it hard enough to get this story out and I haven't even got to the bad part.

"I'm not good at this communication thing," I say. "I'm sorry."

"I'm not good at sharing," says Ava. "I was competitive right out of the womb. Used to scream the place down if I saw Nate with something I wanted. Didn't matter what the thing was. The fact that Nate had it and not me was enough."

"You won't have to share me with Lee," I say.

And then I wonder how true that really is. Lee is my friend, after all. But friends are different from lovers, right?

Ava's still smiling, but it has a knowing twist to it.

"Short of locking you in this place and never letting you out again, I'll have to share you with everyone. Shelby, Nate, the whole Flora Valley Wines team, my family." She pauses. "And Lee…"

She reaches a hand behind my neck and pulls me down to her for a kiss. Her mouth against mine is hungry and urgent, her tongue sending pulses of lust down my body until I'm groaning with need.

And then she pushes me off.

"But I'm the only one you do this with, comprende?" she says.

I can only nod. The blood hasn't come all the way back up to my brain yet.

In one fluid movement, Ava converts from prone into a cross-legged sitting position. How does she *do* that?

"And now," she says, "on with the story. We were up to the part where you met the most beautiful woman you'd ever seen in your life—"

"—until I met you." Better late than never.

"Noted." Ava flips her hand in a shooing motion. "Move along."

I'm aware that a portion of the blood supply that should be back in my brain hasn't made it. It's still down south and sending signals that it wants attention. I know I promised to tell the whole story, but I think I'll stick to the edited highlights. Or lowlights. Definitely more of those.

"So, I finally had dinner with Billy, Lee, Shelby, and Frankie. Lee made me have a shower first and gave me some of her sons' old clothes, Shelby's older brothers. Fair enough, I was rank. Frankie was fourteen and so I was of no interest to her whatsoever. But Shelby kept staring at me across the table until Lee told her to stop. Shelby apologized but said it was because I reminded her of an old dog they'd had who was part Irish Wolfhound, part Leonberger, basically a huge, hairy mutt. Billy laughed and told me this was a compliment. If I reminded Shelby of one of their beloved pets, that meant she thought I was okay. Once I got to know Shelby, I realized this was true, but all I could hear at the time was that I was no better than a mongrel dog."

"You were in a bad place," says Ava. "Hard to see straight."

"Billy asked if I wanted handyman work round the

property. Flora Valley Wines ran on a shoestring budget, so he couldn't pay me much, but I was welcome to stay rent-free in the old workshop. The wood burner stove could be fixed up. He could get a loan of a bar fridge."

"Your very own doghouse," says Ava gently.

"How I saw it, too. My first instinct was to run a mile and get away from these nice, deluded people. But there must have been one last grain of common sense lodged in my head because I said yes."

There was also a grain of masculine pride. Even feeling like a mongrel dog, I'd been taken enough by Lee to want to impress her. To want to know her better. But that's probably not an admission for right now.

"Plus, you had a crush on Lee," says Ava matter-of-factly.

"How did you—?"

"Most beautiful woman? Remember?"

Jesus, all right, got it. No point in tiptoeing around.

"First few weeks, I barely said a word to anyone. Did what Billy asked me. Pretty simple work, kind I'd been used to back home and on Blair's farm. Shelby was busy learning the ropes of the winery from Billy. Frankie was at school, and Lee was doing arty stuff and looking after the garden. They'd say hi in passing but otherwise left me alone. They could see I wasn't starving to death, that I'd bought some clothes and was relatively clean. Looked like I was managing okay, so they left me to it."

"But you weren't managing okay."

"Not even close," I acknowledge.

"Cam, you had PTSD," says Ava. "Didn't anyone tell you that?"

Plenty. But what did it matter? Didn't change anything knowing what I was feeling had a label. Didn't make it better.

"Army wanted to set me up with a counselor," is what I tell her. "But I don't much care for being pitied."

"Ugh," says Ava with feeling. "I know what that's like."

"I underestimated the Armstrongs, though," I say. "They might have left me alone, but they were watching all the time. They knew I wasn't okay, and they also knew that if they tried to help in any obvious way, I'd be out of there quicker than a blink. Like I said before, Billy wasn't a rescuer. He was—"

"A connector." Ava nods.

"One day, about three months in, I was walking past the storage shed and Billy called me over. Some of the wine barrels were broken, and he asked if I could fix them up as he couldn't afford new ones. I knew nothing about barrels but how hard could it be? They're only a bunch of wooden slats held together with metal bands. I'd seen IKEA bookcases that were more complicated. We bundled the broken barrels into the truck and offloaded them at the workshop. And that was the start of a very steep learning curve."

"Let me guess," says Ava. "Making barrels is hard?"

"*So* fucking hard," I say. "I found out later that in the old days, you had to apprentice to a master cooper, to learn"—I make air quotes—"'the secrets and mysteries' of the trade.

Whereas ignorant me was convinced I could learn it all on my own. If it hadn't been for my stubbornness, I would have quit after the first day."

"Billy lit a fire under you."

"There's a literal fire in coopering called a cresset," I tell her. "It warms the staves so you can bend them enough to tighten the last metal hoops and form the final barrel shape. That process is called trussing, in case you wanted to know."

"I didn't, but thanks anyway."

We share a grin, and my memory contrasts this picture with one of Past Cam, scowling, swearing, wrestling with those first barrels. Past Cam was not a happy human...

"You learned, though." Ava's prodding me along again.

"Carried that first successful barrel into Billy's storage shed myself. He looked it over and pronounced it 'pretty good'."

"Ouch."

"Yep, that stung. But stubborn me was like the Incredible Hulk: I could not be stopped. I researched like a madman, got all the right equipment, like a draw-shave knife and the aforementioned cresset. Ordered all kinds of different woods to test them out. And then I made barrel after barrel. Tore my hands to shreds, wrecked my back and got burned more than once."

"By the cresset?"

"Good guess."

Ava smiles. I lean down for another kiss, but she puts her finger across my mouth.

"This is all very interesting," she says. "But we need to skip to Lee. *I* need you to skip to Lee."

Okay. I blow out a breath.

"She came down to the workshop to tell me a load of wood had arrived. American white oak, from a small supplier I'd found in the back blocks of the Appalachians. By now I'd learned how different wines work with different woods. Flora Valley makes pinot noir, and American white oak gives it a creamier flavor. French oak adds a touch of silkiness and spice."

"Lee now," says Ava. "Wood later."

"No, see, the thing is, that's exactly what I told Lee," I explain. "I waxed all poetical about oak when I'd barely said six words to her in as many months. And for the next hour, we had an actual conversation that started with oak and roamed all over, into art, and craft, and nature, and … doing what you love."

"No love," says Ava. "Bad word."

"But that's when I realized," I say, "that I loved making barrels. That I was good at it—finally—and would only get better. I realized I could be a master cooper and do this for the rest of my life. I almost cried."

"Ugh," says Ava, folding her arms. "You and she bonded. Over lumber."

"We did," I admit. "And Lee started coming over regularly. We'd have a beer, and we'd talk. She was patient and a good listener, and she wanted me to be happy. I opened up to her."

"Ugh," says Ava again.

"Don't worry," I tell her. "It goes downhill from here."

I see Ava tense. She's not looking forward to this part, and she doesn't even know what I'm going to say.

And, suddenly, I can't go there. Can't go back to that time, back to that version of me I've spent years trying to leave behind. Back to those emotions: the anger, the shame, the guilt. The fear that I'd ruined everything through my stupid, thoughtless impulse. Again.

"Oh," Ava breathes. She reaches up and cups my face, gently, in her hand. Her bright blue eyes search mine, and it takes every bit of willpower I have to hold her gaze.

"You know what?" she says, and I see a small, so very welcome smile. "I think we've both had enough upheaval these last twenty-odd hours. Weddings, medical emergencies, disturbing cocktail ingredients, hot sex. Why don't we just chill for the rest of the day? Lie here, have another beer. Talk about, I don't know, trussing. Or geese. Or how funny you look on a horse…"

She's giving me an out. I shouldn't, but I'll take it.

"I look funnier sprawled on the ground beside the horse," I say.

Ava laughs. I like the sound.

"I could share some personal stuff about me in return?" she says.

"Such as…?" I know it's good to share, but Ava's right. Last twenty-odd hours have been full-on.

"Such as … I like metal music?"

That I can handle.

"More of a classic rock guy myself."

"I would never have guessed," she says with a grin. "Um … what else? You already know I drive fast, and that I'm impatient, competitive and hate sharing."

I nod. "But you're also kind," I tell her. "And you're honest. I admire that."

Ava's smile fades and her expression grows thoughtful.

"Actually," she says slowly. "I have something way more important to share with you."

"Okay…" I'm wary again.

"I'm starving," she says. "What's for dinner?"

Chapter Thirteen

AVA

I know, I know. That wasn't real sharing. Not after everything he told me ... and almost told me. It took a lot of courage on his part, which only highlights the lack of mine. But we're in a good space right now, a lighter space, which is more what I need.

Trouble is, I do have one more really important thing to tell him, and it is this: I do not like pumpkin. I do not like it in festive pies, nor in a latte with cream and spice. I do not like it in a soup. I think it looks like baby poop. I do not like it baked or boiled. If a meal has pumpkin, then it's spoiled. (Channeling my inner Dr Seuss. You're welcome.)

Cam's been looking in his fridge and pantry for dinner ingredients. He's pulled out a pumpkin. The time to speak up is now.

"I was going to make a jack-o'-lantern with this," he says, "but Halloween has come and gone."

"Shelby and Nate's pigs'll love it," I suggest. Firmly.

Cam gives me a look. "Not a pumpkin fan?"

"If Nate had a plate of pumpkin, I'd let him keep it. Tells you all you need to know."

Cam grins and puts the world's worst vegetable back in the pantry where it can stay until it rots.

"Okay, so I've got macaroni," he says, "and some Monterey jack."

"Milk? Flour? Butter?"

Shakes his head. "Should have checked supplies before I went to Martinburg."

I forgive him. He got me underpants and condoms instead.

"I can eat macaroni with grated cheese on it," I say.

"I'd sooner eat wood shavings," he replies. "Shit. Looks like I'm heading into Verity for pizza."

Verity's one pizza parlor is terrible. The tourists keep it in business, but the locals only go there if they're drunk or hungover or have been on a keto diet for way too long.

Cam's pocket makes a brr-brr sound. We're both clothed again, by the way. Shelby's jeans fit me perfectly, but I've put Cam's flannel shirt back on because it's soft and smells like him. He's also in a flannel shirt and jeans, so we're twins. If twins looked nothing alike and were committing incest. Bad simile. Bad.

Brr-brr. Cam pulls out his phone and immediately, I tense up. But he frowns at it like he's puzzled, so it can't be Her.

"Hello?" he says.

Then he says, "Yup," and "Okay," and "Yup" again. I think I drained all the words out of him.

He looks over at me, and says, "It's your sister. Says they're all having dinner at Nate and Shelby's and do we want to come, too."

"Who's 'all'?" Important question.

A tinny yapping comes through his phone. Izzy heard me.

"Izzy, Danny, Max," Cam relays. "And Jackson."

"No parents?"

Tinny yap.

"Nope," says Cam.

I don't know. Family…

Cam sees my hesitance.

"Ava's supposed to be resting," he says to Izzy.

I hear a peal of laughter. Minx. I know exactly what she's implying.

Cam does too, and his face reddens. Izzy yaps some more.

"Okay. Sure," he says, and ends the call.

"She said we don't have to stay long, and I can put you to bed at a decent hour." He pauses. "She emphasized the word 'bed'. And made 'decent' sound the opposite."

"If we go, there'll only be more of that," I warn him. "My siblings are merciless."

"If we go, there'll be food," he replies.

"Your gas gauge is reading empty, isn't it?"

"I could eat that pumpkin raw. Rind and all."

I blow out a long breath. "I'll change into Shelby's other clothes. If I wear your shirt, we won't get out alive."

"I made stuffed pumpkin!" says Shelby as she opens the door to us. "Ha, no, just kidding. Nate told me how much you hate it."

"What else has Nate told you?" I inquire, eyes narrowing.

"Ooh, that's between me and him," Shelby replies breezily. "Can't break a confidence."

Behind me, Cam stifles a laugh. I'll punish him later.

Everyone's in the kitchen, sitting round the big scrubbed-pine table. The Armstrong family home, now Nate and Shelby's, is all artsy and craftsy-style, exposed timber and shaker tiles. It's got the comfortable shabbiness of a house that's been well lived-in and well loved. It's also full of dogs, cats, and the occasional goose. You have to keep an eye on your food and any loose jewelry.

The four men, Nate, Danny, Max, and Jackson, greet Cam in the time-honored dude tradition of a single lift of the chin. Jackson raises his beer, a gesture also in the dude greeting canon. Izzy observes this and gives me the time-honored Durant eyeroll.

"How've you been?" she says as I take a seat next to her. "Mom is *beside* herself with worry. We almost had to lock her in the cellar to prevent her driving over to Cam's."

"Thanks."

We both know what I'm really thanking her for. There are some things no mother should ever have to see.

I don't want to ask the next question, but I'm compelled to. "What about Dad?"

"Oh, you know," says Izzy. "On the computer. Researching all your symptoms. Sending Doc Wilson email after email because Doc has stopped taking his calls."

"And what does Mitch think is wrong with me?"

"Everything," says Izzy, with a wry grin. "Lyme disease, fibromyalgia, leaky heart valve, brain injury, cancer, of course—"

"Of course."

"Liver failure, overactive thyroid, *under*active thyroid. Oh, and anemia."

"Wow. Hope it's not that."

I've got my poker face on but it's shaky. I've had a lot to distract me from thinking about all the tests Doc Wilson no doubt has already lined up. Now it's right in my face, and I have to say that list of potential diagnoses doesn't fill me with optimism. Feels me with terror, in fact.

Izzy puts her hand on my arm. The younger Durants are much better at physical affection than me and Nate. As long as she doesn't hug me, I'll be fine.

"How do you feel?" Izzy asks softly. "Better?"

"I don't know," I say honestly. "Okay, I guess. Not too tired, but it's been a pretty cruisy day."

"Cam looking after you well?" Izzy raises her eyebrows. The minx.

She bends closer, so she can whisper in my ear. "We're

all super happy for you," she says. "Especially Shelby. Jackson said their mom's been trying to set Cam up with women for years, but it's never worked out."

"That's right," says Jackson.

Seems Izzy's whisper was more of a penetrating hiss.

"It became a running joke in the family," Jackson continues.

"What did?" says Shelby as she dumps a huge casserole pot on the table.

"Mom's failed attempts to give Cam here a love life."

Cam's been talking to Nate. About vineyard handiwork, no doubt, a subject he's very comfortable with. From the way his head shoots up, like a deer hearing a rifle being cocked (or given that it's Cam, a moose), this subject is on the opposite end of the comfort spectrum. I feel for him, but there's no way I'm coming to his rescue. Knowledge is power, and I selfishly want to hear all about the women who failed to win Cam's heart.

Shelby is making room on the table for Max to put down whipped potatoes and wilted greens.

"I remember Mom's crazy artist friend," she says to Jackson. "I thought Mom gave up trying after that?"

"Oh, no, no, no," says Jackson with a huge grin.

"I'm right here," says Cam pointedly.

He is ignored. Jackson begins to count on his fingers. "There was the yoga teacher from Martinburg, the primary school teacher from Santa Rosa, that woman who briefly owned the chocolate shop, Javier's wife's sister's second cousin, a European acquaintance of Ted's who may have been a princess…"

Jackson's onto his other hand now.

"… that financier from New York who bought the old manor and burned it down for the insurance, the rep from the organic food certifying company…"

The Durant boys have contributed nothing to this conversation. Mainly because they've been killing themselves laughing.

"Oh, man," says Danny, wiping his eyes. "I want to know more about the arsonist. That sounds like a really hot date."

Max snorts. "Why didn't the princess work out? I mean, if the shoe fits?"

"That's Cinderella, you doofus," says Izzy. "She was upper middle-class at best."

"Walt Disney and every pre-teen girl would beg to disagree," Max retorts.

"I think Cam was wise to break up with the chocolate shop owner," says Nate. "I wouldn't have a bar of a woman like that."

"Not to mention his close brush with the crazy artist," says Jackson. "And that organics rep was certifiable."

Danny high-fives him.

I sneak a look at Cam, who is leaning back in his chair staring up at the ceiling, wishing, I imagine, that it would fall on top of him and end this torture.

Shelby puts down the salt and pepper, and frowns.

"How come I didn't know about any of these other women? Why is this all news to me?"

"You were busy with Dad," says Jackson. "Learning all that wine stuff."

"Wine stuff?" Shelby gives her brother a look.

He shrugs. "That's why you're running the place and not me."

Shelby pulls out her chair and flops into it.

"Eat!" she says, waving her hands at the food. "I didn't cook it, so it'll be fine!"

"Ted?" I ask.

The whipped potatoes are topped with truffle shavings. Dead giveaway that the food came from Bartons hotel. Requesting that they hold the truffle is like asking for your steak well done: you get put on the Bartons blacklist.

"Yes, Ted had it sent around," Shelby says. "I just had to keep it warm."

"As the New York financier said in court about the old manor," says Danny, causing the shoulders of four out of the five men at the table to shake yet again.

"It's delicious," says Izzy loudly. "Why don't we all enjoy our delicious food in peace?"

"Thank you, Izzy," says Shelby. "It's a good thing Frankie and Tyler had to fly home today. If all the Armstrong kids were here, it'd be like that hollerin' contest they have in North Carolina."

"But you've got me," says Jackson. "For a few days more, anyway."

"You're not staying with Nate and Shelby, are you?" I ask. After their wedding? Talk about a third wheel.

Jackson looks down at his plate. "Nah, I found a place."

"Room for two?" says Danny. "I hear there's a yoga teacher looking for a place to hang her mat."

He, Nate, and Max are in fits again. Someone's going to snort whipped potato out of his nose if he's not careful.

"All right, you horrible lot," says Shelby. "Give Cam a break."

Cam is shoveling food in his mouth like he's entered some sort of contest. His revenge might be to not leave seconds for anyone else, and I wouldn't blame him. There's nothing worse than being the reluctant center of attention.

"I want to hear how Ava's doing," Shelby adds.

Oh, crap.

Time to lie.

Chapter Fourteen

CAM

Jackson Armstrong is a shithead. An immature jerk. A shit-headed, immature, jerk-faced douchebag. A—

Ker-THUNK!

The Dodge hits a massive pothole I failed to see because of the red mist in front of my eyes.

"Could you chill just a little?" says Ava. "You know, so we can make it home alive?"

"Sorry," I mutter, and ease my foot off the gas.

We continue in silence, but I can feel Ava watching me.

"You're pretty good at hiding your feelings in public," she says. "I don't think any of us realized you were *this* salty."

Why not? I want to yell. How would they have liked to be the butt of Jerkson's jokes?

"Was it the content of the teasing?" says Ava, relentlessly. "Or the teaser himself?"

Relentless and perceptive.

There was a time some years back when I had the opportunity to smack the immature douchebag into next week. If I'd actually done it, I can guarantee he'd have learned to think twice before opening his smart mouth.

Regrets. I've had a few.

"Jackson Armstrong needs to grow up," I tell her.

Ava's quiet again.

"I think he's unhappy," she says. "And possibly unemployed."

Who cares? If Jerkson has hit the skids, it'll be all his own fault. Bet he made one too many jokes-that-aren't-jokes and got shown the door by the boss, cheered on by his relieved ex-colleagues.

"Guess we're all fighting our own battles," she adds.

The rage in my head has fogged my ability to think straight. Takes me a couple of beats to register that Ava's voice sounded a little reflective. A little scared.

Shit. I've been so focused on my own grudge that I haven't given any thought to how Ava must be feeling. Like she told the others over dinner, Doc Wilson will be calling first thing tomorrow and the testing regime will begin. She did a good job of seeming unconcerned, suggesting that Doc was only going all out to reassure Ava's mom, who is extra worried after her husband's health scare. Though everyone let the subject drop, the unspoken question left hanging was, what happens if the tests *do* reveal something?

'What next?' is a question Ava and I haven't raised between us, either. And not only in regard to her health. What's next for us? We've been thrown together like two frogs in a pot, and though I'm enjoying her company, I know this can't last. The heat will get turned up and we'll have to make a move. And what will that look like? I'm not in the habit of thinking about the future. A day at a time is how I live my life. But I guess you can't keep hiding from situations that test you.

I pull in outside the workshop. Home sweet tiny home. Ava is yawning, covering her mouth with the back of her hand. It's only nine-thirty, but it's been a long day.

"Straight to bed?" I ask.

She perks up, gives me a wicked grin. "Where else?"

"To sleep," I add. "You need the rest."

"I need this week to be over," she says. "I need to know if there's anything wrong, so I can deal with it and get on with my life. That's what I need. But what I want…"

Ava slides her fingers into my mop of hair and pulls my mouth down to hers, kisses me hungrily. I respond because of course I do. Run my hand up and under her top, cup her breast. Think about how to do it in the cab of the Dodge without freezing our asses off…

She breaks the clinch.

"You're right," she says. "I need rest."

Shit. I'm that weak; I cave the instant my dick gets hard. *Nice work, Hollander. You really know how to stand by your heroic principles.*

But Ava presses her lips against mine again, briefly, softly. And smiles.

"So it's best if I lie there and you do all the work."

And by that, she means…?

Got it. Slow, but I got there.

"Don't worry, I'll reciprocate," she says. "No fun trying to sleep with a case of blue balls."

"How do you know?" I ask as we step down out of the Dodge.

"I have more balls than most." Ava pokes my arm. "Thought you'd have figured that out by now."

Yup, I'd figured it. What I don't yet know is what *I've* got balls-wise. Guess we'll soon find out.

Doc doesn't care for people being tardy, apparently, so Ava and I arrive five minutes before her eight-thirty appointment. Behind the desk is a middle-aged woman who looks like she's seen the person she most hates on Earth, who just happens to be you.

"That's Priscilla," Ava whispers. "She's ornery."

"No shit," I say, very quietly.

"Hi, Priscilla."

Ava approaches the desk while I look for the waiting room chair that's farthest away. It's by the kids' toy box. Makes sense. Any closer and they'd be needing therapy for life. I could be doing Priscilla a disservice, but I've seen friendlier expressions on the faces of serial killers who'd scoop out your brains and feed them to you.

And here's the Doc, bustling out of his office, exuding cheerful authority. I wish I'd met doctors like him when I needed them.

Doc glances over at me and correctly interprets that I'm hiding in the corner.

"You want to join us, son?"

He doesn't have to ask me twice.

With us all safely in his office, door closed, Doc cuts straight to it. "I'm going to start with bloodwork, so get yourself to the hospital and hand this to the lab."

He gives Ava a medical slip, which she takes, reluctantly.

"Do it this morning and I'll have results in a day." Doc spotted the reluctance. "Right now, I'm going to check your vitals."

He heads off to fetch the blood pressure cuff.

"Doesn't he mean vittles?" I whisper in her ear.

"No, son." Doc Wilson has the hearing of a bat. "Vittles —also victuals—comes from the Middle English and Old French word *vitailles*, a corruption of the original Latin *victualia*, which means food or provisions. Vital comes from *vita*, the Latin for life."

Bet he doesn't know what a cresset is. On second thought, I wouldn't take that bet.

Doc takes Ava's pulse and blood pressure, sticks a little torch in her eyes and ears, and presses around her ears and neck, checking her glands, I guess. All of a sudden, I feel queasy. Last time a doctor poked and prodded me, I ... let's just say, it wasn't a fun time. Probably why I haven't been to a doctor since. I switch my gaze to the poster meant for kids, all bright colors and fluffy bunnies, and focus on regulating my breathing.

"You okay, son?"

Doc has the hearing of a bat and the eyes of an eagle.

"Cam?" Now Ava's worried.

I take a big breath in. "Yup, fine."

"You've gone the color of oatmeal," Ava insists.

"Put your head down between your knees," says Doc.

It sounds like an order. I obey.

"Breathe in for four … hold for four … out for four…"

Circular breathing. I know this. Recommended for panic attacks, too. Least I'm not having one of those. This time.

Ava rubs my back. Ironic. She's supposed to be the patient here. Ironic and embarrassing.

The nausea is subsiding. Slowly, I raise my head. Doc hands me a cup of water, but makes no further comment, for which I'm grateful.

"Okay," he says to Ava. "Bloodwork this morning. I'll call you as soon as I have the results."

Ava gives him a quick peck on the cheek. "Thanks, Doc."

Then she takes hold of my arm. Like I'm an invalid needing to be helped out of my chair. I resist the urge to yank it free. That's my fragile male ego talking, and I'm not going down that road again.

"Want to grab some coffee?" she asks when we're safely past the Priscilla gorgon and out on the street.

"Any bars open at this hour?"

It's a joke. Mostly.

"How about coffee and a donut at the Creamery? Buy five, get one free?"

"Sold."

Two donuts down, Ava asks the question I was praying she wouldn't.

"You were okay at the hospital on Saturday night," she says. "I would have thought that was a worse place to be?"

"I was jacked up on adrenaline then," I tell her. "Didn't have time to look around me. Just kept my eyes on you."

"Danny hates needles," she says, obviously trying to make me feel like less of an idiot. "All his breezy charm fails him, and he becomes a sweaty, gibbering mess."

Good. After last night, Ava's brother Danny is second to Jerkson on my grudge list.

Ava fixes me with her blue gaze. She's got a little sugar around her mouth. I reach out with my thumb to brush it off and she catches my hand.

"Cam, this is all part of the PTSD, right?"

There are times I appreciate her directness. This isn't one of them. My feet are itching to move—out of this chair, out of this place, away from this conversation.

"Ava, can we just say that I did not enjoy my stay in the army hospital, and leave it at that?"

She stares at me a beat longer, then drops a kiss on my knuckles, releases my hand. "Sure."

Then she picks up her third donut, offers it to me. I'm tempted but...

"Save it for after the blood test," I suggest.

Ava nods. "You don't have to come. The hospital's a ten-minute walk. I can meet you back here."

Hoo boy. For a moment, I feel winded.

Ava reaches out for my hand again. The urge to run comes back stronger than ever.

"I don't think less of you for disliking hospitals," she says. "I hate hospitals. I hate feeling dependent and I hate not knowing what's going on. And I've only been in the hospital a couple of times with broken bones and concussion, occupational hazard with horse riding. I was in and out in a few hours. Nothing like what you went through—"

"Ava!" I yank my hand away. "Drop it."

It's the first time I've snapped at her. First time I've snapped at anyone for years.

She recoils. Her blue eyes flash.

"Bet you've told Lee all about it," she accuses. "Bet you didn't hesitate about spilling your guts to her."

I regret snapping at her, but that was below the belt.

"Lee didn't push me," I say.

"Oh, so I'm pushing you?" says Ava. "Am I not simply showing you some fucking empathy and consideration?"

The guy behind the counter is looking our way. Guess we're making what's known as "a scene".

"I don't want to talk about it now." Not here. Not with eyes on us. Not while I feel like I'm backed into a corner.

"Okay, you know what?" Ava shoves the one leftover donut back in the box and scrapes back the chair as she gets to her feet. "You go. I'll call Danny and get him to pick me up from the hospital."

Shit. "Ava..."

Too late. She's out the door. The guy behind the counter catches my eye and shrugs, as if to say "Women, eh?"

He's wrong. Only one person to blame for this, and it's yours truly. Doing what I do best, which is react badly when my emotional buttons get pushed.

Lee bore the brunt of that for years. It was true what I said about her giving me time, but she also never let me off the hook. She kept on encouraging me to give things a try and then stick them out, not give up. Lee was positive, optimistic, kind, and relentless. Even when I behaved like an immature shithead. Same way I did just now.

What the fuck, Hollander. Ava *was* showing you empathy and consideration. It's *your* fault you couldn't handle it. It's the same reason you got shitty last night. Sure, those guys might have been jerks, but you overreacted because their stupid jokes reminded you of all the times you'd been an emotional coward. Those women Lee set you up with were perfectly nice (okay, maybe not the arsonist, she *was* a touch insane.) But to spend more time with them would have meant deeper conversation and venturing into emotional, vulnerable territory. So, instead, you dumped them and ran away.

Now, you're the one who's been dumped, and you deserve it.

Ava was right. She does have bigger balls than most, certainly bigger than yours. If you want her back, you'd better make more ballsy choices from now on.

You could start with not being resentful that she didn't leave you that last donut.

Chapter Fifteen

AVA

Being patient, you may have already guessed, is not one of my top skills. Running, riding, driving—moving forward at speed has always been my thing. It's why I'm direct because who knows what might happen tomorrow? Why regret what you didn't say?

Of course, that also works in reverse. What you do say can make everything fall to shit. But dammit, unlike the times when interrogation absolutely is my goal, I wasn't trying to be nosy. Or "pushy", gah! I bet the saintly Lee Armstrong pushed Cam all the time. She just disguised it by being all sweet and nice. I would yell out loud in frustration if I didn't think it might send Mom off the road. Danny wasn't picking up when I called him, and Izzy and Max left for the airport this morning, so I had no choice but to beg Mom to come and get me from the hospital. Which she did, bless her. Unfortunately, her first question to me was about Cam, and where he was.

"Not here," was my short answer.

"Oh." Mom sounded disappointed. "I would have liked to meet him properly."

"He has to go to work. Earn a living. You know, like regular people."

Mom ignored my feeble attempt at class warfare. So, she should. I'm a big, fat hypocrite. I'm running back to my extremely large and luxurious family home. Worse, I'm being driven back by my mother, who's decorated the place in a style she likes to call "country". Us Durant kids joke that she means a whole country. Like one of those landlocked principalities in Europe.

We turn into our tree-lined gravel driveway, and I start to panic. After I walked out on Cam at the Creamery, I pounded the pavement straight to the hospital. Did the admin, had the blood tests, all in a fury that proved a useful distraction. But now, reality's hitting. I can't go back to Cam's, so I've no choice but to stay here and be interrogated by an overly anxious mother and a father who's even less patient than I am. Oh, joy.

Nope. No can do. I'd rather bunk down beneath an overpass.

Reading my mind, Mom says, "Will you be staying the night? Danny's staying on to do some more business, so we can have a small family dinner. You could even invite Cam," she adds, a little plaintively.

Okay. If Mom's under the impression that Cam and I are still tight, I can get away with a few white lies until I can figure out a plan. "I've just come back to grab some clothes," I tell her, as we pull up outside the house. "I'll stay at Cam's for a couple more nights. And I think we have plans for dinner. But thank you for the offer, Mom. I appreciate it."

"Oh." Mom's disappointed again, but she rallies quickly. "Well, I've baked your favorite cookies. Chocolate and salted caramel."

And today is brought to you by ... sugar! Though I'm still hanging onto that last donut. My plan is to eat it while Cam watches in a petty, petty act of revenge. If he ever wants to see me again, that is.

"Come into the kitchen and sit down," Mom insists as soon as we set foot indoors. "I know how blood tests can take it out of you."

"Thanks, Mom." I hook a thumb toward the stairs. "But I'll go pack first—"

"Is that you, Ava?"

Or I'll pack later.

"Hi, Dad."

The most disconcerting thing about my father is how much he looks like Nate. All right, yes, and me. At fifty-nine, his hair is still dark, only partly flecked with gray, and his eyes are our shared bright blue. Mitch's eyes have a quality Nate and mine don't, though. When he fixes you with a stare, you feel like you're being impaled by shards of glacier ice. Judgmental glacier ice shards that target all your weak spots.

"Ray's not taking my calls" is his conversation opener.

"I'm great, Dad. Thanks for asking."

I know I shouldn't rise to it. But there's so often a gap between knowing and doing.

"Your father is concerned about you," says Mom, quietly.

Is he though? Or does he want to control me, like he always has? Does he want to make sure I know everything that I'm doing wrong? I've kind of had enough of people pointing out my flaws today.

But Mom deserves better than to watch me and Mitch scrap. So, I'll keep my cool. Even if it kills me.

"Do you want to talk about it over coffee?" I ask Dad. "Mom's made cookies."

"I'd strongly advise you to reduce both your caffeine and sugar intake," says Mitch. "You should keep your energy levels even. No spikes."

I take a deep breath before I spike him.

"Just one cookie, Dad." We won't mention the donuts. "And I'll have decaf."

Pre-heart condition Mitch would have resented any response that wasn't an unconditional "yessir." But standing on the cliff edge of mortality has made him try harder not to raise his own blood pressure. Still fully capable of raising mine, though.

"Have you seen Ray yet? What does he—?"

"Let's go into the kitchen, Mitchell," says Mom. "Ava can sit down."

Nice emotional blackmail there, Mom. Not that she does it intentionally. Years of living with Dad have honed her ability to influence him in ways so subtle that now neither of them realizes it's happening.

I love our kitchen; it's my favorite room. Because we're (obviously) wealthy, Mom does have a housekeeper, but the kitchen is her domain. She's always been an amazing cook. Mom and Dad's dinner parties are legendary, though us kids suspect that, most of the time, Mom's food only just makes up for Dad's company. Their staunchest friends are the ones who love Mitch despite his intensity. And he can be great company when he lets himself relax. Which is maybe twice a year. For around ten minutes.

Mom, bless her, puts out her cookies, but also some homemade hummus and corn chips. All organic. Dad won't touch anything else.

"I saw Doc Wilson this morning." I launch into it before Dad can. "There's nothing obviously wrong with me, so I've had some blood tests and we'll wait for the results, which should come tomorrow."

"But what is Ray expecting those to show? He must have some idea."

I can see why Doc stopped taking Dad's calls. *Breathe, Ava. Be cool.*

"One step at a time, Dad," I say. "Doc's not going to throw around diagnoses until he has some firm evidence. You know how he works."

Mitch drums on the table with his fingertips. Impatience is strong in our bloodline.

"Did you have a virus before the onset of the fatigue?"

I know why he's asking this question. Dad's heart

condition is called dilated cardiomyopathy. In layman's language, my super-healthy, athletic father got a virus that weakened his heart muscle, and the damaged muscle started slowly being replaced with scar tissue, forcing his heart to enlarge. If he hadn't finally accepted medical intervention, it would have failed. Permanently.

"I didn't have a virus, Dad." And more for Mom's sake, I add, "Honestly, I think I just got plain old worn out."

"You're twenty-seven!" protests Dad. "You should have energy to burn!"

"Mitchell," soothes Mom, "Ray will find out what's going on as quickly as he can. He's never let us down."

She spoons up hummus with a corn chip and offers it to him. Dad's Spartan defenses kick in (eating between meals?!) Then he relents and crunches it up.

A car is making its way toward the house. Danny's home, and if my ears don't deceive me, driving a different car from the one he came up from LA in, which means he must have sold that beautiful Porsche 550 Spyder replica. It's not worth anywhere near the several million an original would fetch, but I'm sure Danny has managed to wrangle top dollar out of some susceptible buyer.

"Is that Nate with him?"

Mom's heard the second male voice, too. The pair are guffawing as they approach, joking around, so it can't be Nate. Nate has a sense of humor, but it's quiet and dry. This second guy sounds more like—

"You all remember Shelby's brother, Jackson?" says Danny, entering the kitchen.

"Good morning, ma'am," Jackson says to Mom. "Sir."

He sticks out a hand to my father, who gets to his feet and takes it reluctantly. Mitch isn't that great with strangers, even ones who've recently become related by marriage.

"Ava." Jackson gives me a smile.

He's looking a little rough around the edges. Maybe he and Danny went drinking after they left Nate and Shelby's last night?

Danny pours two big mugs of coffee, hands one to Jackson. My theory's holding up so far.

"Mom, Jackson's accommodation arrangement has fallen through. Is it okay if he stays here until Sunday? I've got a couple more clients to visit, then we'll both head back to LA."

"Of course," says Mom, ever the gracious hostess.

"Can't he stay with Shelby?" says Dad, unaware that gracious is even a word.

"Dad, Shelby and Nate just got married," Danny says. "Did you and Mom want guests on your honeymoon?"

Mom smiles and takes Dad's hand. "We were so preoccupied that we didn't even notice the blackflies."

"Ginny!" Dad protests, but his mouth twitches upward. Dang. He really has mellowed.

My heart gives a lurch so sudden it sends a knot of nausea up into my throat, and it's all I can do not to let it show. My parents love each other. They're devoted to each other. And sitting here watching them, I wish that I felt that kind of love from them. Okay, more specifically from my father. I wish I felt like he loved me as unconditionally as he loves Mom. I wish I felt like he saw me as a whole being, not just a series of achievements. Not just a venture to be continuously improved. I wish I could talk to him, and to Mom, and to my whole damn family without feeling guarded and defensive. It's why I know I can't stay here now that the possibility of me being ill is out in the open. I'd feel constantly under scrutiny. Constantly judged for falling short.

I felt that way with Cam this morning. When he called me pushy. Attack has always been my best form of defense and I went there without hesitating. I knew the subject was difficult for him, as it would be for anyone who's experienced what he has. His response was not unreasonable. I could have apologized and backed off, but instead I leapt down his throat. Whereas he had cause to be touchy, I didn't. And now I've got what I deserve: a big fat zilch.

My heart lurches again. I don't want zilch! I want Cam, goddammit! Cam, who is kind and gentle and there for me. Whose generosity I threw back in his face, along with a bunch of nasty remarks. It may be too late for me to ever have a great relationship with my dad, but I refuse to give up on me and Cam. Okay, so it'll mean learning to break the habits of a lifetime, but I am nothing if not goal-oriented. Of course, this plan entirely depends on whether Cam's willing to forgive me, but I'll cross that shaky bridge when I get to it.

I notice Jackson looking at me over his coffee mug. In the face of my return stare, Jackson's face reddens, like I've caught him out. I wonder what his story really is. I mean, you'd have to be desperate to accept an offer of accommodation at the Durants, no matter how great Mom's cookies are.

I shift my attention to save him any more embarrassment. "What's the latest car, Danny?" I ask. "Who did you bilk this time?"

"Bilk?" Danny is mock offended. "I made a great trade. The 550 for a 1961 190SL Mercedes. Factory hardtop, Solex carburetors. Been restored once, back in the eighties, and showing its age. But a simple refurb will put fifteen, even twenty grand on it, no problem."

"Hardtop? You mean it's a convertible?"

"Yup." Jackson is grinning. "Me and Dan'll be cruising down the coast highway like Thelma and Louise."

"They drove a Thunderbird," I tell him. "But apart from that, the resemblance is uncanny."

"So, you live in Los Angeles?" Mom asks Jackson.

"No, ma'am." Again, a quick look in my direction. "I'm ... following up some opportunities."

Knew it! He *is* unemployed! Then again, so am I. And I know how much it sucks.

"Jackson's in sales," says Danny. "I'm setting him up with some contacts."

I catch Danny's eye and he gives me the faintest nod in return. A nod that means: I've got it all under control.

I nod back: thank you. Danny may be an ego on legs but he's not *entirely* selfish.

Mitch coughs, pointedly. A signal that he's tired of this

interruption and wants to get back to grilling me about medical stuff. Right. Time to go. Time to face the music with Cam.

"Danny, can you drive me back to the winery? I'll just grab my stuff."

And I hop up from the table before anyone can ask me about viruses, fatigue, blood tests, Cam, or what in hell I'm actually doing with my life.

But Danny says, "I've got a million emails to catch up on. Can Jackson drive you? I've named him on the insurance policy."

"Have you named *me*?" I inquire sweetly.

"No, because I'm not insane."

Danny tosses the keys to Jackson, whose grin now stretches ear to ear. "Take it easy, big fella. She's a feisty little thing and needs to be handled carefully."

Oh, boy. He'd better be talking about the car.

Chapter Sixteen

CAM

I should go to work. Early November's a busy time for vineyards. Got to maintenance check the equipment, clear out the drainage channels, compost the grape pomace—that's all the stuff leftover after the crush, skins, stems, pulp, etc. Javier's crew will be checking the vines for any that are struggling. Got to do that while the leaves are still on; you can't tell when the vines are bare. They'll mark the ones they'll need to remove over winter.

I should go to work. But the fight with Ava this morning is circling in my head like vultures over roadkill. Screeching at me about how useless I am, how weak. It keeps circling and circling and I can't shut it up.

Keeping busy would help. Doing something physical. Like my job.

But I give in to old habits, pick up my phone and call Lee.

And get her voicemail.

I won't leave a message. What would I say? Can I dump all my emotional baggage on you again? Use up all your time and energy when you have a hundred better things to do?

I sit in the Dodge, knowing I should make a rational decision and *go to fucking work*. Instead, I replay the concern I had when she left so quickly after the wedding. Unlike Lee not to hang around and be social. And even though she's told me since that she's fine, I persuade myself that I should go check up on her, while knowing full well that the only reason I'm going is so that *she* can help *me*.

When Lee's husband died, Flora Valley Wines became hers, and she didn't want it. She'd loved Billy with all her heart and put in stupid hours for years to help him keep the vineyard afloat. But when he died, she wanted to be free of the pressure. She wanted time for herself, to take up painting again in a small studio of her own. Preferably by the sea.

Lee was going to sell up, but Shelby, who wanted to run Flora Valley Wines more than anything, persuaded her mother to give her six months to find an investor who'd buy Lee out. And Shelby did. She found an old guy with money and a soft spot for enthusiastic young women and organic wine: J.P. McRae, who brought Nate in to be the new manager. That's how Nate and Shelby met. That's how I met Ava…

I should let Nate know where I am. He's my boss, after all, and he only gave me leave for this morning. I should text Shelby, too, so she doesn't worry. I should absolutely check in on Ava, and apologize, like a grown-ass man.

I do none of these things. I put the Dodge in gear and light out for the coast.

Lee lives outside a tiny village that often gets used for movie locations because it's ridiculously picturesque. Her house is on the cliffs overlooking the bay. It's not unlike my place, in that it's a converted shed. Except where my place is tidy and minimal, Lee's is a messy, gaudy riot. Probably why she can be so calm: she lets all the craziness out, instead of trying to keep it buried inside.

The Dodge isn't a quiet vehicle, and I half expect Lee's door to open as I pull up outside. She wouldn't know it was me; it could be anyone from Flora Valley Wines—Shelby, Nate, even Javier or Doug—who use the truck to run errands and, if they're in the neighborhood, will stop off and say hi. They all miss Lee. She was everyone's friend and confidant. But I was the one who took up most of her time.

The front door stays shut as I get out of the Dodge and walk up. The garage is closed so I can't see if Lee's car is there. It's an EV, of course. She doesn't use it much as the town is a half hour walk away and Lee has always kept fit. Yoga at sunrise and sundown, hiking, swimming. All of which, over the years, she's tried—and failed—to get me into. She *did* succeed at making me see the point of mindfulness. Taking time to look around, focusing on smells, sights, sounds, lettings those sensations quieten down your thoughts. It works for me. When I let it.

I knock. No one comes. I check my phone. No text. No missed call.

What now? Sit in the truck and wait? *C'mon, Hollander. That's stupid. Go home. Go to work. Stop letting down people you care about.*

Then I remember where Lee hides the spare key – under the Buddha statue by the path. Because I should double-check that she's okay, right? Don't answer that.

I unlock the door as quietly as I can. But Lee has these gong chimes hanging just inside the entranceway and immediately they begin jangling in (so Lee once informed me) perfectly tuned pentatonic scale. A harmonious burglar alarm.

I freeze. Listen. No movement. No one calling out "Who's there?" The gong chimes may be in perfect harmony, but they're loud, which means the obvious: no one's home.

The rational part of my brain has finally won. I'm leaving. I'll just grab some water first. Thirsty work breaking and entering.

Lee's house is shaped like the top half of the letter H. Bedroom at one end, studio at the other, connected by a long kitchen and living area with glass sliding doors that open out to a deck surrounded by a pretty, coastal-style garden. Every front-facing room has an amazing sea view. On this November day, it's blustery, and the sea is all choppy whitecaps and crashing surf. I'm drawn to the wildness, the wind, as if it'll clear my head of all the noisy, circling thoughts. I slide open the glass doors and walk out on the deck.

Only to hear a quiet voice say, "Hello?"

Heart thumping, I swing round. Lee's sitting in her wicker egg chair, cocooned in a blanket, red hair spilling out from under a wool beanie.

No, wait. Not Lee. But *so* alike, it's uncanny.

"Sorry." I do my usual mumble. "I'm Cam. Friend of Lee's."

"Ah," she says. "Of course."

This woman is either exhausted or frozen. Every movement seems to be a huge effort.

"You okay out here?" I ask, concerned.

A small smile. She gestures to the chair next to her. "Join me."

I take a seat. This woman not only looks like Lee, she has the same magnetism. I'd always thought it was Lee's warmth and openness that drew people to her, but now I can see a steely quality I'd overlooked. Probably why we all say yes to whatever Lee asks of us.

The other chair has a sloped back and I'm too tall to recline in any comfort. So, I sit forward, arms propped on my knees, hands finger-knitted together because I don't know what else to do with them.

"Lee's-friend-Cam," she says. "She didn't mention you were coming."

Tone's not warm exactly, but it's not judgmental.

"Didn't tell her," I say. "Was passing."

Another small smile. "She did say you come across as a man of few words."

Defense mechanism, I could tell her. Don't engage. Keep your distance. Safer that way. But when it's obviously an effort for this woman to speak, I can't let her do all the lifting.

"Came here to talk to Lee," I say. "Got a few things on my mind."

"Lee's in town. Organizing an art exhibition. A fundraiser." The woman pulls up the blanket so she can check her watch. "She'll be back within the hour."

Then she says, "What's on your mind, friend Cam?"

Maybe it's because I've come all this way. Maybe it's because she looks so much like Lee. I don't even know this woman's name, and I tell her everything. I tell her about my humiliating moment at Doc Wilson's, about the fight with Ava, how I overreacted and snapped at her because any mention of war or PTSD still makes me crazy, even ten years down the track.

"It's like all I've done for the past decade is find ways to hide from it when I should have been dealing with it," I say. "I've hid like a coward because I could. Because Billy and Lee let me."

"Let you?" The gentle rebuke might not have been intended, but I hear it, nonetheless.

"Okay, no, not exactly. They *did* push me..." I feel a stab of guilt about Ava. "But I guess they knew I was the only one who could decide to deal with my mental health, so they didn't push beyond a certain point."

"They were right," she says. "It was your decision."

"Thing is, like people say about alcoholics, you have to reach rock bottom before you acknowledge you have a problem. I've never fallen that far. Because…"

I'm struggling to explain this properly. Fairly.

"Because for the last ten years, you've been cushioned by the Armstrong family and Flora Valley Wines," she says, correctly.

"Not their fault," I say hastily. "Blame lies squarely at my feet. I've been a coward…"

I've run out of talk. Run out of energy. I sit and listen to the crash of the sea below, and the glittery sound of wind chimes. And the blood rushing in my ears from the sudden surge of mortification.

Finally, just as I'm about to curl up in a ball, she speaks.

"Would you have told Lee all this?"

Good question. Embarrassing question.

"Probably not all of it," I admit.

"So, you came here for comfort? For reassurance?"

I want to crawl under this chair like a hermit crab.

"Habit." I'm down to single words, now.

"Well, friend Cam," she says. "I don't know what Lee might say to you, but I'm not in the habit of providing comfort."

She pauses, as if to catch her breath. My nerves are on high alert, waiting.

"Sounds to me like you can't afford to waste any more time," she continues. "You never know what's round the corner and it's not always good. *Tempus fugit* so *carpe diem*, friend Cam. Translation: stop shillyshallying and make that choice. Step up."

Shit. She doesn't sugarcoat at all. She's like Lee's evil twin.

I have to ask. "Who are you?"

"I'm Lee's sister," is the reply I didn't actually expect.

My mouth's fallen open. I shut it.

"I never knew Lee had a sister."

The woman stares at me for beat. "Neither did she."

Behind us, the gong chimes sound off and a cross-breeze rattles the sliding door. Lee's home.

She dumps a tote bag on the floor, then comes right out. She sees me when I stand up and is visibly startled. Can't tell if it's in a good way or not.

"Cam!"

"I called," I say, "but…"

Lee composes herself enough to smile.

"I was in the middle of a hanging. Pictures, not people," she adds.

"Good to know."

Her attention switches from me to her doppelgänger. Her sister.

"You and Debra have met."

"You were right," says the woman whose name I now know. "He's good company."

I am?

Lee steps up to me, briefly touches my arm.

"Thank you for staying here with Debra. I hate leaving

her alone, but I promised ages ago that I'd help with the exhibition."

Little light goes on. That's why she couldn't stay after the wedding. Had to get back here as soon as she could. Exactly how long has her sister been with her? And why hasn't she told anyone? Like Shelby, for example? Her own daughter.

"Debra doesn't mind being left alone," says Lee's sister. Her tone has that "don't pity me" bite.

"I should go," I say. "Due back at work."

"Okay." Lee's distracted. Normally, she'd try to convince me to stay and have a cup of some healthful yet disgusting tea.

"Goodbye, friend Cam," says Debra. "Come again. If you can."

Lee sees me to the door. She's biting her lip. Not her normal calm self at all.

"Cam, I'd appreciate it if you didn't tell anyone about..." She glances back, toward the deck. "Not yet."

"Sure."

I don't tell her that Debra already dropped the sister bombshell. If Lee wants to keep that secret, too, then I'll add it to the list. She's kept enough secrets of mine these past years.

"What did you come to see me about?" she asks. "Everything okay?"

Fair assumption. I only engage with Lee when I need her. All other times we get together, it's down to her. And I did need her. But I got Debra instead.

"Everything's good," I tell her, and smile to prove it.

Lee's eyes suddenly widen. "Oh, God, I almost forgot! Is Ava okay? How is she?"

I don't want to talk about Ava. Partly because I feel guilty as hell, but mostly because I just told Lee's secret sister everything and I'm all talked out.

"She's doing well," I say. "I'll tell her you asked after her."

And that's enough for both of us. Lee's anxious to get back inside.

"Take care," I say.

"You, too," she replies.

And before I'm even at the truck, she's closed the door.

Guess that old adage is true: be careful what you wish for. I came here wanting someone to listen and instead I got resoundingly told. Time's precious. Don't waste any more of it. Step up.

I can start by facing the shitstorm that'll be waiting for me back at work—deservedly so.

And then I can apologize to Ava.

Time's precious. Don't waste it.

I put the Dodge in gear and hit the road.

Chapter Seventeen

AVA

The feisty little Mercedes is red, like all good sports cars should be. It's showing its age, like Danny said, but I can see how fantastic it would look fully refurbished. Danny has good instincts for cars: he can see the potential below even the roughest surface. And he knows exactly how to connect the right car with the right buyer, because he can strip away their rational top layer and see what pushes their emotional buttons. Hint: it's not miles to the gallon.

I pushed Cam's emotional buttons this morning in all the wrong ways. And he pushed mine. But now my head is clear of my initial resentment, I can see our argument was a good thing. The rosy haze of sexual attraction does a great job of blinding us to each other's faults. It's nature at her finest, making sure we procreate before we realize we want to punch each other's lights out. Getting to know each other on a deeper level is where a lot of couples fall apart, but it's the only thing that will keep you together. I'm glad Cam and I had our first fight. When we come back from it, we'll be so much stronger.

At least, that's my hope. Not exactly sure how the coming-back-from-it part will work with Cam because—oh, the irony—I don't know him that well. With guys in the past, I've opted for the direct approach, going straight to the issue at hand. And when my directness proved too much for them, I just saw it as a sign we weren't supposed to be together.

But those guys ... it was never serious. I didn't want a relationship with any of them. Not like I do with Cam. He's the first man I've felt connected to in more ways than physical. He's the first man I've ever thought about spending my future with. Whatever future that might be...

Dammit. I was feeling positive and now I'm anxious again. I need a distraction. Good thing there's one sitting right next to me.

"So," I ask Jackson, "did you quit or get fired?"

This kind of car isn't really made for someone of Jackson's bulk. The driver's seat is pushed as far back as it can go but he's still crammed in. His big mitts are clutching the narrow wheel, and he's driving cautiously like he's afraid the wheel will snap. Or maybe he's just nervous about being responsible for Danny's new car. My question doesn't help. Jackson jumps and the car does a little shimmy on the road.

"Shit," he says. "Give me some warning next time. Ring a small bell. Or cough discreetly."

"No way," I say. "Element of surprise is key."

Jackson blows out a breath—either releasing stress or resigning himself to his fate. My guess is the latter.

"I got made redundant," he says, "along with ninety-nine others so, you know, nothing personal."

"A hundred layoffs. Tidy round number. What was the firm?"

"Tech start-up. Layoffs in San Francisco, Chicago and Phoenix, Arizona. Where I was."

"Why Phoenix?"

"Steve Miller Band," says Jackson. "You know, the song about going to a bunch of cities to get work so he could be with his sweet baby, yeah?"

"Absolutely no clue," I say. "More of a metal fan. Not a lot of sweet babies in grindcore."

"Don't ever tell me what that is."

"Did you get a payout?"

"I got my last paycheck," says Jackson. "Used it to get out of my apartment lease. Landlord wasn't going to budge."

"Capitalism at its finest," I say.

"And before you ask, I have some savings," he adds. "I just don't have a job. Or a car. Or a place to live."

"Does—?"

Jackson lifts one hand off the wheel in the stop signal.

"And before you ask that, no, Shelby doesn't know, and neither does Mom or the rest of my family. I didn't want to be a downer at the wedding. Plus, I still have a tiny bit of pride."

I have another question.

"If you don't own a car, how'd you get here? Bus?"

"Hitchhiked. No serial killers. Obviously."

"Okay. Wow…"

Jackson enjoys a short breather as I process what he's told me. When I quit my job, I had a lot of savings because I've never liked shopping—or owning things, period. I hardly ever went out to restaurants or clubs. I didn't travel except if I was needed at the race venues. Only flew home for Thanksgiving and Christmas because I'd be in deep shit if I didn't.

But even if I hadn't two coins to rub together, I'd be fine. I'm always welcome to crash at the Durant family mansion, where I have everything on tap: a comfortable bed, a well-stocked fridge, my own bathroom. I don't have to contribute to expenses. I do but I don't have to. I can lie around in our peaceful garden, or by our pool. I can borrow a car … usually. In other words, I'm a spoiled little bee-atch.

"You okay?" says Jackson. "I feel like you've still got some tightening to do on those thumb screws."

"Thinking about blood tests."

"Won't ask."

"Wouldn't answer if you did," I tell him.

The corner of Jackson's mouth lifts. "Must try that some time."

"Good luck when I'm around."

And then, all my senses snap into high alert. We're coming up to Flora Valley Wines. Jackson wants to see Shelby, to tell her he's moving to LA. I'm here to see Cam, of course. To apologize. And when he's apologized back, then we can go back to his place, and I can carry him bodily up the stairs to the bedroom. I'm small but strong, and I'll be amped up on sexy hormones. I can totally fireman's lift a two-twenty-pound man. Then I'll throw him on the bed and—

Okay. Getting way ahead of myself here. We pull up in the gravel area outside the main office. I expect to see the Dodge truck ... but it's not there. The rational part of my brain knows that means Cam's probably out on an errand, or one of the other Flora Valley peeps has commandeered it. But my heart still lurches with disappointment. In my usual impatient way, I'd figured we'd get the apologies out of the way in a couple of minutes, and then I'd throw him over my shoulder. Seems I'll have to wait. I hate that.

Jackson turns off the engine and exhales lengthily.

"Remind me never to have a midlife crisis," he says. "Small red convertibles are not for me."

"Danny will happily do all the driving down the coast," I reassure him. "He's Louise, and you're Thelma, remember?"

Jackson struggles out of the Mercedes with all the grace of a bear stuck in a trash can.

"Louise drove them over the cliff," he says, straightening his shirt.

"Yeah, but Thelma got to have sex with Brad Pitt when he was cute."

He nods. "Fair point." Then he pauses. "Um, do you mind not telling anyone what I just told you?"

Jackson's not referring to boning a young Brad Pitt.

"Of course," I say. "Just because I can extract secrets doesn't mean I want to share them. Knowledge is power, man."

"Thanks. I think—"

"Jackson! Ava!"

Shelby's jogging over from the house, waving cheerily. To be fair, Shelby does everything cheerily. Wish I could be more like that.

"Hey, sis." Jackson bends down to give her a kiss.

Shelby hugs him back, and then hugs me. It makes me smile that Nate ended up with a hugger.

"Hey, do you know where Cam is?" Shelby asks me.

That question does not make me smile.

"He's not here?"

"No…"

Shelby frowns, perplexed. It obviously isn't like Cam not to turn up when expected. Ever reliable, that's Cam Hollander. On every day except today, it seems.

"I called him, but no answer," says Shelby.

I have a bad feeling about this. About where Cam could be. "Nate might have asked him to do something," Shelby adds, filling me with the sweet air of relief. "I'll find out."

She calls Nate. A short conversation and too many "love you's" later, Shelby says, "Nope, Nate has no idea where he is, either."

The sweet air of relief turns noxious. My bad feeling becomes a conviction. Cam's with *her*. And he doesn't want anyone to know.

"Oh, well," says Shelby, who can put a positive spin on mutually assured destruction. "Come on in the house. I'll put the coffee on."

Jackson shudders. I know why. The strength and consistency of Shelby's coffee is legendary.

"The Black Death," he says. "Make mine a double."

"Did you and Danny get wasted last night?" asks Shelby.

She hooks her arm in her brother's, and they start walking toward the house. I hang back, not sure what I want to do. I had my plan and was feeling good about it. Positive. Upbeat, even. Now, I'm back where I was this morning, bubbling in a stew of resentment, with an added splash of hot spicy jealousy.

I hate him. I hate her. I hate myself for feeling like this.

"Ava, you coming?"

Jackson has noticed I'm not following them. Cam may have been right about him being a frat boy jerk, but I don't care what Cam thinks: Jackson Armstrong's been good company for me, and he could do with some moral support. I don't think he'll tell Shelby why he's moving to LA, but if he does, he could use a friend with him. And so could I.

"Coming," I say.

Nate enters the kitchen just as Shelby's pouring coffee out of a battered old percolator that looks like it marched to the sea with General Sherman. He's holding two big paper bags, one that looks like it's full of—

"Donuts!" says Jackson. "My man!"

"Cracker Café's finest," says Nate. "And as I guarantee

no one here's eaten lunch yet despite it being well after two, I also have pulled pork sandwiches with coleslaw and spicy pickle, even though Iris knows I hate spicy pickle."

Iris runs Verity's diner, The Cracker Café. She's proud of her hardscrabble Florida roots and there's a giant stuffed alligator on the diner wall, which she may or may not have killed with her bare hands. Even though Shelby insists that Iris is cranky with everyone, Nate's convinced she holds a special loathing just for him.

"I *lo-ove* spicy pickle," says Shelby, with an erotic lowering of her voice that, judging by the alarm on Jackson's face, has not gone unnoticed. "Give me yours right now."

"Guys," says Jackson, "should we leave you alone?"

Nate brings plates for the sandwiches and donuts. "Spicy pickle isn't everyone's idea of an aphrodisiac, and that group includes me, so don't panic."

He sits and immediately stares at me. "How are you doing, sis?"

I reach for a sandwich. May not eat it, but better not be rude.

"I survived the Mitch interrogation," I say.

"Has Dr Google told Dad what you have?"

"Everything, apparently. Including anemia."

"You don't want that," says Nate.

"No, because then I might pass out on the living room floor in front of my parents. How embarrassing."

"What's this?" Jackson's all ears.

"Nate got seriously iron deficient," says Shelby.

"Fainted—"

"In a manly fashion," Nate interjects.

"Mom called it the day before," Shelby goes on. "Said he needed a good steak."

And Lee Armstrong needs a stake through the heart. She's a succubus, and she's stolen my man.

Jackson mistakes my sour look for being sad about this medical talk. He shuffles his chair closer, so he can put his arm around my shoulder and give me a squeeze.

"Eat your spicy pickle," he says. "It'll cure anything."

I can't help but smile. And I don't move away. It's quite comforting having Jackson's arm around me. He's the human equivalent of a weighted blanket. I don't even mind that he's stuffing a sandwich in his face with his other hand.

Shelby reaches over and opens Nate's sandwich, so she can purloin the pickle. Nate shakes his head.

"What's mine is yours, husband," she says, and piles the extra pickle on her own sandwich. "Don't fight it."

"Pickles, sure," says Nate, "but I refuse to share your heartburn."

"Might not be heartburn," Shelby warns. "Maybe take a match to light when you come up to bed."

Jackson guffaws. Really, he does—a big, hearty explosion of laughter. Shelby starts to laugh, too, and bits of sandwich fall out of her mouth. Nate's still shaking his head but he's smiling. The humor is completely contagious, and now I'm laughing, too. I lean toward Jackson and we both sort of collapse onto each other.

Which, of course, is when Cam walks in.

Chapter Eighteen

CAM

I might have mentioned before that when Nate arrived to manage Flora Valley Wines, he and I didn't exactly hit it off. Nate told me later he was jealous of how fond Shelby was of me, and that prompted some incivility on his part, which he apologized for.

Got to admit, I couldn't figure why he had any reason to be jealous; a blind man could have seen how Shelby felt about him. But right this minute, Nate, I take back any criticism I ever had of you. Being jealous turns you into a crazy person. A chest-beating, Tarzan-yodeling maniac who wants to tear a person limb from limb. One person in particular. If you can't guess who, you haven't been paying attention.

"Cam!"

Shelby greets me first. She's swallowing a mouthful of sandwich, so it's a little muffled. "Where have you been?"

She doesn't sound too stern, but when I came in, everyone was in fits of laughter, the kind it's hard to stop.

Nate's expression is less amused. Waiting to hear what I've got to say for myself.

All the way on the drive back, I rehearsed what I'd say. How I'd apologize to everyone, but particularly Ava, for my shitty, immature behavior.

But now, I'm feeling indignant, like *I'm* the victim here. It's not my behavior that's questionable, it's theirs. You know who I mean – Jerkson and Ava. He's basically embracing her and she's letting him. All my intentions to apologize fly out the window, helped along by the toe of my boot.

"I went to see your mom," I tell Shelby.

Because I have one eye on Ava, I see her immediately stiffen. And the jealous maniac who's taken me over twists the screw another notch.

"I was worried about her."

But it's not Ava who looks upset. It's Shelby.

"Why? Is she okay? What's wrong?"

Shit. What an idiot I am. It wasn't that long ago that Shelby's dad died, and she'll be extra anxious about her mother. I've just triggered her grief and worry. For no good reason except petty spite. I'm an idiot and an asshole.

"She's fine," I say quickly. "Totally fine."

Too quickly. Shelby's suspicious.

"Cam? You'd tell me, right? You wouldn't make some stupidly loyal promise to Mom to keep me in the dark?"

Well, not about *this*...

I shake my head. "She's fine. Nothing wrong at all."

"Good to hear," says Jackson.

He was laughing the hardest when I came in. Not even the hint of a smile now. Lee's his mother as well, I remember too late.

"Cam?" Nate's on his feet. "Can I have a word?"

When the boss wants a word, it's never good. But I deserve whatever verbal kicking he's about to give me, so I better harden up and take it.

He leads me outside and closes the front door.

"I promised the truck to Doug," he says. "You said you'd have it back by eleven."

"Yeah. Sorry." I'm looking down, scuffing my boot in the gravel, like a sulky kid.

"Cam, what the fuck?"

Surprised, I lift my head. When Nate's in boss mode, he's crisp and professional. Never raises his voice. Never swears.

"What's going on? Why were you so worried about Lee that you had to drive all the way to her place?"

Not in boss mode. Concerned husband mode. Can't fault him for that. I feel I owe him some honesty in return.

"I freaked out at Doc Wilson's," I say. "Didn't know who else to talk to."

Nate lets out a slow breath and rolls his shoulders as the tension eases.

"You could have called Lee instead," he says.

I could and should have.

"And Lee really is okay?"

She has a secret sister, but apart from that. "Yeah."

"Because I don't think Shelby would cope if her mother got sick," Nate says. "Given that she had a whole breakdown after her dad died. You know—you were with her then."

I was. Didn't think about that when I was being a petty asshole. Between her grief and running around trying to keep Flora Valley Wines afloat, Shelby got poleaxed by depression and, one day, couldn't get out of bed. All her friends and family rallied round, and with their help and some medication, she recovered. But we all know that those mental scars never fully heal. You'll always be vulnerable.

"Lee's not sick," I say. "But she does have some stuff going on. Nothing bad. Just … complicated."

Nate gives me a look.

"You did make some stupidly loyal promise, didn't you?"

He got me.

"It's nothing bad," I say. "I swear."

"Okay…" Nate blows out another long breath, looks me in the eye. "And Ava has nothing to worry about? Shelby's always wondered … whether you and Lee…"

Seems directness is a Durant genetic trait. But I guess when you're protecting the ones you love, you can leave no stone unturned. Or skeleton closeted.

"Lee and I are friends," I say.

Nate's a few inches shorter than me. Most men are. But right now, it's me who feels small. Secrets weigh you down, bend your back. Diminish you.

"Cam, Shelby cares about you," says Nate. "Ava does, too. And I care about them. I don't need to say more, do I?"

No, sir, I almost reply.

I hand him the keys to the truck. For Doug. To whom I also owe an apology.

"I'll get to work," I say to Nate. "You can dock my pay for the day."

"Not going to do that," he says, "but composting can wait. I'd rather you went back in and made things right with Ava."

He sees my hesitation, and his mouth twitches.

"She won't kill you," he says. "Mild to moderate injuries is my guess."

"Can I kill Jackson instead?"

"Shelby cares about her brother. Refer to my previous point."

This is why Nate is the boss. He's got what it takes to have hard conversations without flinching. Nate has backbone. So does Ava. Time for me to have it, too.

"Do you want me to ask Ava to come out here?" says Nate. "So you can talk to her on your own?"

He's trying to be helpful. But it feels like he's calling out my cowardice.

"Nope," I say, and mumble-add, "thanks."

"If it's any consolation," says Nate after a beat, "I was so jealous of you, I used to refer to you in my head as Survivalist Ken."

My eyebrows lift. "Like ... Barbie and Ken?"

"Yeah. The perfect couple."

"Ken has no dick," I point out. "Just a plastic blank."

"Really? Huh…" Nate frowns. "What about Action Man? Surely he—"

"I'm going back inside," I say.

"You do that." Nate's pulled out his phone. "I'm googling 'naked Action Man'."

As I turn away, I hear a startled yelp. Guessing Nate might need to re-think his search terms.

Back in the house, I inhale the distinctive lingering smell of Shelby's coffee. Like tar and burned BBQ with a top note of the biofuel they make from old cooking grease. Shelby's coffee puts hairs on your chest and probably the inside of your lungs. But I breathe it in anyway because my heart's starting to pound. It's only ten steps from the front door to the kitchen but I feel like I'm taking that last, long walk from death row.

Jackson and Ava are up at the kitchen counter helping Shelby wash the mugs and plates. All three of them turn when I enter. Only Shelby smiles.

"There's one donut left over," she says. "Want it?"

The three I had this morning haven't gone the distance.

"Sure," I say.

Shelby reaches into a drawer, retrieves the donut from inside a saucepan, and hands it to me.

"I hid it from Jackson," she explains. "For his own good."

"Hey," he protests. "You're not the boss of me."

"You're not the boss of you either," says his sister, "when it comes to donuts."

I take the opportunity to slide a glance at Ava. She's staring right at me, a cool look on her face. Dammit. She's so beautiful and I am such an asshole. Not sure I can make it up to her. Not sure if she'll let me.

Jackson and Shelby are still bickering. I move closer to Ava.

"I'm sorry," I say to her. "I fucked up."

"You did," she replies. "Big time."

The donut frosting is melting. My fingers are getting sticky. But she doesn't seem angry. Not on the outside, anyway.

"So…" I venture cautiously. "On a scale of 'I'm open to an explanation' to 'the snake pit is too good for you', how would you rate your current position?"

Ava's still giving me no clues. Remind me never to play her at poker.

"Did you know," she says, "that the Gaboon viper produces the second-largest quantity of venom of any snake on the planet?"

"Which snake produces the most?"

"The one I'm stocking your pit with, obviously."

She's either deadly serious or there's a faint glimmer of hope. The frosting from the donut is oozing down my fingers. I don't dare move, though—this feels like a critical moment. Better think carefully about what I say next.

"I don't mind snakes so much. Camel spiders now…"

Jesus, Hollander. Words are not your special talent.

"Are they those huge hairy desert things that can run really, really fast?"

"Top speed's only about ten miles an hour. And they're not *that* big. But they're still fucking terrifying."

"Bet you wouldn't want one in your sleeping bag."

Am I imagining it, or did she just move a little closer?

"I've seen battle-hardened soldiers scream in falsetto when there's one three feet away," I tell her, "let alone in the same bed."

Ava holds my gaze for a moment. She's still got her poker face on, not even the tiniest tell, far as I can see. Then she glances down at my hand.

"Seems like you're in a bit of a mess there," she remarks.

The donut frosting is pink, with sprinkles. And it's all down my fingers now and halfway to my wrist. I lift my hand, ready to run it under the tap. Ava grabs it. Sticks my index finger in her mouth. Sucks all the frosting off it. Slowly.

Jackson and Shelby must have left the room. Or they might be right behind me making rabbit ears. Can't tell. Don't care. Have to focus.

"No snakes?" I ask, super quietly, just in case this is all a dream and I wake myself up.

"Cruel to have someone of your size landing on them."

She wipes a sticky sprinkle from the corner of her mouth and sucks it off her own finger. I'm having a coronary.

"I suppose you have to go back to work," she says.

My gratitude for Nate knows no bounds. I owe him. I owe everyone. By some miracle, I'm being given a free pass, a second chance. Better not fucking blow it, Hollander.

"I've got the rest of the day off," I say. "Want to ditch this donut and go to my place?"

"Good idea."

Ava still has hold of my finger. She brings it to her mouth.

"Though I'd just like to finish this frosting."

Chapter Nineteen

AVA

Okay, so I'm a sucker. Literally. Cam and I should be sitting down right now and setting things straight. We should be talking, not making a furtive dash for hot make-up sex.

But I saw his face when he came into the kitchen and caught me leaning on Jackson. He was incandescent with jealousy. I know jealousy can be an unattractive quality when it's all about control and possession. But Cam's not the controlling type, and it gave me a small buzz to see how much me being in proximity to Jackson bothered him. You only get bothered if you care.

And when he came back into the kitchen after talking with Nate, he was genuinely contrite. Whatever brain fart made Cam drive up the coast, I believe he regrets it. And we will talk about what happened today. We will get things straight between us. But first, hot make-up sex it is!

I'm not exactly sure how to say our goodbyes tactfully,

but when I look around, there's no one there. For their sakes I hope they left when Cam came back indoors. The mental image of me sucking Cam's finger could scar them for life.

"Doug's got the truck," says Cam. "You okay to walk?"

Little does he know I have plans to fireman's lift him up to the bedroom soon as we arrive.

"Prefer to run," I say. "But no more chat. Let's go."

I open the front door only a crack and peer outside. Can't see anyone, but that doesn't mean they're not lurking.

"Okay," I tell Cam. "Move fast until we reach the safety of the trees."

"Who's after us?" he asks.

"No one who values their life," I reply. "Right. I'm making a break for it."

And off I scoot, across the gravel, past the office, through the garden and into the trees that line the property. There's a gate here, and a rough path that takes you to Cam's workshop. It's on the other side of a big stretch of vines, so the walk is maybe twenty minutes. Not long. Unless you're insanely horny.

I expect Cam to be right beside me, but I'd forgotten what Shelby had told me: that Cam's not built for running. She said his preferred speed is that of geological features forming. An exaggeration, but not that much. He's still ambling across the gravel. Miles behind me.

And what's this? Is that a goose I spy, waddling up to him, making shouty honking noises? Does he stop, so he can rummage in his pants pocket and hold out a handful of dried corn kernels for said goose? Why, yes, he does. He even takes time to pat it on the neck when it pecks at his hand for more. I don't dare yell at him to shift his ass, because that will undoubtedly bring one of the vineyard crew our way. So, I hang by the gate, insane now with impatience as well as horniness. Until he finally arrives.

"Remind me never to agree to a three-legged race with you," he says. "I'd fall flat on my back first step, and you'd drag me the whole way along the ground."

"Yes, and we'd still win," I say, and smack him on the rear like a horse. "Come *on*."

"Anyone tell you the story of the old bull and the young bull?" he says, still traveling at an inch per hour.

"Nope." I'm walking in circles, dashing forwards and looping back to him.

"It's kind of sexist, so I'll skip the details," he says. "Lesson is: conserve your energy and you'll go the distance. If you know what I mean."

I pause. "Is that a promise? Or a dare?"

Cam takes advantage of my temporary halt to bring me into his arms, a place I am happy to be brought. I wrap my own arms around his waist and look up at him.

"A promise," he says. "I owe you."

He bends and kisses me for … who knows, I lose track. When he breaks it, I find I'm on tiptoes and clutching a fistful of his shirt. And, amazingly, no less horny.

I glance around. We're in a group of trees through which we can see the vines. We can also see quite a few vine workers, but they seem super busy. Not looking in our direction at all.

"No," says Cam, the mind reader. "I'm not taking you up against a tree. It's too damn cold."

Is it? I'm quite warm myself. But I guess there is a chill in the air.

"Come on," he says, like I haven't been repeating those *exact* words for the last hundred years.

Another century later, we arrive at his workshop. He fishes the door key out of his pocket—not the same one he keeps the dried corn in—and lets us in.

Instead of rushing upstairs as soon as the front door clicks shut, like I would, he walks into the kitchen area, pulls two tumblers from the shelf, and fills them with water.

"Important to hydrate," he says, handing me one.

Fortunately, I decide against making a joke about how moist I am already. Too crass. And it involves the word "moist".

After we've drunk our water, he says, "Need the bathroom?"

"Cam," I warn.

"Means we won't be unnecessarily interrupted," he says.

I go to the bathroom. When I come back into the main house, Cam's leaning against the counter, smiling.

"Do I need to floss, too?" I ask.

He pretends to hesitate, and I begin to mock beat him. "Go! Up! Now!"

"Okay, okay!"

He's laughing now. And, because he wants to remain alive, he's moving up the stairs with me following with both hands pressed against his rear. I work out that if he stopped, I couldn't budge him—so much for my fireman's lift fantasy. But I've got more fantasies where that came from, and I intend to live some out right now.

As I start taking off my clothes, I realize I've left the overnight bag I brought from home in Shelby and Nate's kitchen. But they'd know better than to bring it over? Right?

"Did you lock the door?"

Cam's unbuttoning his shirt. "Uh-huh."

I can tell from how dark his eyes are that he's not fully focused on my question. But now that his shirt is off, and his naked torso is on full display, I'll have to trust him. No way I'm wasting good hot make-up sex time running downstairs to check.

Off come his jeans. Then his boxer briefs. And there he is —one hundred percent in the buff. Muscled, golden, *very* ready, and all mine. Shit, better finish getting my clothes off. I got distracted.

Now, we're both naked, standing about a foot apart, taking each other in. Of course, I make the first move, but before I can get my hands on him, he says, "Wait."

"What?" I say. "No! Why?"

"I…" He's finding the words. "I thought I'd fucked up so bad I'd lost you and … I'd just like us to lie on the bed and … take our time."

My current fantasy was him lifting me up and carrying me around, like they do in raunchy romantic movies. But I can adapt. Taking our time sounds good. Though I'm guessing I might have to adjust my idea of how much time, to fit Cam's and not call it after twenty seconds.

We lie on top of the covers, side by side, face to face. Cam traces his finger around my cheek, over my lips, my jawline, my neck, the dip in my shoulder blade. It's way more intense than I expect, like his fingertip is electrically charged, creating a trail of tingling heat. It's all I can do not to shiver; I don't want him to stop because he thinks I don't like it. I love it, but it's also agony. Every inch of skin he touches releases a hot surge of desire. I'm *aching* for him, desperate for him to enter me, fill me up, fuck me. I could wrap my leg over his right now, slip his hardness into me and end this torture.

Cam's finger starts heading south, down my arm, skimming the curve of my breast. I can't help it, I grind myself against him, and he catches my hip, stills my movement.

"Soon," he says.

How soon? I want to yell. Soon is not soon enough!

Breathe, Ava. Be in the moment. Not everything has to happen at a million miles an hour.

Gently, Cam pushes my hip, coaxes me onto my back. I pull my leg up, seeking some friction, some release, and he catches that, too, runs his palm up my thigh, slowly, lightly, almost hovering above my skin. I can feel goosebumps lifting, seeking out the heat. His hand glides over my belly and up toward my breasts. Now *two* areas of my body are competing for his touch. My breasts crave for him to cup them, run his thumb around my nipples, and put his mouth into action, too. My southern region demands the same attention, from his hands, his mouth. It's pulsing down there, hot and frantic, like it's on the verge of orgasm, and I don't think I can take much more. I mean, how long has it been? An hour? The length of the Cretaceous period?

Maybe it's time to reverse this. See how he likes it.

I shift onto my side, push him not so gently on the shoulder so he'll roll on his back. May as well have shoved the two-ton Dodge.

"Come on," I say. "Fair's fair."

"I'm not done yet," he says. "Barely halfway."

Halfway? Hell, no!

Because I'm sneaky as well as impatient, I slip my hand down to take hold of his cock. I find that usually accelerates proceedings. But Cam's way ahead of me, catches my wrist.

"Lie on your front," he says. "It'll be worth it. I promise."

Okay, fine. I roll over on my stomach, lay my head on my arms, and wait.

As an athlete, I've had more massages than I can count. I like them firm—dig those thumbs right into the sore spots, thank you. No pain, no gain. So, when Cam starts tracing his finger across my shoulders again, I get antsy. Not enough pressure! Too feathery!

But the way he's doing it— rhythmically, purposefully, creating patterns like he's drawing on my back—I start having the weirdest feeling. A tingling that's in my *head* as well as my body, like the goosebumps are rising inside of my *skull*. My whole being is flooded with what I can only describe as a sparkly shiver coming in waves that are more and more intense until—holy heck—what the *fuck?*

I think I just had an orgasm in my brain.

Cam's mouth brushes my ear. "Don't move," he whispers.

And his hand slips down to stroke my ass, softly, before his fingers delve between my legs, sliding into my hot, wet depths and over my clit, rushing me like a runaway train to a matching full body orgasm that I swear makes me float right up to the ceiling and gently back down again, like a contented feather.

Who knows how long later—the entire Mesozoic?—I'm roused from my trance by a rustling of foil, and Cam murmuring, "Now okay?"

"Absolutely," I murmur back. "But just so you know, I'm not moving. Can't even open my eyes."

His soft laugh. "I can work with that."

A change in air pressure, and Cam is holding himself above me, arms straight on either side. I lift my rear up a little, so he has easier access, and then I gasp as Cam slides inside me up to the hilt. This position is so lazy for me but so good. My thighs are clamped together making the fit extra tight and Cam's cock feel huge. I'm guessing he likes it, too— the repeated mutter of *"fuck"* being a small clue. He begins to thrust shallower, but he has no chance of making this last because by now, I've managed to slide my hand underneath and find my own center of pleasure, which is quick to respond. I plummet over the edge and drag him with me, and we're so loud that any squirrels in the trees outside will have dropped their acorns in fright.

"Shit…"

Cam's arms are trembling. He rolls off before his arm muscles give out completely and he crushes me under his weight, then lies on his back, his chest still heaving.

My neck is getting cricked, so I shift onto my back, too.

"Where did you learn that?" I say after we've both caught our breath. "The drawing on the back thing?"

"Uh…"

I sense embarrassment.

"Let me guess," I say, "the yoga teacher?"

"Uh, no," says Cam. "It was YouTube."

"Wha-at? Get outta town."

"I was looking for mindfulness videos and found these others. People whispering, brushing hair, mixing paint, all kinds of stuff. They're supposed to calm you, even give you a pleasant tingling feeling."

That's an understatement. I must check these videos out.

We lie quietly for a while more.

Then Cam says, "I'm sorry. About … driving to Lee's. After our argument, I needed someone to talk to. Wasn't thinking straight."

"And?"

"And … what?"

"Did you and Lee talk?"

He's silent for a moment. Long enough for me to know he's figuring out how to fudge the truth.

"We didn't," he says. "She was out, and so ... we didn't get the chance."

I roll on my side and prop myself up on my elbow so I can look him right in the eye.

"Cam," I say, sternly. "What are you not telling me? Because it's absolutely obvious you're holding something back."

"Are you saying I'm a shitty liar?" He offers me a weak smile. I'm having none of it.

In the heat of my glare, Cam winces, rubs his thumb across his forehead like he's got a headache.

"Shit..." He breathes out the word.

"What?" Patience be damned!

"Lee has a secret!" he almost shouts. "And I promised I wouldn't tell anyone."

"A secret."

Cam's still flustered. "It's nothing bad. She's fine—"

"Oh, good."

His brown eyes are pleading, but I'm not going to be a sucker twice in one day.

"Ava, if I could tell you, I would," he says. "But—"

"I'm an ace secret keeper," I remind him. "You've seen my poker face, right?"

"Yeah." Another weak smile. "Had me pretty convinced about the snake pit."

"It's still an option. Believe me."

Cam sinks his head back onto the pillow and screws his eyes shut. Bad luck, buddy. Just because you can't see me doesn't mean I've disappeared.

When he opens them, he seems calmer. More resolved.

"Ava, if I made a promise to you, would you want me to keep it?"

An entirely reasonable question that I completely resent him asking.

"Of course," I say. "But it doesn't change the fact that I'm still pissed about you making one to Lee."

He nods slowly. "Okay…"

"Or that I'm doubly pissed that you went to see her after our argument."

He's still nodding, like one of those plastic dogs on a car dashboard.

"Old habits," he says, more to himself than to me. "Sometimes you're not aware of how much of a hold they have on you until it's too late."

Damn. He's right. Here I am, after all my good intentions, going full frontal again because he's pushed my emotional buttons.

I knew we should have saved the hot make-up sex until after the talking. Then again, we've now had our second argument, so maybe that warrants another round?

Ava. No. Calm those hormones and focus on what's important.

"You know, today I vowed to be honest with you," I tell him. "I also vowed to apologize for being an attack raptor. That's *my* bad ol' habit. Merest hint of a threat and I go straight for the soft parts."

"Whereas all I do is run and hide," says Cam. "These days, anyhow. Wasn't always like that."

"Two sides of the same coin," I tell him. "Fight and flight. Both mean we're avoiding facing up to whatever's making us uncomfortable."

"Shit…" says Cam. "You're right."

"Doesn't mean I have a clue how to do things differently," I admit. "But I'm willing to try."

I press my face into his shoulder, brush it with a kiss. He smells so good, like sex and sweat and the smokiness of Fall.

"We could start by sharing one secret each," Cam suggests quietly. "Not that one—" he adds, as I raise my head looking eager. "One of our own secrets."

I give a mock shiver. "Sounds terrible, but okay."

And then I say it before he can. "You go first."

Chapter Twenty

CAM

"No fair," I protest. "You took advantage."

Ava laughs. "Of what?"

"You're quick and small, and I'm big and slow."

She looks smug. "No backsies."

Shit.

"Is this how it works in your family?" Might as well try a few delaying tactics. "You snooze, you lose?"

"No, we fight to the death," Ava replies. "It's like *Highlander*"—she drops her voice down to a dramatic register—"*there can be only one.*"

Then she pokes me in the shoulder.

"Stop procrastinating. It's my turn after you, and I hate waiting."

Okay. Guess it's show and tell time…

My breath has quickened, and I can feel my heart thumping. It's all I can do not to throw off these covers and make a naked dash for freedom into the woods. Old habits coming to test me. Old fears coming to haunt me.

I've pushed people away for years because I'm afraid they'll despise what they see when the curtain's pulled back. When they see the real Cam Hollander. But I know Ava's right about talking. I know the cost of bottling everything up. I'm about to share a prime example of that.

I bet Ava has never done anything really bad. She might have pissed a few people off in her time, but I bet she's never betrayed a trust, and so badly that no matter how often they say they forgive you, you know you can never fully make amends.

Can I let Ava see that side of me?

Guess there's only one way to find out. Can't be worse than being chased by a camel spider. Least, I hope not…

"This involves Lee," I tell Ava.

Her mouth tightens. "Figures."

"And no one knows, except her and me."

She's got the poker face on. Can't tell what she's thinking. No distractions. I've got to do this now or I never will.

"I've told you how Lee and I got to be friends," I say. "She'd come to the workshop, we'd have a beer, talk. I started to open up to her. Tell her what it was like over there, in Afghanistan. What I saw. What I did…"

Ava drops a quick kiss on my shoulder. Her mouth feels extra warm, I realize, because my skin now feels cold. It's what guilt does to you. I recognize it all too well.

"I didn't exactly blurt it out all in one go," I say. "Took

months before I could talk about the worst of it. Lee was patient—"

"Ugh," says Ava.

"—up to a point," I continue. "But she could tell the difference between me talking about stuff in a way that was helpful, and me wallowing in self-pity, using my experiences as an excuse not to move on. I didn't make that distinction, and I resented her making it for me. Things got … heated."

I don't want to tell her this next bit, but I have to.

"I put my fist through the workshop wall. Well, not through. Against. Punched the shit out of it while Lee watched. Split my knuckles. Blood everywhere."

"Ouch," says Ava quietly.

"Picked up some barrels I'd made and smashed them on the floor, Incredible Hulk style." I cringe at the memory of Past Cam. "Acted like a child. A big, dumb toddler full of anger I couldn't control. Didn't want to control."

Ava seems subdued, withdrawn. Don't blame her.

"Lee didn't try to calm me down. Knew there was no point. She waited until I was so exhausted, I had to sit down on the floor. She fetched the workshop first aid kit and handed it to me. I thought she was going to patch me up and when she didn't, I … started to cry."

Fuck. So much for it sounding better when you say it out loud.

But Ava says, "Not surprised. All the adrenaline was leaving your body, dumping you into a big low. Been there, done that."

She adds, "And if you're thinking, 'but you're a girl', you can take a flying leap. Happens to all of us, no matter how strong we think we are."

I wasn't thinking that. I was thinking about the last time I cried. In a hospital bed. After I'd made sure I was alone because I couldn't bear the shame of it. Me back then had no idea how real shame could feel.

"Cried and cried," I say, in hardly more than a whisper. "Until Lee came over to me, put her arms around me. And I…"

Can't go on. Feels like I'm choking.

"Oh," says Ava. "Shit."

She's figured it out.

"How … um, how far did it go?"

"Not far at all," I say. "I kissed her, and she pulled away immediately. But … that's not the point. It shouldn't have gone anywhere. I shouldn't have even tried."

"No," Ava agrees. "You were in a bad state, but still … Lee was someone's wife. And she wasn't coming on to you. Just trying to give you comfort."

Every word is like a cigarette being stubbed out on my bare skin.

"But"—she says after a pause—"it didn't destroy your friendship with Lee, did it?"

"No…"

"She forgave you."

I have so many objections to this line of reasoning. Sure, Lee forgave me. Lee still considers me a friend. But Lee also knows who I can be when I'm at my worst, and whenever I look at her, I still see that person, and Lee sees him, too. We both know who, deep down, I really am.

And now, so does Ava. Who's gone very quiet.

"If we were all condemned to be judged by our worst mistakes," she says, "and never given a chance to redeem ourselves, we'd be fucked, wouldn't we?"

"Depends on the mistake, don't you think?"

"Okay, sure, if you're Jeffrey Dahmer and you murdered and ate people, then you deserve the condemnation. But if you were him, you're probably not interested in redeeming yourself, either. Right?"

I feel kind of like I'm walking into a trap.

"So … wanting to be better makes up for the mistake? That what you're saying?"

Ava shakes her head. Not disagreeing, more figuring out how to express her thoughts.

"We can't undo the mistake," she says. "And we have to face any consequences and not avoid responsibility, *but* we can also choose how that mistake defines us from then on."

Definitely a trap. Or that scene in *Indiana Jones and The Last Crusade* where the Nazi has to pick which cup is the holy grail. He chose—poorly.

"I don't know how to let it go," I tell Ava. "I can't see how I can present myself to the world as a good man, a dependable man, when I know what's behind that. It's not just what happened with Lee, it's the war, and the fact that I've been running and hiding for ten fucking years…"

Shit. I can feel tears pricking behind my eyes. Fuck that. Crying sucks ass.

Ava's cheek is resting against my shoulder. I can feel her soft breath on my bare skin. Long, even breaths, in and out. Ava is calm. She's not upset. Can't tell you how much I admire her for that.

"You really think you're not dependable?" Ava asks.

"I'm worried I won't be," I say. "When it counts."

To her credit, and my relief, Ava doesn't wheel out a response like "Don't be an idiot." She might be thinking it, but she doesn't say it.

What she says is, "Who have you let down since then? And ducking out of second dates doesn't count. We've all done that."

There goes that answer.

"No one, I guess," I say, reluctantly. "But that doesn't mean I won't."

"True. It doesn't," says Ava. "We're all capable of acting on our worst impulses, and there's always a risk that we might. But the future's in the future, pardon the obvious. Why worry about what might happen? Why not focus on what we're doing today?"

I hear Debra, Lee's secret sister, scolding me. *Stop waiting and step up. Now's good.*

Can I do it? Can I put the past behind me and live in the now? Stop running and face my fears head on?

"I mean, all things considered," says Ava. "Today's been pretty okay. I give it a solid B."

"B!" I object. "In my humble opinion, that was some A-plus sexual hijinks back there."

"Yeah, but you scored a big ol' D-minus for running off

to Lee's. But you did get bonus points for your company at Doc Wilson's ... and for the donut frosting."

It suddenly occurs to me that I've already done it. I've already faced my biggest fear. I told Ava everything and the world didn't end. In fact, we're making jokes. Bantering. How the hell did that happen?

"You're the best thing that's happened to me, you know that?" I say. "Thank you."

"Well, don't be so hasty. You haven't heard my secret yet."

Ava's smiling but there's a twist to her mouth, and a plea in her eyes.

She feels the same way I did. Afraid that revealing the secret might change everything ... and for the worse.

And I realize that whatever she tells me, my feelings for her won't change. Ava is the best thing that's happened to me, and I don't want to hide anymore.

"Spill," I say gently. "I'm here for you."

"Okay." She sits up, loosens her shoulders, and puffs out breaths like she's on the starting line of a running race. "Okay..."

Good thing I've had a lot of practice being still and quiet.

"Okay." Ava draws herself up tall. Then starts to speak at a million miles an hour. "I quit my job at the racing stables before I was fired for non-performance, and I wasn't performing because I was constantly exhausted for no reason that I could see. I went to a doctor, and they gave me iron tablets and told me to eat more so I did, and nothing changed. *Nothing.* Just as I was starting to properly freak out, Dad got sick so I had this perfect excuse to run on home, and because everyone was so busy with him, and then with Shelby and Nate's wedding, I could fly under the radar and avoid letting on that there was anything wrong. Thought I'd managed that fine, but Mom has eagle eyes and she ratted me out to Doc Wilson, and then I passed out at the wedding, and you know what's happened since."

She pauses for a quick inhale.

"But that's not my secret. My secret is that I'm terrified. I'm terrified that my life is over because I have some shitty debilitating illness that'll either kill me or make me a burden to my loved ones for the rest of my probably shortened life. I'm terrified that you and I will never get a chance to have a proper relationship because you'll be carrying me around because I can't walk and showering me and doing other things that I won't mention because they ick me out. And you'll be miserable, and I'll be miserable and humiliated, and it will suck so hard that whole galaxies will be pulled into its sucky black hole. Or I'll be dead. Which, right now, sounds like the way better option."

"I—"

Nope. Not finished.

"I hate being pitied. I hate, hate, *hate* the idea of being dependent. I hate the thought of being dead, despite its practicalities. I hate thinking about any of this because it scares the living shit out of me and I especially hate talking about it, so I'll shut up now."

She folds her arms tight across her chest and hunches

her shoulders almost to her ears, giving her the look of a pissed punk-rock vulture. It's funny but it isn't.

I reach my arm around her and coax her stiff body against mine.

"You know, some of the kids I do therapy riding class with are seriously physically disabled." I'm not sure this is the right thing to say, but I've started now. "But they know how to experience joy. I've seen it. I've seen them amazed by what their bodies can do, even when they can hardly do a thing. I've seen them frustrated, too. Lashing out. It's hard. It's a day-at-a-time life. I'm in awe of all of them. And everyone who loves them and gives them the care they need with dignity and respect."

Ava says nothing, but her body has lost its stiffness.

"If Doc Wilson has bad news, I'd be honored to care for you," I say. "Plus, you're super light, so I can carry you around until I'm creaky and old."

There's a long pause, and I worry I've gone too far.

"I'm going to wipe my own ass as long as I'm able, though," she says.

"Noted."

"And I'm not dead yet," she adds.

"Undeniably true."

Ava slides her hand down to parts of me that are also undeniably alive and responsive.

"So now we've got all our secrets out in the open and the world didn't end," she says, with a wicked smile. "How do you feel about improving that B score?"

Chapter Twenty-One

AVA

I wake up to Cam gently nudging my arm. Roll over in the hopes it's all on again only to find he's sitting on the side of the bed. Holding out my phone.

"Doc Wilson," he says.

Shit. Any lingering sexy embers have been doused with cold water.

I scramble into a sitting position. "What did he say?"

Cam pushes the phone at me. "That he wants to talk to you."

I almost wriggle my hands away, like a kid who doesn't want to touch something gross. But I'm not a kid. I'm a grown-ass woman. I need to grown-ass woman-up.

"Hey, Doc," I say, breezily as I can.

"Morning, Ava."

He has such a reassuring voice. I wish it was working on me.

"I got the results of your blood tests—"

Cam's expression is tense. No doubt so is mine. I put Doc on speaker, so we can both hear.

"—and nothing leaps out."

I should feel ecstatic, except that Doc's tone tells me there's a "but" coming.

"I'd like to do an MRI, to rule out anything like multiple sclerosis—"

"Multiple sclerosis?"

Cam and I stare at each other, wide-eyed. I almost thought that by letting all my terrors out into the open last night, they might prove to be nothing but phantoms. But this is very real.

"Is that a possibility?" I'm amazed at how calm I sound, when I've actually broken out all over in a cold sweat that's making me shiver.

"Highly unlikely," says Doc, "but you know me. I like to be sure. The MRI will also check for any parasites that didn't show up in the blood, and anything else that shouldn't be there."

"Such as?"

"Tumors, cysts, inflammation, bleeding. None of which I expect, but as I say—"

"You like to be sure."

Shivering's getting worse. Cam picks up his shirt and drapes the soft, warm flannel around me. I clutch it tight and breathe deep, in and out.

"Okay, when?" I ask Doc.

"Got you booked for three this afternoon at Martinburg General," says Doc. "Made the assumption you'd be free."

"You assumptioned correctly," I tell him, then add, pitifully, "Will you be there?"

"You don't need me to hold your hand," he says. "An MRI is completely painless. What about the big fella? I realize he'd rather be a cat in a roomful of rocking chairs than in a medical environment, but he seems fond of you."

I glance up at the big fella. His jaw has a rigid set to it, and his skin's a little ashy.

"He'll totally come with me," I tell Doc. "He's super pumped."

I end the call, and collapse on the bed in a fetal position. Cam sits down beside me and strokes my back until I have the wherewithal to haul my ass into a sitting position.

"Fuck," I say shakily. "What a fun afternoon *I'm* going to have."

"I'll be there," says Cam.

His jaw is set like it's been wired.

"Seriously, you don't have to."

"I'll be there."

"Thank you." I kiss him with my cold, shivery lips.

"There's one upside," I add.

"What's that?" He doesn't look convinced.

"After it's over it won't be too early to go to a bar."

I know Cam will feel bad about asking Nate for more time off, so I call my big bro while Cam's in the shower.

"Multiple sclerosis?" says Nate. "Jesus, Ava."

"Doc says it's highly unlikely," I reassure him, even though I'm the one that needs it. "He's just being thorough. But it might be parasites. Three cheers for the little guys."

"I'm guessing you're not going to tell Dad," Nate says.

"So he can stand over the MRI operator and tell them how to do their job? Sure!"

Nate's voice shifts into professional mode. "You know, I shouldn't really give Cam time off. After yesterday's no-show."

"Could also be tumors," I say. "Or internal bleeding."

I can practically hear Nate pinching the bridge of his nose. "Fine," he says.

"We thought we'd go to The Silver Saddle after," I say. "Want to join us?"

"The idea being that a few shots of tequila will kill any parasites?"

"You should have been a doctor," I say. "That's first-class medical advice."

"I don't usually go drinking on a Tuesday," says Nate the self-disciplinarian. "But as it happens, Shelby's catching up with her friends at the Saddle this evening, so…"

"See you at five with your line-dancing boots on," I say, and end the call.

The Silver Saddle actually has a sign that says: LINE DANCERS WILL BE THROWN OUT ON THEIR ACHY-BREAKY ASSES. But I never miss an opportunity to wind Nate up.

Cam comes back into the bedroom. I know he won't like what I just did so I dive straight in for a confession to get it over with.

"I asked Nate to give you time off."

Yup, he doesn't like it, but I can see he accepts that it's done.

"I'll make up the hours," he says.

"He's also meeting us at The Silver Saddle after. Along with Shelby and her friends."

Not thrilled about that, either.

"Which friends?"

"I did not ask. The usual, I guess?"

Shelby's best friends in all the world are Chiara and Jordan. It's like the witches of Eastwick only gigglier.

"Jackson?"

Damn. I forgot that Jackson and Danny aren't leaving until the end of the week. Poor Cam. This whole day is now packed with things he truly hates: hospitals, socializing, and Shelby's big brother.

"Maybe." I screw up my face in apology. "Can I make it up to you with tequila sex afterwards?"

He doesn't answer. Starts gathering clean clothes. He's going to work. Leaving me.

"See you at the office at two thirty?" I sound so needy I almost gag.

He's fully dressed now, bar his work boots. I'm faced with a day on my own, with nothing to do but think about a three o'clock appointment that might reveal ... what?

"You okay?"

Cam's brown eyes show concern like nobody else's. And the truth is, I'm not okay. But that's my problem, not Cam's. He's doing more than enough.

"I'm good," I say pretty convincingly. "I've got plenty to keep me occupied."

Cam bends, kisses me softly but intently. I don't grab onto him, which shows great restraint on my part.

"See you at two thirty," he says.

And off down the stairs he goes. I check my phone. It's eight forty-five. Only five and three-quarter hours to wait. Or in real terms, ten zillion years.

Guess I could walk into Verity, check out the job posts. The temporary ones, at least. But it's eight miles and I know that kind of exercise would wreck me. What I don't know is why. And like I said when I was being grown-ass woman honest with Cam last night, that makes me terrified.

I've never had to deal with anything medical that was truly serious. I've broken bones and I've been concussed and that's it. Okay, a few degrees the other way, I might have been paralyzed or killed, but I wasn't. I was laid up for a while, which, of course, I bitched and moaned about. But because my riding job meant I had to be in top form, I followed the doctors' advice and bounced back.

Until the day all my bounce left me. Flat as a balloon with no air. And no job.

You know, I really did think that a couple of weeks bumming around in my parents' house scarfing Mom's cookies would fix me right up. When it didn't, when I stayed tired right down to my bones, I truly believed it was better not to tell anyone. They were worried enough about Dad. No need to add me into the mix.

And as soon as Dad was on the mend, Nate announced

he was getting married. More distraction! If I hadn't fainted at the wedding, I might have been able to slide under the radar for a whole bunch longer.

Ha! Who am I kidding? Mom had already spotted that I wasn't at my best. She knows me too well, being my mother and all. And she'd shared her concerns with Doc, so it was only a matter of time before they staged an intervention. I would have objected and deflected and told half-truths, and everyone would have got super cranky. Then Nate would have piled on. He fights dirty so he'd have brought Dad into it, and...

Okay, so in hindsight, it was a good thing that I fainted at the wedding. Saved a lot of Durant family aggravation, which is several levels above normal family aggravation. And of course, big plus, it meant I got together with Cam.

Cam, who's coming with me today even though he hates hospitals and doctors' offices and anything medical.

All we talked about last night was showering and getting up and down stairs—domestic stuff. But what if I have something that means hospitals and medical treatment are a regular thing? How could I dump that on Cam, force him to go through it when it's so triggering for him? PTSD is a serious condition; what if it got worse because of me? Nothing's worth sacrificing your mental health for. Not even a person you care about.

I'm a pragmatist and know I'm getting ahead of myself here. But not so far ahead that it's unrealistic. I'm also a planner—love me a good plan. So how should it play out if the diagnosis is that kind of bad? What would be best for both of us: me *and* Cam?

It's nine fifteen. I've got five and a quarter hours to come up with something. Because right now, I sure as heck can't think of any scenario in which Cam and I have a happy ending.

Chapter Twenty-Two

CAM

I collect the Dodge keys from Nate at the office. He hands them over with a grim look and I brace myself. Okay, so Ava is his sister and technically, I didn't ask for more time off, but I know this is pushing it. I have responsibilities to Nate and Shelby, too. Don't want to let anyone down anymore.

"If the news is bad," Nate says, "can you ignore all Ava's instructions and call me straightaway?"

"I ... don't know if I can make that kind of promise," I tell him.

"Then send me a text," says Nate. "I'll take the heat if she finds out."

Shit. I know I'd make the same request if I were in Nate's shoes. But…

"It won't be my news to tell," I say. "Sorry. I know how you feel."

"Fuck," says Nate, but I can see he accepts my stand.

"Well ... encourage Ava to communicate as fast as possible. She's proud and stubborn and won't want to, but she's got a whole family worried about her, so do what you can ... please," he adds after a beat.

Nate tends to bark out orders when he's stressed. Shelby's having an influence on him. Like Ava's having an influence on me.

As neither of us is the bro-hugging type, I nod. Nate hands me the keys. Conversation concluded.

It's twenty minutes to my workshop from the Flora Valley Wines office if you walk, three if you drive. I pull up at my place at two thirty-one, expecting Ava to be waiting outside in her usual impatient fashion. But the front door is shut and there's no sign of her. I think about hitting the horn, but her nerves are probably already frayed to the max, so I set the brake and get out. Open the front door ... she's not in the main room, either.

"Ava?"

And there she is. Walking slowly down the stairs. With the exact same grim expression I just saw on her brother.

Anxiety kicks me in the guts. What's happened since this morning? Has Doc Wilson had a second look at the bloodwork?

Ava walks up to me and leans her head on my chest. "Fuck," she says. "I don't want to do this."

Relief. But also a mental slap across the head. Stop making it all about you, Hollander. It's Ava you need to focus on.

"It'll be over soon," I say. "And then I'll buy you a beer."

"And curly fries?" Her voice is muffled by my shirt.

"Double helping."

Ava raises her head and breathes in deep.

"Okay, let's go," she says. "But set the child locks in case I decide to make a barrel roll for freedom halfway."

We make it to Martinburg without incident. Also without conversation, no doubt because both of us are concentrating on keeping our breathing regular. And I'm winning right up until we pull into the hospital grounds. Then I feel my heart start to race, and my hands shake a little on the wheel.

"How you doing, big guy?" says Ava.

"I'm good," I manage.

She lightly punches my shoulder.

"It'll be over soon," she says. "Then beer and fries. Double helping."

I give myself another mental head slap. If she can do this, so can I. We can do this together.

Ava and I lock gazes and nod, like we're about to jump out of a plane. Outside the Dodge, she takes hold of my hand, and we both know it's for my comfort as well as hers. We set out for the hospital doors.

The next however-many minutes happen in a blur. It's like I've been sucked into a tornado and all I can see are specks whirling in a black mist. After they take Ava away, I manage to find the waiting room, but I can't look at my phone or skim an out-of-date magazine. All I can do is sit and try not to pass out or throw up.

It's been ten years since my time in the army hospital,

but I guess the triggers never really lose their power. *Or, says a voice that sounds a lot like Lee's, it could be that you've never properly faced the trauma. You've buried it in a hole, and now it's climbing out of the earth like a zombie intent on snacking on your brain.*

Okay, so that last part sounded more like Ava. But at different times, she and Lee have both given me the same message: if you don't deal with it, the pain will never go away.

I can hear Lee's voice telling me how trauma affects more than our mental state. You hold it in your body, she'd say. You need to find ways to release it, gently and slowly. You need to get in touch with your whole self if you want to be fully well.

"Well, well…"

Wait. I *can* hear Lee's voice. What the—

"How are you, friend Cam?"

Not Lee. Debra. The secret sister. Sitting in the chair beside mine. No longer wrapped up in a blanket but still wearing a lot of clothes: big wool sweater, scarf, and hat, and what look like ski pants. It's got to be eighty degrees in the waiting room. I'm sweating in my flannel shirt and only part of that's nerves. This woman really feels the cold.

"Uh, I'm…"

Nope, I've got nothing. My brain is fried.

"The hospital not your favorite place," she says. "Mine neither."

Somehow, her presence is pulling me out of my funk. Maybe she's having the same effect on me that Lee always did—calming, regulating. Or maybe it's just the shock of an unexpectedly weird coincidence. Whatever it is, my mouth opens and words start coming out.

"Why're you here?" I say, and then scramble to add, "If you don't mind me asking?"

Debra waits a moment before answering. "Did Lee not tell you?"

"Uh, no. We ... haven't caught up."

Another longish pause. Can't read her at all. Mostly because there's not a lot of her face to be seen between hat and scarf.

"I'm dying," she says.

Fuck, that's...

Fuck.

"Yes, the ultimate conversation-stopper," Debra says, with a small smile. "But it isn't as if I have a lot of time to beat around the bush."

"I'm sorry," I say.

All she does is nod. I'm embarrassed. Cliché Cam.

But before I can come out with something even clumsier, Debra says, "Why *you* here?"

"Came with Ava," I reply. "She's having an MRI. She's ... the girlfriend I told you about."

The recollection of spilling my guts to Debra makes my insides curl up, but luckily, she keeps the conversation right on track.

"Are they looking for anything specific?"

Strange that, despite us veering into medical territory, I'm not feeling queasy anymore. Maybe Lee was right, and I felt bad because I bottled things up. Now I've got someone to talk to, who probably knows a lot about medical procedures, I feel steadier.

"Ava's doctor says it's a precaution. She's been exhausted for a while, and the bloodwork didn't pick up anything."

"Well, let's hope the MRI doesn't either," says Debra.

I should be asking Debra more about what's going on with her, but now the worries I've been holding back are shoving questions out of me.

"But what could it be if the scan doesn't show anything? Is it normal to be so tired?"

"Is she a driven person?" Debra asks. "Competitive?"

"If those qualities have dials," I reply, "Ava goes up to eleven."

"Then it could be burnout," she says. "None of us have endless reserves of energy. If we don't replenish, we'll soon have nothing left."

"But she told me she loved her job," I say. "She loved riding, loved the high-pressure environment."

"Burnout isn't necessarily about overdoing things you find hard or stressful," says Debra. "In fact, it happens most often when we do too much of the things we excel at."

I think back to my early days making barrels. When I finally got good at it, I went for broke. Made barrels from dawn to dark until both Billy and Lee told me to stop being so fucking stupid. I finished off the barrel I had on the go and then slept for two days. I think Debra's onto something.

"Are you some kind of therapist?" I ask her.

She lets out an unexpectedly loud shout of laughter. People turn to look at us, some not so kindly. Debra ignores them all. Guess when you're dying, it's a waste of time caring what other people think.

"I'm a person who left no stone unturned in the quest to find out what was wrong with me," she says. "But before that, if you're in any way interested, I used to be a high school English teacher."

She sees me screw up my face and smiles wryly.

"School not your favorite place, either?"

"I stuck it out."

Mainly because my older sister Blair made me.

Debra smiles. "I used to inflict *Waiting for Godot* on my students," she says. "There's a moment when Estragon says, 'I can't go on', and Vladimir replies, 'That's what you think.'"

Her smile fades and she withdraws into her chair. I won't ask what the heck *Waiting for Godot* is because that's what Google is for. I should ask her about herself, if she needs anything, if she and Lee need help at home. I can hardly ask about what's going to happen next because she's told me. And I'm guessing there's nothing anyone can do about that.

"Hey, big guy."

Shit. Ava's right in front of me. I didn't see her come in. She looks okay, a little pale.

I get to my feet. "How did it go?"

"They made me stay still the whole time," she says. "I hate staying still."

"Any…?"

"Nasty discoveries?" She read my mind. "Scan has to go to an expert first. They'll read it and contact Doc Wilson."

"More waiting," I say.

"Yup…"

Ava moves in for an embrace. I wrap my arms around her and kiss the top of her head.

"Too bushed for beer and curly fries?" I murmur.

Kind of hoping she'll say yes, but it's her call. She's the one who's had a rough time. All I've had to do is sit and talk to—

Hell. Debra. I should introduce her. Which will be complicated, but I can hardly pretend I don't know her.

I look back over my shoulder, trying to think how to explain this to Ava. But Debra's not there. I peer out through the doorway. No sign. Guess she wanted to avoid complications, too.

Luckily, Ava doesn't notice any of this. She raises her head from my chest, and says, "Yes. Beer and fries, yes. And a burger. And a jug of margaritas. And—"

"And I've got work in the morning."

"Killjoy," she mutters, but with a smile.

"But I'll be the sober driver," I tell her. "Just as long as you don't force me to dance."

Chapter Twenty-Three

AVA

The Silver Saddle is a typical Western-style bar with a jukebox, pool tables, and a lot of wood paneling. It's owned by Brendan, who gave up truck driving, which he hated, to become a bar owner, which, if you didn't know him well, you'd think he hated, too. Brendan is brawny, dirty blond and tattooed, like he's an extra in *Sons of Anarchy*. Who knows, he might be. Rumor has it he's dating an actress who lives in LA. No one in Verity has ever seen this woman, so it could be a ruse to keep people with biker fantasies at bay. That and Brendan's manner, which Doc Wilson would describe as surly. "Customer service" isn't a phrase that Brendan puts much stock in. You'll get good food and beer, but you'll get it within Brendan's timeframe, which is dictated by whether he judges you okay or an asshole. Bear in mind that everyone starts as the latter and has to work their way up. Want to leave a bad review on

TripAdvisor? Go for it. Might first want to make sure your life insurance premiums are up to date.

Shelby and Nate are already here in the big corner booth, along with Shelby's besties, Chiara and Jordan. Rumor also has it that Jordan had a big crush on Brendan until she found out about the actress. Now, she's giving him the cold shoulder, and only comes into the bar because Verity's one other licensed establishment, Bartons hotel, doesn't serve beer. Okay, that's not strictly true. You can order a German fermenting lager at forty-five bucks or splash out on a limited edition vintage Danish brew that costs a mere hundred. Or you can come to The Silver Saddle and drink what you're given.

In my case, an ice-cold IPA that Cam's just set in front of me. Cam and Brendan are like non-speaking brothers from another mother, so he never has to wait long. He slides into the booth next to me. I love the feel of him next to me, but I can sense tension. Cam would rather be back in the hospital waiting room than in the spotlight that Chiara, Jordan, and Shelby have just (metaphorically) shone right in his eyes.

"How are things going with you and Ava?" Chiara asks.

"Uh," says Cam. "Ava's right here..."

"I can see that," says Chiara, as if she's humoring a slow person. "I want to hear it from you."

There's a pause.

"Good," he says.

Minimum viable answer. Risky move.

But Chiara's obviously feeling merciful.

"Glad to hear it," she says. "Keep on doing the right thing now."

From anyone else, that would sound like encouragement. From Chiara, it has an undertone of menace. I have no idea what she does with her life other than work reception at Bartons hotel. International jewel thief? Head of KAOS or SPECTRE?

Whatever, she could not be more different from Shelby's other best friend, Jordan. Where Chiara is dark and elegantly spiky, Jordan is all blonde, tanned bounce. Nate once described her to me as having the personality of a pile of Labrador puppies in the body of a 1950s pin-up. She can also drink like she's competing for the World Beer Pong Championship. I like her very much.

"These guys just told me that you fainted at the wedding!" Jordan says to me. "Are you okay?"

"There was a whole ambulance crew in the barn, bae," says Chiara. "Ava got carried away on a stretcher. How could you have missed that?"

Jordan blinks, accessing memory data files. "I was ... dancing?"

"Who with?"

"Javi's cousin," says Shelby. "You know, the one who's the underwear model?"

"How can you know this when Jordan doesn't?" Nate asks a very fair question.

"Probably had my eyes closed," says Jordan.

"You didn't want to look at the underwear model?" I inquire.

"I let the music take control," says Jordan. "You know? Like the song?"

We all stare. Her shoulders do an embarrassed little shimmy.

"Don't at me," she says. "I'm a very tactile person."

Ever practical, Nate brings us back on track. "Jordan's key question was: is Ava okay?" He stares hard at me. "Are you? How was today?"

I'd prefer never to think of it or mention it again. But unlike Chiara, Nate won't let me get away with a one-word answer.

"Ever had an MRI?" I ask them.

Group-wide shaking of heads.

"My advice? Try to avoid it. Unless you like being trapped in a narrow tube and forced not to move or swallow."

"You can't swallow?" says Nate.

"Not when the machine's on. They do give you a panic button to squeeze, though, so they're not completely heartless."

"I don't mind tight spaces," says Jordan. "But I hate keeping still—"

Relentless Nate steers the conversation back to me. "And what did the MRI show?"

I shrug. "Got to wait until they review the scans."

"Doc Wilson will call tomorrow," Cam chimes in unexpectedly. "And then we'll call you."

Wow, assertive.

He places his arm around my shoulders. And protective. I like it.

Nate likes it not one bit. "Okay, but surely they—"

"Burger and fries."

Two big hands lower two big plates in front of Cam and me. Double cheeseburger. Curly fries with a hint of cayenne. My appetite has been nonexistent today but suddenly I'm starving. Besides, shoving food in my mouth is a great way to avoid more talk.

"Everyone got what they want?"

Brendan has Chiara's trick of adding a hint of threat to a routine statement. Everyone nods. If anyone does have an additional request, it can wait.

"Another beer, Jordan?"

Brendan never asks twice. I catch Shelby widening her eyes at Chiara, who's become as inscrutably alert as a cat.

"No, thank you." Jordan's tone is clipped and formal. And she keeps her head turned to one side.

A man's gotta know when to walk away, as the song goes, and Brendan does just that. Back to the bar, where he ignores the customers angling for service, and proceeds to polish a whole tray of glasses. I know this because he's in my line of sight. And I have no shame when it comes to staring.

"It's been two months," says Shelby to Jordan. "What if he's broken up with the actress by now? You'll never ever know if you never talk to him ever again."

"Lot of 'never evers' there, Shel," says Chiara. "And he hasn't broken up with the actress—"

"I don't care," says Jordan with a toss of her head.

"*She* broke up with him."

Definitely head of KAOS or SPECTRE.

This news does not cheer Jordan.

"They broke up?" she says with a hiss. "And he didn't tell me?"

"Wait." Nate's frowning. "I might have the wrong end of the stick here, Jordan, but I was under the impression that you and Brendan had never gone out. Not even once."

He's treated to scorching stares from Jordan, Chiara, and his own dear wife, Shelby.

"That", says Chiara, "is beside the point. As you well know."

Nate's face says he knows no such thing and has no idea why they're mad at him. He turns to Cam for backup, but Cam holds up both hands in the surrender pose.

"Sorry, man," he says.

"It's not rational," Nate insists.

We can all recognize the last gasp of a man who knows he's outgunned. I fire the final shot to put him out of his misery.

"And were you completely rational when you fell in love, brother dear?"

Shelby lays her head on his shoulder. "He wanted to be, didn't you, honey bunch?"

"*Honey* bunch?" Nate rolls his eyes to the ceiling. "Jesus, fine, I give in. Stop torturing me."

Shelby kisses his cheek and smiles sweetly. Once again, I think how hilarious it is that uptight Nate fell in love with a woman who wears her heart permanently on show everywhere, not just on her sleeve. You're never in any doubt about what Shelby's feeling. Never ever, as she might say.

And then I sneak a look at Cam because I realize I'm worried about how *he's* feeling right now. We didn't talk about anything medical on our drive to the bar because I was bushed and needed a power nap. I didn't even acknowledge that he'd hung in there in the hospital waiting room. I'd half expected him not to be there, and I should have thanked him for going the distance, but again, super tired. The burger and fries have given me a bit more energy, but that will probably be canceled out by the beer. So, it isn't likely we'll have a coherent conversation between now and tomorrow morning.

Tomorrow morning is when I should hear from Doc Wilson. Maybe. Depending on when the specialist gets to my scans. And then, what kind of conversation will Cam and I have?

"You okay, Ava?"

It's Nate. Of course it is. Oldest brother has always felt responsible for the rest of the Durant clan, and he's extra vigilant when it comes to changes in our moods.

I feel Cam hastily shift around so he can get a better look at me. I don't want to see the concern in his brown eyes because, right now, it will do me in. I focus on Nate instead, because I've had lots of practice keeping my poker face intact around my family.

"I'm good," I lie. "Just tired. It was a long afternoon."

"We should go," says Cam. He sounds a little guilty, as if he feels to blame for over-taxing me.

"No!" I protest. "I've got another helping of curly fries to eat yet, remember?"

A new voice enters the fray. "Did someone say curly fries?"

"Jackson!" says Shelby. "Danny!"

She's happy to see the late arrivals. Judging by how tense he's suddenly become, Cam not so much.

"Room for two little ones?" says Jackson, gesturing to the booth.

"Absolutely not," says Chiara. "I need my space." She waves her hand. "Go fetch some chairs."

Obedient as a big hairy dog, Jackson grabs a chair in each hand, and flops down into his. Danny, being a highly competitive Durant, stays standing, a tiny power play he'll never win because it's obvious Chiara couldn't give two hoots whether he sits, stands, or does backward handsprings around the room.

To make it look like he has an actual valid reason for staying on his feet, Danny says to Jackson, "What can I get you?"

"Not fussy, man," says Jackson. "Any kind of beer'll do." He adds a slightly embarrassed, "Thanks."

My guess is Danny's been paying for everything, which he can easily afford, but I understand why Jackson has mixed feelings. No one likes being beholden. Or broke and needy. Once again, I'm reminded how lucky I am. Or spoiled, depending on how you look at it. Though I hope I've never taken my good fortune for granted.

Jackson says to Shelby, "Hey, I thought I'd go visit Mom tomorrow. Want to come?"

I feel Cam jump a little beside me. And I try not to think too hard about what that might signify.

Shelby makes a glum face. "I can't. Too busy."

Her expression goes from glum to concerned. "Is she okay, do you think? I've been texting her and she seems fine…"

Jackson flicks a look at Cam, and I feel the same tiny jolt go through him. What's going on? Is it the secret he's keeping for her? Or is it that Lee Armstrong always has that effect on him? I don't like either of those options, so I drink more of my beer. It's going straight to my head, so I'd better eat more fries, too. Oh, mine are gone. Cam's stopped eating his. I'll steal those.

"I'm sure Mom is fine," Jackson reassures his sister. "But I don't know when I'll be back this way, so I want to see her before I go."

Shelby looks glum again. "Don't stay away too long."

She reaches across the table and steals the last of Cam's curly fries. "You know, sometimes I wish the world wasn't so big," she says with a sigh. "I wish I had my family closer."

Nate and I raise an eyebrow at each other at the same time. Family is awesome, we're both thinking … but a little goes a long way.

Speaking of: brother Danny's been up at the bar for

longer than it should take to order two beers. I check out what's happening. Simple: Brendan is ignoring him. Danny's LA vibe probably reminds him of his ex-girlfriend. Or he's in the mood to punish someone for Jordan's continued coolness.

"Uh-oh," says Chiara. "I think your brother's about to click his fingers. That will not go down well." She places her wine glass on the table. "Time for an intervention."

She hustles Shelby and Nate out of the booth so she can exit, which she does with long-legged elegance. She strolls up to the bar like a catwalk model, places her hand on the small of Danny's back, and whispers in his ear.

"What's she saying?" I ask Cam. "Any guesses?"

Cam briefly shakes his head. He seems to have sunk into a fully non-verbal state, and it's starting to bug me. I know Cam doesn't socialize well, but all I can think about is that all *he's* thinking about is Lee Armstrong. One mention of her and he withdraws inside himself like a freaking hermit crab.

I'm tired; my brain is beer-fuzzy, and my emotional buttons are worn from being pushed. If I don't act now, I'm going to get super cranky. Last thing I want to do is have a big ol' fight on the way home.

I nudge Cam's arm. "Time to go."

That was the right thing to say to rouse him. He's on his feet, holding out his hand for me. I slide out of the booth to say my farewells.

"Take care, Ava," chorus Shelby and Jordan.

"Call me," says Nate, doing his best not to make it sound like an order.

I turn to Jackson, expecting one of his usual cheerful remarks. But he's staring up at Cam, who, reluctantly I can tell, is returning his gaze.

"Anything you want me to pass on to Mom ... to Lee?" Jackson asks him.

He's not smiling. His tone has more than a hint of challenge. What's going on here?

"Nope," says Cam.

His tone is like a shove in the chest. Seems the big ol' fight might not include me.

But turns out I'm the only witness. Jordan and Shelby are yakking away with Nate caught between them (which he secretly loves). And here's a ruffled Danny back with beers, followed by an amused Chiara. Jackson lets his gaze linger on Cam for a beat and then he turns away to greet Danny, and rib him about being a city slicker. The moment passes.

Cam takes hold of my arm, not hard but harder than usual, and steers me away. We get in the truck and Cam starts it up with a roar. He's furious and I've no idea why. And you know what? Right now, I don't give a shit. I'm tired, I'm scared, and I'm fed up with Lee Armstrong still pushing Cam's buttons. Cam promised to be here for me but part of him is still absent, far away with her.

I want to thump him on the arm. I want to yell at him. But, of course, I do the worst thing ever. I start bawling my eyes out.

Chapter Twenty-Four

CAM

Shit, Ava's crying.

I pull the truck over to the side of the road, shut off the engine. Ava's wiping her eyes furiously, and I can't tell whether she's crying because she's angry or angry because she's crying. I hesitate. Should I hug her or leave her alone? And then I berate myself. I'm doing it again, running from emotions. Get a grip, Hollander. You aren't the one hurting here.

"Hey," I say softly. "What's up?"

"*Everything!*" she replies, her voice hiccuping with sobs.

Not much to go on. But I can't let her do all the work.

"You're worried about the MRI results?"

She nods a little. Then covers her face with both hands and shakes her head.

Okay, Hollander. Think. What else could she be upset about?

Right...

"Me and Jackson," I say. "Yeah, that was … not cool." I add, "Sorry," even though what I want to say is, "He started it!"

But it seems I've struck out on that guess, too. Ava's still shaking her head. Slowly now, like she can't believe I'm being such an idiot. What else? I hardly said two words to anyone all evening. Chiara asked me how things were going with Ava, and I was honest about that. Maybe I could have said more but that's not my style. It's why I hardly responded to Jerkson's parting shot, either, that stupid pointed question about—

Ah, fuck…

I can see how Ava might think that clash was all about Lee. It wasn't. It was about Jerkson getting up in my face, and for no reason other than he enjoys being an annoying shitheel. He only ever tries to wind me up when there's a crowd of friendlies to keep him safe and laugh at his shitheel jokes.

"Jerkson is a fucking idiot," I say without thinking.

While the red mist has been rising in front of my my eyes, Ava's calmed herself down.

"He asked you that question for a reason," she says, with only the hint of a hiccup. "And you got all touchy for a reason. And all I can think is there's something more you're not telling me about Lee frigging Armstrong."

Though it doesn't feel that way, it's a fair accusation. Thing is, being honest will highlight further examples of my least-praiseworthy behavior. I haven't told Ava how I acted after I tried to kiss Lee. But if I don't, this answer won't make sense.

"Jerk— Jackson has always had issues about my friendship with Lee," I say.

I'm glad the Dodge's interior lighting is subpar. I don't want Ava to see how red my face is getting.

"I don't blame him," I say. "He's the oldest brother and even though he acts the clown, I think he feels a responsibility to the family. To make sure everyone's okay."

Ava's quiet, listening, but in the dark, I can't tell what she's thinking. I plow on.

"After the ... incident ... in the workshop between me and Lee, I was a mess. Never felt so ashamed. I mean, she and Billy were my friends. They'd been nothing but good to me, and I'd abused that. Abused their goodwill and their trust, and all because I couldn't get my act together. I let myself be ruled by anger and frustration. Only other time I've felt that bad about myself was during the..."

No. Don't want to go there. Not yet.

"Anyway," I say. "I was so desperate to make amends, I made it worse. Hung around the house and the office, offering to do odd jobs or errands, anything to be useful to Lee and Billy. Billy saw that I was agitated but he was a practical guy, so he took me at my word and gave me work to do. Lee tried to keep things normal, but after a while of me hanging around like a bad smell, she was forced to give me the hard word. She was polite but firm, told me to back off. And Jackson overheard..."

Which is probably why he still gets under my skin. Saw me at my weakest and worst.

"He came down to the workshop later that day and confronted me. Demanded to know what was going on between me and his mom. Course, I told him it was none of his fucking business, and he came at me swinging. And for a moment there, I was ready to pound him into the dirt. But my inner Doc Banner took over from my Incredible Hulk, and I let him hit me. Right in the jaw. Rookie mistake. Probably first time Jackson had hit anyone, and he didn't know to aim for the soft parts. Split his knuckles and almost broke his hand. Game over."

I'll skip the part where I fetched the same first aid kit Lee had used for me.

"I got us both a beer and told him there was nothing going on between me and Lee. He accepted it because he'd run out of fight, but he never fully believed it. That's why he had a go at me tonight."

Even if it's only a few seconds, the time spent waiting for Ava's response seems to drag on forever.

When she finally speaks, her voice is quiet, subdued. "It's tough feeling like you always fall short."

Not exactly sure who she's referring to here. "Are you talking about Jackson or me?"

I see the flash of a smile. "All of us, dummy," she says.

Can't take offense—she's correct. When it comes to how humans work, I am dumb as a post.

Because while I can see why her remark might be relevant to me and Jackson, I can't see how she can group herself in with us. Far as I know, before she got sick, Ava succeeded at everything she put her mind to.

"When have you ever felt you fell short?" I ask her. "You were a college track champ, a star horse rider. You—"

"*Were*," says Ava. "That's the key word. I was. I *used to be* those things. What am I now?"

I know this question. Know it well. For seven years, I had the answer: I was a soldier. I was a good soldier, too, capable, strong. And then I wasn't. I didn't see the end coming the way it did. Thought the odds were high I'd be injured physically, but I never considered the real damage would happen to my mind, my spirit. It was like I'd been erased, like chalk on a blackboard, rubbed down to nothing but dust. If it hadn't been for Billy and Lee, who knows what might have happened to me? At least now I feel like I have a home, and some kind of purpose, even if it is just making barrels and fixing stuff. But it took a long time for me to get there.

I'm starting to understand what Ava means. When you have to rebuild your life from scratch, it can seem an impossible task. And it's even worse for her, because of the uncertainty around her health. She's in limbo, which probably feels more like purgatory.

What comfort can I offer her? It's not like I'm the greatest example of how to get your life back on track.

But maybe that's not what's needed here. Maybe all Ava needs now is the comfort of knowing she's got support…

"Hey, this might be stupid idea," I say, "but do you want

to come with me to the therapy riding class on Sunday? Maybe help out?"

"Do I get to watch you ride?" she asks with a quick smile.

"Hell, no," I reply. "I walk alongside. And keep well away from the parts that bite and kick."

"You never did tell me why you volunteer there," she says. Not accusing, just curious.

Hoo boy. There's a very good reason for that. It's the secret. The biggest one I have. Question is: do I have the courage to go there?

"It's a long story." And before she can speak, I add, "But I'll tell you if you want to hear it."

Ava's quiet for a moment. "This is about the war, isn't it?"

Every part of me constricts, like I'm being crushed by an invisible weight. I'm struggling for breath. My fingers have the steering wheel in a death grip.

"Cam." Ava's hand is on my arm. "You don't have to do this now. There'll be another time. I can wait."

But I can't, is my sudden realization. I can't have this ... *darkness* ... inside me any longer. I've held it in for ten years and that's way too long. Even though I'd like nothing better right now than to crawl into bed with Ava and lose myself inside her, I *can't* wait. The time is now.

"I want to tell you," I say. "I need to. If that's okay...?"

Since we've parked up, the temperature in the Dodge has been steadily dropping. I'm about to turn the engine back on, crank up the heat, when Ava says, "Do you have any cocoa?"

"Uh…" I think hard. "I do, yeah. Pretty sure."

"Itty-bitty marshmallows?"

"All out of those," I admit. "Slug of bourbon instead?"

"Now you're talking," she says. "Drive on. Alcohol-laced bedtime drinks await."

I was kind of joking about the bourbon, but as we hit the road again and I realize what I've promised, I'm beginning to think that one slug will definitely not be enough.

Chapter Twenty-Five

AVA

Some people like to rage when they're jealous and let their other half know exactly how they feel. Me, I prefer to put jealousy in a Tupperware container and store it at the back of the refrigerator. I might throw it out or I might re-heat it later. All depends.

This evening, being at a low ebb all around, I was definitely close to tossing my jealousy on the barbecue and flaming it. Glad I didn't. It might be embarrassing to burst into soggy tears but it's better than a shouting match. If I'd shouted, then I probably wouldn't be getting bourbon cocoa. Marshmallows would have made it perfect, but you can't have everything.

I shouldn't be making jokes, but that's my schtick when I'm uncomfortable. This is a huge deal for Cam, and a pivotal moment in our relationship. I want to be there for him, but I'm also afraid that I won't have what it takes to give him what he might need. The Durant idea of therapy was seeded in our dad's motivational comments, including such gems as "Excuses are for losers" and "Pain is weakness leaving the body".

But I'm leaping ahead, impatient as always. Right now, what I can and should do is shut up and listen. Whatever comes next, we can deal with it at the time.

Cam closes his front door behind us and moves immediately to light the woodburning stove. I watch him as he places the hewn logs and kindling inside and sets it all alight. He does it efficiently, with practised ease, and once again, I'm struck by how comforting it is to be around a man who knows how to do practical stuff well. When you've spent your life focusing only on competitive activities, it's humbling to realize how limited your abilities really are. I can run, and I can ride and look after a horse. That's it, folks. Don't rally round me when the zombie apocalypse strikes.

He stands up. His expression is … strained, taut. And I suddenly feel super guilty, like I emotionally blackmailed him into this.

I step forward and slide my arms around his waist, rest my head on his chest. I can see why they make sheets out of flannel. It's so soft and relaxing. Well, it would be relaxing if I couldn't hear Cam's heart thumping. Strong but probably a little too fast.

"You don't have to," I say. "Tell me, I mean. We can just drink our cocoa cocktail and go night-night."

"You keep giving me an out." There's a bite in his tone which is very un-Cam. "Do you not want to hear it?"

A fair question. I'm telling myself I'm being kind to Cam by not forcing him to dig back down into the dirt of his worst memories. But maybe it's my feelings I'm putting first? Maybe I'm the one who's afraid?

Shit. That's the truth right there. Cam's story—I *am* afraid of hearing it. I'm afraid because it's about when his life changed forever, and not for the better. Yes, okay, he finally found his place, but it took years, and after tomorrow, when I get the results of the MRI, I might learn that years of struggle are ahead of me, too. Cam thought he was mentally strong until he got broken. How will *I* fare? How strong will *I* be?

"Ava?"

Cam's waiting for me to answer. Have I got what it takes to hear his story? I guess there's only one way to find out…

"Is it too cold to sit under the stars?" I ask.

That was not what he expected to hear. "Uh … I could grab some blankets?" he says. "And a bench seat from the workshop?"

"You do that. I'll get busy brewing cocoa."

Cam's shaking his head, half-smiling, like the evening suddenly got strange but he's okay to roll with it.

"Bourbon's in the top cupboard under the stairs," he says. "Next to the emergency survival kit."

"I like your priorities." I grin and hurry him along with a wave. "Go. Blankets. Seating. Before the night sky clouds over."

When I head outside with two steaming mugs, Cam lets me sit on the bench before wrapping a big soft wool blanket around my shoulders. He also gently slides a hat onto my head.

"Short hair's not much protection from the frost," he says, tugging it down over my ears. "You need a woolly mane like mine."

"Some men don't like women with short hair," I say.

Cam sits down beside me. "Some men can't see past their own ego to what's really important."

I hand him his mug of hot cocoa. "It's got a ton of cream, sugar, and alcohol in it. I suspect it'll taste like those really bad liqueurs we used to drink in our teens."

"Ugh, yeah," says Cam with a shudder. "That bright green melon one. Same color out as in."

"Ee-yew!" I protest. "Okay, on that note, I'd better test this concoction out…"

I take a sip of the hot cocoa.

"Not bad," is my verdict. "If I do say so myself."

Cam doesn't look convinced, but he also takes a sip.

"Shit," he says. "That is good."

"All the food groups: fat, sugar, alcohol, and Hershey's cocoa powder."

We're happy making small talk, though we both know we're putting off the moment of truth. But it's a beautiful night, why not enjoy it? Cam's workshop is in a small clearing, so the sky is a patch of velvet black above us, framed by a lattice of moon-touched branches. Still, dark, and deep, like a Robert Frost poem. The stars are strewn all over like the sugar I may have accidentally spilled on Cam's kitchen counter. The longer you look, the more stars you see: great swathes of them, reaching farther and farther outwards, all the way to infinity.

"Gives you perspective, doesn't it?" says Cam. "The universe is so big we don't even feature so much as a pin prick."

"You know, we should find that comforting," I tell him. "Because no matter how badly we mess up, in the grand scheme of things it's not important at all."

"Still hurts though. Even if the universe doesn't care…"

Cam's voice is quiet, distant. The moment of truth. Best not put it off any longer.

"What happened?" I ask softly.

He's propped his elbows on his legs, bent over, staring at the ground, both hands wrapped around the mug of cocoa. It's too dark to see his expression, but I do catch the corner of his mouth rising in a wry smile.

"It's the shortest story I'll ever tell you. Happened in the blink of an eye. You wouldn't think it'd have such an effect, but it did."

My urge is to reach out and touch him, but I don't want to interrupt the flow. I think it's best if I just sit quietly and let him take however long he needs.

"I was the ideal soldier," he begins. "Mainly because I never thought too hard about anything. Took each moment as it came, followed orders, did what had to be done. Liked the camaraderie of my platoon but never got too close to anyone. Didn't see the point when tomorrow they might be gone. If I'd ever been asked to describe myself, I'd have said I was pragmatic. But the truth is I was self-centered. That's the trouble when you enlist young: you haven't had time to get over your teenage self-absorption, the conviction that the world revolves around you. And I was lazy," he adds. "Army rules meant I hardly ever had to think for myself. I never had to consider the consequences of my actions because I was just doing a job. I believed those above me knew what they were doing, and if it was okay with them, then it was okay with me..."

Cam's assessment of his young self seems overly harsh to me. But it's his story. He has to tell it as he sees it.

"We were stationed at a base in Eastern Afghanistan, and I'd never taken much notice of what was around us. Which was locals—mothers, fathers, kids—trying to get on with their lives. I didn't bother to notice them because they were outside the scope of my job. They weren't relevant. Then, one day, a bunch of insurgents decided to attack the base. Fired on us with no warning, overshot ... hit the local village..."

Oh no. I take a sip of cocoa because I need the comfort. But I don't really taste it.

"We were sent out to help," Cam says. "First thing I saw was a little girl and a scrappy mule, both of them lying in the dust, the mule screaming and flailing, its back leg shot almost clean off. The little girl was trapped underneath, and I could see she was badly injured, too. But there was no way I could lift that animal while it was in that state. So, I shot it in the head, put it out of its misery. As it flopped down lifeless, I caught the little girl's eye. She can't have been any more than nine years old, and the fear on her face... She began to struggle under the dead weight of the mule but there was no way she could escape. I bent toward her, but she screamed at me. I'll never forget that sound, so full of rage and pain and terror. I realized she thought I was going to shoot her, too…"

Cam cricks his neck, takes a breath.

"All this happened in no more than two minutes. Me running up, me shooting the mule, the girl screaming. But in those two minutes everything changed. I looked outside my small narrow world for the first time, saw what I was part of. Saw what that meant…"

He's gone completely still. Lost back in the moment. I feel sad, and I feel angry, too: how many young people like Cam have gone into war with no real idea about what it might be like, only to have the truth be so traumatic they never fully recover? Most people enlist because they genuinely want to do good in the world—fight bad guys, help keep peace—but it's never that simple, is it? War's chaotic, full of gray areas. A mess.

I can see now how easy my life has been. I've never really been tested, not in any meaningful way. Maybe that's why I needed to hear this story: to prepare me for what might be required of me after tomorrow.

I'm assuming Cam's done, but amazingly, he pushes on. "Next moment, or so it seemed, I woke up in the army hospital. Apparently, a big fucking mortar shell exploded close by, and I was incredibly lucky it didn't blow me to bits. Still, I had internal bleeding, broken bones, concussion. I was in the hospital a good long while."

He turns to me. The faint moonlight casts deep shadows on his face.

"You're probably wondering about the little girl," he says. "Truth is, I can't tell you. There were a lot of civilian casualties that day. I like to imagine that she was saved. But in my heart of hearts, I know she never got to live her life."

All the things I want to say to him—it wasn't your fault, you did the best you could—they might be true but they're no help at all. So, I say the only thing that's left.

"I love you," I tell him. "And I'm so glad you're here with me now."

He doesn't respond. He doesn't have to. Not yet. I rest my head against his shoulder, and we sit there listening to the quiet sounds around us in the cold, starry night.

Chapter Twenty-Six

CAM

Ava's alarm wakes me up out of the deepest sleep I've had for a good long while. I lie with my eyes closed, waiting for her to hit the snooze button, but the alarm jingles on. I should probably be grateful that you can't program your own sounds into an iPhone alarm, otherwise no doubt I'd be serenaded by some kind of death metal riff. If death metal has riffs.

Still jingling. Either Ava is still sleeping as deeply as I was until a minute ago, or she's not in the bed. Nothing for it. I have to exit the last stages of dreamland and come back to the real world. And punch that phone into submission.

She's not in the bed. I listen but can't hear any noise downstairs. I rub my eyes to get myself fully awake. Soon as I do, the memories of last night come flooding back, and though the bedroom is warm, I start to shiver. I've only told that story to two people. First time, I told Lee, and now I remember how much it hurt. It was like I'd woken up in the hospital all over again, knowing the pain in my body was the least of it. Lee urged me to go to therapy, but the prospect of reliving that moment once again, and in front of a stranger ... I couldn't do it. And it's taken me years to work up the courage to tell it again.

Maybe that's why Ava's not in the bed. Maybe she woke up and realized what a total disaster I am, and made a run for it.

Come on, Hollander. That's your self-pity talking. You know Ava isn't the running type. If Ava has a problem, she's upfront about it. And besides, last night she told you she—

Shit. My sleep-fuzzed brain is slow to kick into gear. Did Ava really say those words? If so, did she mean them?

"Hey."

Ava elbows open the bedroom door, a mug in each hand. I sincerely hope they contain coffee. Hot cocoa suited the mood last night, but this morning, I need a big kick of caffeine.

I sit up in the bed, take the mug she offers me. Black coffee. Smells strong. Outstanding.

Ava slides in next to me. She's wearing nothing but my flannel shirt, and her bare legs are cold against mine. She blows on her mug before taking a sip. I can feel my whole body tense up, waiting for her to speak.

Takes me ten seconds to crack. "Last night? Did you ... did I hear you say...?"

Ava turns to me, eyes questioning. "Was I talking in my sleep? Did I mention parrots?"

"Parrots? No..." I'm dying here. "Before that. When we were outside..."

She blows on her coffee mug, frowns as if trying to recollect. I start to have the tiniest inkling that she's messing with me.

"You said you loved me." There. It's out.

"Oh, *that*..."

Her blue eyes are sparkling with amusement.

"Goddammit, Ava!" I'd thump her with a pillow, but I don't want to spill my coffee.

She laughs out loud, then gives me a sideways look.

"And do you remember what you said?" she asks.

No. After that, I don't remember saying anyth—

Right. Shit. I am so fucking slow sometimes.

I look her straight in her laughing blue eyes and say what I should have said many hours ago.

"I love you, too."

"Good," she says with a smile.

And then her smile falters a little, and she dips her head down to her coffee mug, blows again, but doesn't sip.

The last fuzz of sleep leaves my brain, and everything is suddenly crystal clear. Today's the day Ava finds out her MRI results. And I haven't even mentioned it. Okay, so telling Ava I love her is important, but this is important and urgent.

"Doc called yet?"

Ava turns to me with a faint smile. "It's eight in the morning. Not even Doc Wilson can hustle people along that fast." She shrugs one shoulder. "I'd say noon at the earliest."

I recognize that tactic. Setting your expectations as low as possible, in the hope of keeping disappointment to a minimum.

"Doc is a hustler," I say. "He won't allow you to wait a minute longer than you should."

Ava holds her coffee mug tight and breathes in. "I know," she says on the exhale. "But what do I do until then? Every one of those minutes is going to be like an hour."

And I have to leave her to go to work because I have to. I've used up all my favors in that regard.

But then, every cloud…

"Why don't you come with me to the vineyard?" I suggest. "It's mostly maintenance work, so kind of boring. But you could hang out with Shelby … and Nate, I guess."

"Busy, busy Nate," Ava says with a wry grin. "Though being busy isn't all bad."

She sounds a little wistful. I wish I could offer her something better than a morning watching me check tanks and tinker with the tractor. I wish I could make all her worries go away.

"Okay, I'll come," she says. "But first, something very important."

My gut clenches. Is she about to revisit last night? I don't honestly think I've got the strength.

Ava reaches over and sits her mug on the floor by the bed. Then, in one quick movement, she pulls the flannel shirt up and over her head, so she's entirely naked. The blood that's overheating my brain does a U-turn and rushes south. I place my coffee mug on the floor, too.

But just to be sure…

"The important thing is sex, right?"

Ava smiles. "I love that we prioritize clear communication in our relationship."

She shifts closer, and runs her hand over my abdomen, causing every muscle to jump like they've been wired into the mains.

"And I love you, too," she adds. "But no talk now, only this."

Ava bends her head and runs her tongue up the length of my—

Whatever limited ability I had to talk before, it goes right out the window.

As soon as we pull up outside the vineyard office, Nate strides over to meet us.

"Well?" is his greeting.

"Nice to see you, too," says Ava. "And no, nothing from Doc. Time to practise the virtue of patience, big brother."

"Good thing that runs in our family," he says with a grimace.

"I thought Ava could hang out here today," I say. "Maybe give Shelby a hand with … whatever she's got on?"

"Did someone say my name?"

Shelby's walking toward us, carrying what looks like ... I don't know, a straw voodoo doll?

"It's a corn dolly!" She waves it at us. "I made it!"

Ava says what I'm thinking. "Why?"

Shelby looks down fondly at the doll in her hand. It's very basic, with two straight out arms and no face. I guess love is in the eye of the beholder.

"Mom used to make corn dollies at this time of year," she says. "She used to do a whole Fall display, with straw bales and wreaths and fairy lights. Made the vineyard look so pretty."

"She did all that for our wedding," Nate reminds her. "I hope you're not going to ask her to do it all over again?"

Shelby's not listening. She's lost in the warm fuzzy world of nostalgia. I wish she'd snap out of it. All this talk of Lee is the last thing I need. Last thing Ava needs.

"Mom even made a scarecrow one year that looked just like Cam."

Goddammit.

"How did she make it look like Cam?" says Ava.

I can't tell if she's amused or irked.

"It was tall with bushy hair," says Shelby. "And it was wearing a flannel shirt."

"That describes one in every three men around here," says Nate, who is definitely irked. Maybe he's on edge, worried about Ava. Or maybe he's put out that no one's made a scarecrow that looks like him. I mean, it's quite an honor.

Shelby waves her creation at Ava. "Do you want to help me make more dollies?"

Seeing Ava's face, she adds, "Or you could arrange some pumpkins?"

"Corn husks it is," says Ava. "Lead me to them."

I watch her walk off with Shelby. I know rustic crafts wasn't how she expected to spend the morning, but I'm glad she'll have company.

I turn to see Nate giving me a hard stare.

"Doc definitely hasn't called?" he says. "There's nothing you two are keeping from us?"

"Nothing," I try to assure him.

"Because you've got a track record of making promises around secrets."

Man, Nate is wound up tight this morning. I could take offense at his tone, but I understand where he's coming from. And he's right.

"Doc hasn't called," I say. "We know nothing. I swear."

Nate rubs his hand over his hair. "Sorry," he mutters. "I've had both my parents in my ear all day every day since this started. Somehow, they're convinced I'm the one who should be in control of the situation. I'm starting to think Shelby and I should skip town and start a new life under assumed names."

"It's okay, man," I say. "This is tough."

Nate takes a deep breath, blows it out. "Mom and Dad—Dad especially, no surprise—keep talking about what we should do if Ava has got multiple sclerosis. I know they want to reassure themselves she'll be looked after no matter what, but it's grinding me down. The only thing worse than feeling useless is feeling afraid and useless. I almost wish Ava had got something obviously bad. You know, like gangrene. Or Ebola. Then at least we'd know by now."

What can I say? I'm totally with him. Not knowing sucks balls.

"Guys?"

It's Shelby, calling at us from the house. She sounds anxious.

Nate and I exchange a quick look and start walking, fast. Looks like the waiting might be at an end.

Chapter Twenty-Seven

AVA

I've never had to wait for big news like this before. When I applied for the exercise rider job at the big racing stable, I had no doubt I'd get it. You could call that arrogance, but I knew I was exactly what they wanted because I'd done my research. And I killed it in the interview. So, waiting for them to phone me and offer me the job wasn't stressful. I wasn't anxious one bit. Now, I wish I had been, so I'd be more prepared for this morning. To make the time pass faster, I throw myself into making corn dollies. Two down and now I'm on to number three. Okay, so the arms are crooked on that one and this one's skirt is all ragged, but what's important is that I am pumping them out. I am a corn-dolly-making machine.

I check the time again. Exactly three minutes and twenty-five seconds have gone by. It's official. Waiting makes me insane. Even Shelby is giving me worried looks, and she's the one who decided to decorate the vineyard with corn husks and gourds.

When my phone rings, I have a new appreciation for the cliché about your heart leaping into your mouth. My heart's now firmly lodged in the back of my throat, which is probably why I want to throw up. I tell you, this better not be someone selling me cryptocurrency. My screech of rage will burst their eardrums.

Phone says "Doc". Goddammit, I've waited so long and now I'm not ready. But Doc's a busy man and if I don't answer now, he might—

"Hi, Doc," I say.

"How are you keeping, Ava?"

Doc sounds bright and cheerful. But that's his default setting, so I won't read anything into it.

"I'm ... okay, I guess?"

Depends on what he says next, of course.

At that moment, Cam and Nate hustle into the room, followed by Shelby, who obviously went to fetch them. I've got three sets of worried eyes staring at me, and I imagine my worried eyes are staring right back at them.

"Well, looks like you are," says Doc. "Okay, that is."

"Okay..." I echo unconsciously. I'm not quite processing what he's saying.

Fortunately, Doc's not a time waster.

"The MRI showed nothing to be concerned about," he tells me. "So, between that and the bloodwork, we can rule out any life-threatening conditions."

Oh, thank God. I cup my face in my free hand. I'm too numb to even feel relieved.

"But—"

Oh, shit.

"The level of fatigue you've been experiencing is not normal," Doc says. "The best-case scenario is that you're burned out. The worst is that you have myalgic encephalomyelitis—"

My-*what?*

"—otherwise known as chronic fatigue syndrome. Now, you haven't mentioned any body aches and pains, so I'm hopeful it's not the latter because there's no cure."

"No cure?"

I shouldn't have said that. In unison, Cam, Nate, and Shelby all gasp. But I don't want to interrupt Doc, so I flap my hand at them to indicate that it's nothing fatal.

"Currently no cure for chronic fatigue syndrome, no," says Doc. "But if it is that, then we can put a plan in place to manage your symptoms."

"Does this mean more tests?"

"Nope, it means doing what you Durants hate most—waiting and seeing."

Doc knows us too well.

"You need a proper period of rest and recuperation, with a stable routine, emotional support, good nutrition, no alcohol."

Yikes.

"And if it's burnout, you should come right in a month

or so. If there's no improvement in that time, and if no other symptoms arise, then we'll assume it's chronic fatigue."

"So—a month?"

Shelby gasps again and claps her hands to her face. Cam and Nate go pale. I should have put the call on speaker.

"That doesn't mean I only have a month to live," I tell them. "I'm not dying."

"Fuck's sake," Nate breathes out.

Shelby keeps her hands over her face. Cam closes his eyes and tilts his head to the ceiling.

"I'd like you to see a nutritionist," Doc rolls on, oblivious to the three heart attacks he's inadvertently caused. "And it might be a good idea to get one of those doodads that monitors your sleep, pulse, and blood pressure."

A doodad. Right.

"Come and see me in two weeks, Ava. And do not overexert yourself. You hear me, Little Missy?"

"I hear you, Doc. Two weeks. Be chill."

Doc sighs. "You Durants will be the death of me," he says, and ends the call.

My hand flops down in my lap, like the phone suddenly weighs a ton, and I let out a long pent-up breath.

Surprising no one, impatient Nate is the first to speak.

"Well? Jesus, Ava, what did he say?"

"I need a doodad," I tell him.

Wrong time to make jokes. Nate looks like the anger guy from the movie *Inside Out*.

"Sorry, sorry," I apologize. "Everyone, pull up a chair. Here's the deal…"

They all sit, and I tell them what Doc just told me.

"We need coffee," declares Shelby after I'm done, and bustles over to the kitchen counter.

"Doc said *good* nutrition," Nate calls after her.

Shelby's coffee has been known to double as an engine degreaser.

And black coffee is all I've had today, so Nate probably has a point. I'll pass.

It occurs to me that Cam's said nothing. His posture in the chair is more sprawled than seated, like he's dropped into it from a height. I catch his eye and give him an "Are you okay?" look. A slow smile breaks, and he starts shaking his head, as if to say he has no idea what the hell just happened. I know exactly how he feels. This is surreal. But guess what? I'm not dying!

I'm not dying and all I might need to feel like myself again is a month of rest. This I can do. Oh, yes. I can eat properly, and get enough sleep, and not drink.

Okay, maybe two out of three. Two-and-a-half if I stick to beer.

I get up, shake out my tense muscles and hop round behind Cam so I can hug him from behind, bury my face in his woodsmoke hair, nuzzle his neck. He pushes back his chair and pulls me onto his lap. Kisses me hard, and I kiss him right back.

"Ava."

Nate's voice has the effect of a sluice of ice water.

"Yes, Nate," I reply from Cam's lap.

"I know I'm being a huge buzzkill—"

"Never!"

"It's my superpower, I embrace it," says Nate. "But you should call Mom and Dad. They've been worrying themselves into a state."

"And calling you on the hour every hour."

It's not a question. I know our parents. Mom will be polite and "just want to know if anything's changed", while Dad will be demanding, like it's ridiculous that a whole hour has passed without someone providing him with an answer.

I think about talking to Dad and my heart sinks. As I said, when we were growing up, his mantra was every variation along the line of "No excuses". Unless we had a broken limb or a fever that required hospitalization, we had to keep going. Weakness of mind or body was not to be tolerated. "No pain, no gain, shut up and train" was another of his motivational gems.

His attitude didn't change even when Doc diagnosed his heart condition. Dad was convinced he could beat it on his own, with pure living and supplements sourced from rain forest fungi or whatever. Took him weeks to accept that surgery was the only option.

Now, he's mellowed a little, but I know that he still worships at the altar of self-discipline. If I tell him that my illness is potentially nothing but fatigue ... I can almost feel the coldness of his response from here. I can feel his disappointment in me the way I always have. Even now I'm a grown-ass woman who should be thrilled she's not dying, I find myself falling back down into a slump.

But it seems Nate's been reading my mind. "Dad will be happy you're okay," he insists. "Remember how he was after I passed out that time? He didn't give me shit because it was *only* anemia."

Shelby is back with the battered coffee pot. I swear, there's a black film on the outside of it, like the coffee is strong enough to seep through the metal.

"Mitch adores all you children," she says. "Of *course* he'll be happy."

Shelby has known our dad all of a few months. Plus, she believes everyone is as nice as she is. Which they are when they're around her. Wish I could have the effect on Dad.

She pours Cam a coffee that steams in a way that suggests it's become sentient. Cam pulls the mug toward him absent-mindedly, and frowns.

"Your dad would give you shit for not having a serious illness?" he says to me.

I wriggle off his lap and onto the next chair, and shrug. Still not able to be fully honest about this subject.

"I'm probably projecting," I deflect. "Dad always drove us pretty hard, and I hear his voice in my head a lot."

"You too, huh?" says Nate with a small smile.

"I get it," says Cam, nodding. "My sergeant could clean a rifle just by shouting down it."

"Oh, boy…"

That's it. Everything has caught up with me. I fold my

arms on the table and rest my head on them. Not good manners, but I am done.

"I can call Mom and Dad if you like," says Nate.

He's such a good brother. I think I'm going to cry.

Nope, Ava, pull yourself together. You've been given a reprieve. This is your newly minted life to take charge of, so do it.

I sit up and grab my phone. Head out of the kitchen for some privacy, and to give them all a break. Call Mom first because I always do. Talk to her, and then, briefly, to Dad.

When I come back into the kitchen, everyone stares.

"It went fine," I tell them. "But I have some bad news."

"Jesus, what now?" says Nate.

"We're all having dinner at Mom and Dad's this evening." I turn to Cam. "Including you."

Chapter Twenty-Eight

CAM

I was raised on a farm. We didn't own it; my dad was the manager. Grew oats, barley, and corn. Got by. Just. People think of Wyoming as cattle rancher country, but there are plenty of other ways to scratch a living out of the land. Blair worked after school as a checkout operator to save up for her first horse. Worked that job right through to graduation, on top of all her farm chores, so she could pay for her horse's upkeep. Back then, I thought she was crazy working so hard, wasting her teen years, when she could be out there, hanging with the boys, having fun. What I didn't realize was that, unlike me, Blair could look further ahead than the next day. She'd set her life goals when she was fourteen, and nothing and no one was going to prevent her achieving them.

I'm not exactly sure when goats came into the picture, but she's turned them into a thriving business. Goat milk, cheese and yogurt, all farm fresh and top quality. She used to sell direct off the farm but that got too busy, so now she sells her products into high-end grocery stores. Blair feels a little conflicted that only well-off people can afford her wares, so she also supplies free milk and cheese to the local mission and women's refuge. Blair's not wealthy, but her life is rich. She's happy.

Which is a long-winded way of saying that I did not grow up with money. We weren't desperately poor but there were no luxuries. Our family friends were people like us. Blair and I didn't know any rich kids and even if we had, we'd have avoided them. We were like reverse snobs, looking down on kids who'd never known what it was like to have calluses on your hands and dirt under your fingernails. Who had fancy cars and clothes, and more hi-tech gadgets and gear than they could ever use. Who'd go on to high-paying jobs because their parents knew their bosses. We were a little envious, of course we were, but that kind of life didn't sit right with us. To me and Blair, it seemed rich people had only one priority: protect their wealth, and if that meant leaving the poor and vulnerable to scrabble in the dust, tough luck. To me and Blair, that attitude was pure D wrong.

Thing is, I've never been able to test that belief because I've never spent one minute in the company of rich people. Until now.

"What do I wear?" I ask Ava. "And what do I bring? Flowers? Some wine?"

"Relax."

Ava's grinning. Glad my social anxiety amuses one of us.

"No one in the history of the world has ever relaxed when someone's told them to relax." I try not to sound huffy.

"Fair," agrees Ava. "Okay, I'm wearing jeans and a long-sleeved tee, both black, naturally. Fully casual, which is what everyone in my family expects from me. You should wear whatever you feel comfortable in."

"I'm not going to feel comfortable, no matter what I wear," I say. "Prospect of meeting your parents terrifies me."

"And you have good reason," says Ava.

Great.

"But I'll be there," she adds. "And so will Nate and Shelby. You'll have protection."

Way to make me feel like a coward.

Ava slips her arms around my waist. "Don't fret. Nate and Dad will probably start arguing, and everyone will forget you're even there."

"You're not helping," I tell her.

She hugs me tight. "You'll be fine. Seriously. They will love you as much as I do."

I want to believe her. I really do. But this is way out of my comfort zone. As I get dressed in my one good shirt and jeans, it occurs to me again how sheltered my life has been here at Flora Valley. Billy, Lee, Shelby, all the crew, they accepted me as I am, an unsociable loner. Okay, Lee did have a try at influencing my love life, but she never scolded me when it didn't work out. Maybe she should have? Maybe everyone's been too easy on me, and more enforced socializing would have done me good. Made me more confident.

Too late now. I'll have to face the Durant lion's den with what minimal social skills I have. And hope I don't get mauled.

"Ready?" says Ava.

"Nope," I reply.

"Me neither," she says. "Let's go."

I think my nerves are under control until we round the last corner of the Durants' driveway (or tree-lined avenue, whichever you prefer). Outside the house is Nate's gray Ford pick-up, but also a red Mercedes sportscar.

"Oh." Ava sounds guilty. "I forgot. Danny and Jackson will probably be at dinner, too. They don't leave for LA until the weekend."

That's all I need. Dumb and Dumber, world's shittiest comedy duo.

"I'll keep Jackson under control," says Ava.

She read my mind. Or possibly my body language. My hands are clenched so tight I'm having trouble letting go of the steering wheel.

The front door of the Durant mansion is shut, and I stop, expecting to have to knock. But Ava pushes it open, waltzes right in. I hesitate, but not too long because she's almost out of sight. This place is so big that if I don't have a guide, I might never see daylight again.

I follow Ava into a spacious living room. My first impression is that it's been decorated by someone with good taste and a big budget. But I don't get a chance for a good look around because the room is full of people, and they're all staring at me.

"Mom, Dad," says Ava, "this is Cam Hollander. My boyfriend."

Boyfriend is right. I feel about sixteen years old, turning up to take my girl to the prom. Being scrutinized with a cold eye by a father who knows exactly what I've been doing with his daughter and is of the opinion that medical castration should be the norm, not the exception.

What makes it worse is that Ava's dad has blue eyes just like hers, only glacial. And a mouth set in a line so straight you could rest a spirit level on it.

He holds out his hand. "Mitchell Durant."

I take it and try to match the pressure he exerts. Not too hard, but firm enough to show he's no pushover. Ava's dad is the same height as Nate, about six feet. Shorter than me, but right now I feel like I'm shrinking under his gaze.

"Good to meet you, sir," I say.

"And I'm Ava's mother, Ginny."

Thank God, a friendly face. Ginny Durant is a fine-looking woman, with blonde hair that looks expensive and a smile that's pure sunshine.

"It's so nice to finally meet you, Cam," she says, taking

my hands and giving them a squeeze. "We're so grateful for everything you've done for Ava."

"I'm grateful for everything you've done *to* me," Ava mutters quietly enough so that—hopefully—only I can hear.

"It's my pleasure, ma'am." Could be speaking to both of them. Though Ava would object to being called "ma'am".

"And, of course, you know Nate and Shelby," says Ginny. "Have you met my middle son, Danny, and Shelby's brother, Jackson, who's our guest?"

I think I hear Mitchell Durant harrumph, but he could just be clearing his throat.

"Cam knows everyone, Mom," says Ava. "So could you please, *please* offer him a drink?"

"I'll get drinks," says Nate. "Beer, Ava?"

"No, thanks." She makes a glum face. "Doc told me no alcohol."

"Finally," says her father. "Alcohol is a destructive poison. Your body would be better off with Class A drugs as long as they were pure."

Nate brings me beer in a glass and hands it over with a murmured, "Let the games begin."

Ava starts chatting away to her mom. My gaze wanders over to Danny and Jackson lounging in the corner. Jackson nods coolly and with a hint of "fuck you". My blood rises. If he gets into it with me tonight, swear to God, I'll—

"Puff?"

Shelby's in front of me with a plate.

"Salmon and dill," she adds. "Delicious but crumbly. Here. Take a napkin."

I do my best to juggle the beer glass, napkin, and canapé. This is why I don't socialize. It requires a level of multi-tasking that I am one hundred percent not up to.

And this, of course, is the exact moment Mitchell Durant decides to engage me in conversation.

"Nate tells me you were in the army?" is his opening.

"Yes, sir," seems a safe response. "Infantry."

"See combat?"

"Afghanistan."

Mitchell Durant nods slowly. "Rough?"

"It was, sir," I remember to add.

I'm worried this conversation has been a total bust, but Ava's dad nods again, claps me briefly on the shoulder and says, "Thank you for your service." Then he walks away.

"See?" Ava's beside me in an instant. "He likes you!"

"How can you tell?"

"He made an effort to talk to you," she replies. "Usually, he just stands and glares."

I bend and whisper in her ear, "Am I going to make it out of here alive?"

She laughs. "Sure. Unless you choke to death on a salmon puff."

Ginny calls out from the doorway. "Dinner's ready, everyone. Please come and take your seats."

I drop the canapé in my empty beer glass and leave both on a side table. Although on second thought, if I shove the salmon puff down my throat and die right now, I won't have to suffer through dinner.

Too late. Ava's taken my arm in hers and is steering me onwards. I just hope it's not my head that gets served up on a platter.

Chapter Twenty-Nine

AVA

Mom's really pulled out all the stops tonight. Dinner is a feast. Sliced rare roast beef, gratin potatoes, baked squash with goat cheese, and Brussels sprouts, a vegetable no one would hate if they tried it Mom's way: caramelized with chestnuts. Delicious. Dad doesn't eat meat, of course, but the vegetable dishes are a meal on their own. Mom always buys organic, and from local growers whenever she can, so everything's fresh as it can be. Dad's finicky tastes are our gain.

The table setting is beautiful, too, with the fancy gold-rimmed dinner service Mom usually only brings out for Christmas, and a centerpiece of artfully arranged sprigs and berries. There's a cluster of cutlery and glassware by each plate setting, and across from me, I see Cam survey his with a look of bemusement and faint terror. If I stretch my leg right out, I can just kick him in the shins. He looks up, startled, and I mouth, "Watch me." He nods, but I can tell he's still freaked out. I feel bad for subjecting him to this social torture but it's not like I had any choice. Mom is sweet and gentle but when she makes up her mind to cook for you, she will not be denied.

"Mom, this is incredible," says Danny. "Rumors of Ava's death should be exaggerated more often."

"Danny!" Shelby protests.

She's seated between him and Cam, while I'm between Nate and Jackson. Mom and Dad are at each end, with Mom nearest the kitchen.

"It's bad luck to joke about things like that," Shelby scolds. "We should do something to counteract it, like—I don't know—burn some sage?"

"Or how about we keep the matches *away* from the dried herbs," suggests Nate firmly, "and let Mom say grace so we can eat?"

Mom's always liked to kick meals off with a short prayer of thanks, even though Dad thinks religion is an irrational superstition. Which is ironic coming from a man who believes refined sugar is worse for you than exposure to uranium.

After we've all murmured "Amen", Nate takes charge of the wine while Mom directs the filling of plates. I'm pleased to see she urges Cam to have more. He's taking small portions to be polite, although I know his hunger gauge must be running on the redline. But Mom has three sons, and she knows how much men really need to eat. She won't rest until his plate is piled high.

Shelby swirls the wine in her glass and sticks her nose in

to inhale the bouquet. I forget sometimes that she's Flora Valley's head vintner. Her sunny personality, and the fact that she looks like she just graduated high school, can deceive people into underestimating her. But when it comes to wine, Shelby knows her stuff. Nate, too. That's why they're such a good match.

I glance across at Cam, who's focusing all his attention on clearing his plate. I realize we've only known each other for four days, all of which were spent in a heightened state of worry that I might be seriously ill. Okay, I still might have chronic fatigue, which will suck, but it's not fatal and I trust Doc when he says we'll have a plan to manage it.

But ... manage it where? I can hardly move in permanently with Cam—his house barely fits *him*. And what will I do here for a job? Can I even hold down a job if this tiredness is permanent? I can't expect Cam to support me. Can't expect Mom and Dad to, either, though I know they wouldn't hesitate. Now Dad's health scare is over, they're looking forward to the next phase of their life together. They don't need me as a third wheel.

I reach out for my wine glass to find that Nate has filled it with sparkling water. It should be a minor disappointment, but I feel hot tears sting the corners of my eyes. Dammit. This is a happy family dinner, a celebration. I am overemotional but I will not cry, not even a little snivel. Take a deep breath, Ava. That's it. In ... and out...

"You okay?"

Jackson speaks softly by my ear. I nod, not trusting that my voice will be steady.

"Might be the adrenaline finally leaving," he murmurs. "When you've been in fight or flight mode for a while, the landing can be a bit bumpy."

I take another deep breath and compose myself enough to look him in the eye.

"Are you speaking from experience?"

"Who, me?" Jackson half smiles. "Happy-go-lucky Jackson Armstrong?"

"That'd be a yes, then."

"Fall down twice, get up three times, that's my motto," he says. "I repeat it to myself while I'm lying in the dirt. I'm sure it'll have the right effect one day."

Everyone else at the table is talking away to each other—Dad and Nate, Mom and Danny, Shelby and Cam. Okay, Dad and Nate are probably arguing but the point is, no one's listening to me and Jackson.

"Just because you haven't found your niche yet doesn't mean you won't," I say, trying to ignore that I'm being a big ol' hypocrite. "You've got a lot going for you."

"True," he says, spearing a potato with his fork. "I have all my own teeth for one."

"Don't run yourself down," I object. "You do have a lot going for you. You're smart, you're funny, you get on great with people, you're—"

"A coward," he says. "First to run when the going gets tough. That's me."

He raises his voice just enough. The whole table stops talking and stares.

Shelby's the one to break the silence.

"Jackson, that's not true. It *isn't*."

"Sister, you're a sweetheart," he says, "but you've got a short memory. Who left you to carry the load when Dad died?"

"Well … everyone," says Shelby matter-of-factly. "You, Mom, Tyler, Frankie … you all left."

"Okay, but who was the oldest? Who should have taken over? Or at least stayed long enough to make sure the vineyard was in good shape?"

"Isn't it a bit late to rehash this?" says Nate, ever practical. "It all worked out. Shelby and I got together, and Flora Valley Wines has a great future. What else matters?"

"Character," says Dad.

My heart sinks. Once Dad gets on his high horse, it'll take a magnitude ten earthquake to unseat him. Next to me, Nate stiffens in his chair, and across the table Danny screws shut his eyes and starts to massage the bridge of his nose. Oh boy, here we go.

"When I assess a potential company to invest in, my first step is not to examine the books," Dad says. "It's to examine the CEO. What manner of person are they? What values and principles do they live by? How strong, in short, is their character? That tells me more than any spreadsheet."

This is all my fault. If I hadn't been such a crybaby, Jackson would have kept quiet. Regrets, I've had a few.

"And the mark of true character", Dad says, killing us by degrees, "is the ability to remain present and focused in times of difficulty. To face trouble and stay the course. Courage—that's the gold standard of character."

"Dad—" Nate's about to protest, bless his cotton socks.

But Jackson gets in before him.

"You're quite right, sir," he says to Dad. "Courage. That's the real test of a man."

I can't tell if he's a little drunk, or if he's simply decided he has nothing left to lose. Whatever the case, I'm steeling myself. Feels like this is about to get ugly.

Jackson looks around the table.

"So let me be courageous," he says. "Let me tell you the truth about myself. I'm broke. I'm unemployed. I have no home. I have no prospects. I've relied on the kindness of you all to help me out, prop me up, and I've no idea if I'll ever be able to repay you."

He pushes back his chair and stands. "I've never done a single thing of note in my whole thirty-two years. The one time I tried to stand up for someone, I failed."

His gaze is now firmly fixed on Cam, who, I notice, has tensed up. His chest is out, jaw set, and the hand that's resting on the table is starting to curl into a fist.

But Jackson shakes his head. "I tried to fight for someone's honor and got put on my ass. Cam knows. He was there. Pretty useless, huh, Cam? Couldn't even throw a punch."

I see the tension in Cam's body release, but he doesn't say a word. None of us does. This is raw despair we're witnessing, and no one here is quite sure what to do about it. Physical ailments, that we can handle. Emotional, not so much.

If there was a moment where we could offer comfort, it's

lost. Jackson's shoulders slump, and with visible effort, he pulls himself upright again.

"I've overstayed my welcome," says Jackson. "Thank you for dinner, Mrs Durant. Dan, thanks, but I'll make my own way now."

And he walks out of the room.

"Jackson, wait!" Danny starts to get up, but Cam beats him to it. Lays his hand on Danny's shoulder, eases him back into his chair.

"I'm the one he needs to speak to," Cam says.

He catches my eye, and I nod. He's right.

Cam heads out the door. Now there are only six of us at the table.

"That young man needs a purpose," says Dad.

His tone is softened and kind, which is so unusual we all turn to stare at him.

"Not everyone is lucky enough to have clear direction early on in life," he continues. "Shelby, I hope your brother can use this low moment as a springboard to better things. He has potential."

I exchange a look with Danny that says: okay, who are you, and what have you done with the real Mitchell Durant?

"Thank you." Poor Shelby is almost in tears. "Why didn't he *tell* me that things were so bad?"

"Because he didn't want to ruin our wedding," says Nate. "Plus, he was ashamed and embarrassed." He makes a face. "And we all know *that* feeling, don't we?"

I automatically expect Dad to disagree, but he sits

quietly with the rest of us. And suddenly, all the barriers I've built between us – yes, *I've* built – come crashing down. I get out of my chair, round the table to where he sits and hug my dad hard from behind.

"Love you, Dad," I tell him and kiss his cheek. "You're a great guy."

Dad swivels in his chair, so he can face me. I see a small frown and a small smile.

"I love you, too, Ava," he says. "I don't say it enough, I know."

He turns to look at Nate and Danny. "I love all my children. You boys, Izzy and Max. And I'm so proud of you. You've become better people than I will ever be, and for that, I'm thankful every single day."

The tears I was holding back are busy dampening my cheeks and I'm not ashamed. Even Nate is a little moist-eyed, and Danny's mouth is opening and shutting like a stranded fish.

"Love you, too, Dad," Danny manages. "And you, Mom."

"We couldn't have better parents," says Nate. "Thank you both for everything."

Now we're all dabbing our faces with napkins, and fair enough. The Durant family has expressed more heartfelt emotion in the last two minutes than we have in the last two decades. Let's hope it won't be another two decades before we find the nerve to do it again.

Finally, Mom speaks, and her voice is a little shaky.

"Nate, honey," she says, "I think this would be the perfect time to top up everyone's wine."

"Including mine," I add quickly. "Red wine prevents heart attacks, Dad," I tell him before he can object.

I retrieve my glass and hold it out to Nate. "Consider this medicinal."

Chapter Thirty

CAM

Damn, this house is big. I remember Shelby telling me that Nate and Ava's dad made all his money from venture capital, but that the house had been in their mom's family since it was built in the late 1800s. Right now, I'm thankful the place has some age because the creak of Jackson's tread on wooden floors is the only way I can tell where he's heading. I follow the sound upstairs and along a hallway, peering into bedrooms until I spot him. He's pulled a shabby sports bag onto the bed and is about to shove in a handful of clothes.

He pauses briefly when sees me in the doorway but keeps going, grabbing more clothes from a chair, forcing them into the bag. I realize I've got no idea what to say to him. I've never had to counsel anyone before. I've always been on the receiving end, listening to other people who took the time to speak kindly to me. People like Lee…

"Did you go visit your mom?" I ask. "You said you were going to."

No response. Jackson disappears into the en-suite bathroom, comes back with a toothbrush, shoves that in with the clothes and yanks the zipper shut hard. Bag slung over one shoulder, he walks to the door, finds me blocking his way.

"Come on, Cam," he says wearily. "Let me leave with *some* dignity."

"How are you planning to travel? You don't have a car."

"On foot," he says. In his self-mocking way, he adds, "The exercise will do me good."

"It's November," I point out. "Couple more hours, the temperature won't be much above freezing."

Jackson blows out an exasperated breath. "Cam, please get out of the way. There's nothing you can do for me."

I pause before suggesting what's just come to mind. "How about I drive you to Lee's?"

He raises a wry eyebrow. "Run home to Mom, is that what you're suggesting? At the tender age of thirty-two?"

I know how it seems to him, but the more I think about it, the more I'm convinced that Lee is the person Jackson needs right now. My theory, just forming, is that Jackson's been feeling like a failure for years. All he ever wanted was for his parents to value him, to believe in him and take him seriously. He saw them treat others that way, including his sister and even strangers like me. He played the clown because that's how he got people to notice him, but all that did was peg him in their minds as a joker, a lightweight.

Once you've got that reputation, it's hard to shake it off. So, you keep up the clowning, and after a while, it's who you think you are. You're convinced you're not—and never will be—a person of substance.

I don't believe Lee has any idea how her oldest son really feels, because Jackson's so good at putting on a happy face. He's done it all his life. Time for him to tell the truth to the one person whose recognition he wants above all others.

"Your mom would be glad to see you."

"You think?" says Jackson bitterly. "She didn't hang around to catch up with me after the wedding. Didn't invite me up to her place."

There's a reason for that, but it's not mine to give. And for a moment, I hesitate. If I drop Jackson on Lee without warning, she'll have no choice but to reveal her secret. To be honest, I don't know why she wants to keep knowledge of Debra from her kids, but I did make her a promise.

But Jackson's her son. He needs her. I figure that comes first.

"Your mom has stuff going on," I tell him. "She's fine, don't worry," I add, as concern creases his face. "But ... her life's a little complicated right now."

"And she could tell *you* but not me and Shelby?" says Jackson, with a hint of anger that's not unwarranted. "Not her actual blood relatives?"

I raise my palms. "I'm sorry. I don't know why she did that."

Jackson gives me a hard look. "You and Mom. You said you never... Was that true?"

I meet his eye. "Upon my honor. Your mom has been a better friend to me than I've ever been to her but that's all we are—friends."

He pulls on his ear. "It's just that ... you've never had a proper girlfriend, until now. And it's now that Mom's started acting weird."

Okay, I can see how he might make that connection. Bogus as it is.

"I'm a fucked-up loner," I say. "You know that. You made enough jokes about my failed dates the other night."

To his credit, he's embarrassed. "Yeah. Sorry, man. Best way to deflect attention from yourself is to place someone else in the spotlight. Worked, too."

"Glad I was good material," I say grimly.

Corner of Jackson's mouth twitches. "Yeah, that arsonist joke really brought the house down."

"Don't start."

His smile fades, and he bends his head, toes his shoe along the floor as if he's working out an invisible equation.

When he looks up again, his expression is unhappy but resolute.

"Okay, take me to Mom's," he says. "It's only one night. I'll hit the road in the morning."

I nod. "Meet me at the truck. Ava can get a ride home with Nate and Shelby. Give me a minute to make my goodbyes and I'll see you out there."

At this time of night, it's a pretty quick trip to Lee's. Quiet, too. I'm not much of a talker and Jackson, who usually is, sits with his head turned away, staring out the window into the dark.

I start thinking about Ava. Tonight was meant to be a celebration, her family and me, all of us grateful that she doesn't have a life-threatening illness. I'd been so hung up about meeting her parents that I hadn't thought past dinner. But now I've got time, and I can see that I'm missing out on a chance for the two of us to celebrate together. Just Ava and me, alone. In the warmth and comfort of my bed. By the time I get back, she'll be asleep, and I won't want to wake her. She's been through the ringer these past few days. She needs a good night's rest.

Tomorrow morning … that's a different story. A whole new day that will feel like the start of a new stage in our relationship. It occurs to me that I have no clue what it might feel like not to have Ava's health hanging over us. We've been in this worried bubble, almost frozen in time, waiting. Not that I'm complaining. I love Ava, and to my amazement, I think she actually loves me back. But we haven't talked about our plans, not a bit. I don't even know if she intends to stay.

And what do I want?

This is a question I've never truly asked myself. When I was fifteen, I decided the army was for me and I went to it without a second's thought that there might be other paths to go down. The years I was in the army, I lived from day to day. No point in making plans when you have so little control over your fate. And when that career abruptly ended, I was lost. All my bearings were gone. I had no sense of who I was, or what I had to offer the world, if anything. It's taken me almost ten years to get most of that back, but I still live day to day, job to job, barrel to barrel.

That's why I've never had a steady relationship. I couldn't picture a future. Couldn't see ahead to a time where I somehow became a partner, a husband, maybe even a father. None of that seemed like it could ever become real.

Does it now that I've met Ava? Now that I've allowed myself to love without holding back, for the first time ever in my life?

I glance across at Jackson. Still staring out the window. My guess is he's wondering why everything's going downhill for him. He's young, smart, and capable, so why hasn't luck gone his way? At his age, he should be rising the career ladder, buying a house, getting married, having kids. Living the middle-class American dream…

But who knows better than me that the universe doesn't give a damn about your dreams? The best-laid plans can be upended in a second, your life exploded into a million pieces, with no certainty that you can pick them all up and start again.

The Dodge's rumble is loud enough for Lee to hear it coming. When we pull up outside, she's in her open front door, waiting. I get out first and her expression is puzzled and concerned, as it might be at this hour. But then the passenger door opens, and Jackson steps reluctantly onto the driveway. Lee flicks me a quick look of inquiry and I nod, but I'm only confirming what she already knows. Her son needs her help. She goes to meet him, as he stands there, hangdog, and puts her arm through his and leads him inside. I think they've both forgotten about me, and that's okay, but Lee looks back over her shoulder as they walk through into the house, smiles a thank you. I wait until the door shuts before I get back in the truck.

With Lee's support, I believe Jackson can pull himself out of this hole. He'll find a direction and set a new course. One full of possibility and achievement.

And if I can believe that, then I've got no excuse not to put the same faith in myself.

Chapter Thirty-One

AVA

"I feel so guilty," Shelby wails for the five hundredth time on the drive back to the vineyard. "I should have realized there was something wrong."

"How?" says Nate. "From our wedding day right up until tonight, he's been all jokes and smiles."

"But you don't know Jackson like I do! I should have looked closer."

My turn to comment. "If someone's determined to hide how they're feeling, they can usually manage it."

"Especially if you're a Durant," says Nate. "Our poker faces are legendary."

"Except you totally have a tell," I say.

"I do not," Nate retorts. "That's just a pathetic tactic to unsettle me. Give it up. You'll never win."

"See, Shelby?" I say. "This is an example of a healthy brother and sister relationship."

"Stop trying to cheer me up," Shelby sniffles. "I'm worried."

"Cam's taking Jackson to your mom's," says Nate. "He'll be in the best possible hands."

"But Mom's been acting weird, too!" Shelby wails again. "Nobody tells me anything!"

Nate catches my eye in the rearview mirror, signals a silent "Help."

"Shelby, I've spent the last two months pretending I'm fine," I tell her. "If I hadn't fainted at your wedding, I'd still be pretending. Sometimes you have to wait until people are ready to talk."

I'm thinking about Cam. How many years did it take him to talk about the war? And what was the cost to him of keeping it all bottled up? Secrets are like tapeworms. They consume all our energy and grow bigger and bigger. Then we either fade to a shadow of ourselves, or it's like that episode of *House M.D.* when he rips the giant white worm right out of that girl's stomach. Okay, apologies for that image. But sometimes letting a secret out is the scariest thing we can do. Because what if we gather the courage to express our darkest fears and doubts, only to have them confirmed? How do we come back from that?

Then Nate says out loud the question I asked myself over dinner but have refused to think about since.

"So, what's the plan for you and Cam?"

He's not to blame for me being triggered. All he wants is to steer the subject away from Jackson. But triggered I am because I have no answer. Cam and I haven't talked about the future. And the more I look at it, the more impractical it seems.

"We've been together four days," I say. "Barely enough time to spell plan, let alone make one."

Shelby lets out a happy sigh. "It would be *so* great if you and Cam got married."

Nate's distraction tactic worked, and Shelby's no longer fixated on Jackson. But I would super appreciate it if she dropped this particular subject, too.

"Just because you and Nate got hitched," I say, "doesn't mean it's right for everyone. I might not even want to get married."

"The cake would be pretty funny," says Nate. "The groom figure twice the height of the bride."

Luckily—for him—Nate doesn't continue with the jokes. He's noticed Shelby has her phone out.

"Shel, do not call your mom or Jackson," he says. "Give them space."

"But—"

"Call Chiara and Jordan instead. They're your best friends. That's what they're for."

"They won't have answers," says Shelby, but I can tell she's willing to be swayed.

"No, but they'll listen to you for hours," says Nate. "And that's the next best thing."

"You're so smart, honey bunch." Shelby bats her eyelashes at him. "I love you so much."

"You", he says, as we pull up outside Cam's place, "are walking a fine line." He leans over and kisses her. "But I love you, too."

I may vomit. And not just because I ate a second helping of Mom's tarte Tatin.

Nate looks back over his shoulder at me, and his silly lovesick smile morphs into a look of concern.

"Sis, are you sure you're okay here on your own? Do you want us to wait with you?"

I shake my head. "There's barely room for two."

One of the many barriers I can see between me and a future with Cam.

I hop out of Nate's pick-up and walk around to his window, which he rolls down. Shelby's already nattering away on her phone. It's good to have friends. It's good to have brothers, too.

"Thanks for the ride," I say to Nate. "And thanks for caring."

Nate blinks, surprised. Fair enough. He and I don't exactly have a track record of being emotionally demonstrative in our family. Nate and Ava, the robots.

"Well, turns out I might love you, too," he says. "Look after yourself. And call me tomorrow."

"Night, Ava!" Shelby breaks off in mid-natter to wave goodbye. Then into the phone she says, "Yep, we're dropping her off at Cam's. I *know*, super cute. Oh, absolutely at the vineyard. Imagine a winter wedding. So pretty..."

Nate rolls his eyes at me. "I'll head it off at the pass. Don't worry."

He waits until I'm safely inside Cam's house before

driving off. When the noise of the pick-up finally fades, the silence crowds in on me. The place is cold, and I don't know how to light the fire. Which means I can't even make myself a cup of hot cocoa. Cam and I are so different. I can't see any way to fit into his life without disrupting it completely. And maybe demanding more from him than he can give.

Cam didn't say when he'd be back, so I have no choice but to go to bed and lie there until whenever. The irony is that having been impatient all my life, recent events have forced me to get used to waiting. Guess that's what happens: life tests you, and you either rise to the challenge or you don't.

Just to be clear, I want to rise. Very much. But that's no guarantee that I will.

I'm roused from sleep by the sound of the front door shutting. The click is barely audible, so part of my brain must have stayed awake, listening. Now, every sense is on high alert, trying to figure out when Cam will come up to bed. I could go downstairs but that might seem needy. If Cam and I are going to start talking about our future, then I want us to be honest. I don't want one of us to agree to anything because they feel obligated.

I try to identify the sounds. He takes off his boots and hangs his jacket. Runs the kitchen tap—glass of water is my guess. Door out to the bathroom creaks open and shut, and after a couple of minutes, opens and shuts again. Then … silence. For *ages*.

Dammit, he's probably gone to sleep in an armchair so

as not to disturb me. I try to summon him with mind power but no dice. Nothing for it. I'll have to go down.

Cam is in an armchair but sitting in the light of a hurricane lamp set on the table, leafing through what looks like a compact photo album. He looks up when he hears me on the stairs.

"Did I wake you? I tried to be quiet."

"I was only half-asleep," I say.

The room is still freezing, and I shiver. He shifts the album onto the table and pulls off the blanket that hangs over the back of the armchair. Opens his arms, inviting me onto his lap, and when I'm settled, he wraps the blanket around me. I'm like a swaddled child but it's kind of nice. Comforting.

"What's the album?" I ask.

"Blair's wedding. Everyone who went got one as a souvenir. Plus a piece of cake, but I already ate that."

He reaches for the album. I straighten out my legs so he can lay it on my lap.

"Oh my," I say. "How old were you again?"

"Just shy of eighteen. And yes, I really was that skinny. Army training put thirty pounds of muscle on me."

I turn a page. "Your sister is beautiful."

"You mean she looks nothing like me," says Cam, but I can hear the smile.

"Same eyes," I say. "Same thick hair, only blonder."

"It's silver now," he tells me. "Blair started going gray in her late twenties. Didn't bother to dye it. Suits her."

I crane my neck to look up at him. "When was the last time you saw each other?"

He makes an embarrassed face. "Two years ago?"

"She's in Oregon, not Antarctica," I point out.

"I call," he says. "But yeah…"

I don't know exactly why he decided to get this album out, but I feel its significance. Old photos show past us, before we started down our current paths. Our younger selves, full of promise and energy, but also with absolutely no idea of what's about to hit us.

"We could take a trip to see her?" I say the next bit quickly before I have second thoughts. "And, maybe, go on to visit your parents in Wyoming?"

"Cut through Idaho?" he says. "Home of the potato?"

It's not a no.

"Without potatoes there would be no curly fries," I say. "They're a legendary vegetable."

Gently, Cam lifts the album off my lap and puts it back on the table. He wraps his arms around me, and I feel his breath warm my ear.

"I really want to make this work," he murmurs. "If … you do."

It's like I've been suddenly filled with light, the kind that swirls and sparkles. If Cam didn't have his arms around me, I'd float up to the ceiling like a balloon.

"I absolutely do," I assure him. "Is it okay if I have no clue how?"

He laughs. "Happy to take my chances."

"Wow, them's fighting words," I say. "Maybe we're not so different after all?"

"We are," he says, "but that's good. If you were too much like me, we'd never have met. We'd both be hiding behind a bush somewhere."

I'm all warmed through now. I wriggle free of the blanket and do a one-eighty turn so I can straddle his lap and face him.

"I know one thing we're perfectly in sync with," I say.

The hurricane lamp light is low, but I can see his eyes darken. He slides his hand up under my T-shirt and I shiver again, this time with pleasure. I kiss him, my tongue tasting his, little bursts of flame with every touch. His thumb brushes my nipple, and the flame engulfs me. I can feel his erection pushing at his jeans, and it would be the work of a moment to unbutton his fly and guide him inside me. But this armchair … it's not built for two.

"If I can't walk in the morning, I want it to be for good reasons and not because I got a cramp," I tell him. "So, snuff out that lamp, pardner, and let's hurry on upstairs."

Chapter Thirty-Two

CAM

After sex like that, I should be sleeping like a satisfied log. Ava fell immediately into dreamland, and I can feel her breathing steadily beside me, her arm crooked on my chest, palm resting on the spot directly above my heart.

I should be sleeping but my brain won't shut up and let me. Now that I'm committed to making it work with Ava, I can't stop thinking about how. What needs to happen, and when? My thoughts start small, with the idea of extending my house so we'll have more living space. Pretty soon, I've designed us a three-bedroom mansion with en-suite bathrooms, a country-style kitchen and open plan living/dining space, and a double garage for both our vehicles. Then I move outside, where I build stables and an exercise yard for Ava's horses, a swimming pool for the summer, and a vegetable garden complete with potato patch.

Of course, then I realize I've only been thinking about

the two of us. What if Ava and I have kids? We haven't talked about having a family, and to be honest, I'd never even remotely considered I could be a father. But now Ava and I are together, I'm letting the idea in, turning it over, testing it ... and finding that I like it very much. I want to be a dad. I want kids and dogs and chickens, maybe bees. Could buy some goats from Blair, start the Flora Valley arm of her business...

Rein it in, Hollander, before you're certified as insane. Your income is enough to keep you in decent boots and real coffee. It's not enough to afford even a fraction of the above. And a mortgage is out of the question. You don't have a decent credit rating because you've never taken out a loan and never had a credit card. Your barrel customers cover the payments to your suppliers. Even though you've never missed a rent payment, you are what's known as subprime. Can't even get a stupid loyalty card from Old Navy.

Billy would have vouched for me to the bank. But I have too much pride to ask Shelby and Nate, my current employers. I'd say the same applies to Ava when it comes to her family. Not that her dad seems like the kind of guy who showers his kids with cash. A bootstraps man is my impression of Mitchell Durant. Expects his children to make their own way in life. Ava had a good job in Kentucky but if she does have chronic fatigue, she'll only ever be able to work at a job that's undemanding and with limited hours. Neither of us will be raking in the big bucks.

So where does this leave me and Ava? I can't see the two

of us living in my tiny house long-term. Guess we'll have to look for a bigger place. If we can find one we can afford...

I've been out here, alone in the woods, for almost ten years. Surrounded by the smells of wood, fire and smoke, and the hot metal tang of machinery. Outdoors, the scent of pine and leaf mold. Breeze bringing the occasional musk of fox and the last few grapes fermenting on the vine. Birds nesting in the branches. Black-tailed deer cropping between the trees.

It's home, is what I'm saying. *My* home, when for a long while, I thought I'd never have one again. It's hard to picture being happy living anywhere else.

Go to sleep, Hollander. This line of thinking is unproductive. You're in love, you and Ava are a team, so make the most of it. Don't fall at the first set of obstacles. Take on the world together. You know that'd be Ava's attitude, so even though you are her opposite, why not try being more Ava? Channel her fierceness and drive. See where that takes you.

As if she senses she's on my mind, Ava stirs and mutters something that sounds like, "But the parrot *likes* black." For a crazy moment, I imagine her in a black wedding dress. It would be just like Ava to...

Wedding. Why didn't that thought enter my head earlier? Got crowded out by the dogs and bees and goats, I guess. And the kids. Not the goat kind. I leaped ahead to a settled life before I considered what might come well before that.

I test this new idea, too. And I'm good with it. As long as we don't invite too many people. I'm not good with crowds.

Go. To. Sleep.

Careful not to disturb Ava, I stretch out my arm, feel around for my phone. Roll my head so I can check the time. Five-fifteen. Only an hour or so until the alarm goes off. Guess that's better than no sleep at all.

Ava stirs again and slides her hand down to rest on my hip bone. Close enough to make part of me stir. I have the dumb idea to wake her. At least, I'd know it was dumb if all my intelligence didn't now reside in my erection. That's giving the idea a double thumbs-up.

But just as I move to gently shake her shoulder, the sound of my phone pealing makes me leap like a startled cat. Ava bounces off me as she's jolted awake, and she scrambles to sit up just as I fumble for my phone.

"What, what?" she says, breathlessly, at the same time as I answer.

"Hello?"

"It's Jackson," is the distracted-sounding reply. "Sorry to call this late. Or early—"

"Jackson, what…? Are you okay?"

Ava is fully alert now, kneeling next to me, seated on her heels.

"Yeah, yeah, I'm fine," says Jackson. "Mom asked me to call. Don't panic, she's fine, too."

I breathe out.

"But Debra's been transferred to the hospice. She doesn't have long. She'd like to see you."

"*Me?*"

"And Ava. And Shelby and Nate. I'm calling Tyler and Frankie, too."

The other Armstrong kids. The whole family. Debra's family. Learning about their aunt's existence for the first time.

"Visiting hours start at eight," says Jackson. "Sorry, gotta go. Gotta get hold of the others."

"Thanks," I tell him, but he's already ended the call.

Ava's looking at me with wide eyes. The room's quiet enough for her to have heard everything.

"Who the fuck is Debra?" is her very fair first question.

"Let me make coffee," I say, trying not to beg. "And I'll tell you everything."

As you might guess, brewing coffee and explaining to Ava is not a straightforward process. We're interrupted by Shelby calling me to make sure she's understood Jackson correctly.

"I have an *aunt*? Mom has a *sister*? No one tells me anything!"

Then by Nate calling me.

"This was the stupidly loyal promise you made to Lee, right? Could you not have given us even a little hint? Shelby's beside herself."

Then by Nate calling Ava.

"Should I go, too? I mean, I'm related by marriage now, but..."

Then by Shelby calling Ava.

"You and Nate have to come! It can't be only me, Cam, and Jackson...!"

Then by Jackson calling me back. "Okay, so Tyler and Frankie are on their way. They'll drive from the airport. Hope they make it in time…"

Then by Shelby calling Ava again.

"Can we pick up you and Cam so we can all go together? I need everyone's support…"

Then by Nate calling me again.

"I've asked Doug to manage the vineyard while you, me, and Shelby are all gone. This time of year, things are supposed to get easier…"

Finally, our phones go quiet.

"Ugh," says Ava. "My ears are buzzing. And my heart is racing, though I'm pretty sure I only managed one sip of this coffee."

"I'll make us refills," I offer.

She's sitting on an armchair in that pretzel-legged yoga position that I haven't a hope of managing even partway. When I take her cup, she gives me a searching look. I hesitate, not able to read her mood. Worried that she seems a little subdued.

"You met Debra," she says, "when you drove that day to Lee's."

"Yup."

"And Lee asked you to keep Debra a secret," she says.

"Yup, again."

"How did you feel about that?"

I sense a question under the question, but I'm not sure what it is. Best to answer honestly and go from there.

"Conflicted," I tell her. "Lee didn't share her reasons why. And sometimes secrets do more damage than good."

Ava nods, but her smile seems to be all for herself.

Then her smile fades. "But you kept it anyway. Would you do anything Lee asked of you?"

And there it is. The question under the question.

"Lee's never given me any cause not to trust her," I reply, cautious but truthful. "And she's done a lot for me with no thought of return. So, yes, I feel like I owe her. But I wouldn't put her before you. Never."

Ava pulls her knees up and hugs them.

"If it was Lee on her deathbed, you'd drop everything, wouldn't you?"

"Of course," I say. "Unless you were on your deathbed, too. Then, I don't know… I guess I'd do a lot of running between wards."

Ava buries the lower half of her face in her knees, but not so quick that I don't catch her grin.

"It's a big deal," I say. "I truly hate running."

Outside, a faint rumble signals Nate's pick-up approaching. Ava sighs and hops off the chair.

"Show time," she says. "Better get dressed."

Between phone calls, neither of us has managed to pull on a full set of clothes. I ditch the coffee cups in the sink and move to Ava for a last embrace.

"Honestly," I say, "if it wasn't so cold out, I'd suggest we go like this. Everyone's so stressed, they'll never notice we're half naked."

Ava laughs and hugs me tight. "Nate will notice and he's two minutes away from knocking on that door. If we're not ready, he'll stress even more. And then we've got to endure a forty-minute drive with stressed Nate to Martinburg."

"Good point," I say. "Let's go fetch us some pants."

Chapter Thirty-Three

AVA

I've never been around anyone who's dying before. Dad's mom died suddenly of a brain aneurysm when he was only a kid (which could explain a lot) but Grandpa Durant is still fit as a fiddle at eighty-two, and Mom's parents are spending their later years, and their kids' inheritance, backpacking around the world. Last time we heard from them, they were contemplating climbing mountains in Patagonia, so unless they get caught in an avalanche, I'd say they're good for a few more years yet.

Okay, so a couple of months back there was a possibility that Dad could die when he stubbornly refused surgery for his heart condition. But he finally saw sense and now he's healthier than most men half his age. The last funeral I went to was our great-uncle Milton's. I was fourteen and in the peak of my goth phase, and thus full of outrage that it was a closed coffin. Possibly why that was the last family funeral I can remember attending.

In short, I don't know what to expect and there's no opportunity to ask. The drive to Martinburg is dominated by Shelby on speaker phone to her siblings, the four of them coming up with ever-more outlandish theories as to why their mom's kept her only sister a secret all these years. I see Nate's knuckles tighten on the steering wheel, but he knows that the Armstrong kids need this chance to connect and vent, and the only faint sound of protest he makes is when Shelby's brother Tyler suggests that Debra was stolen as a baby and brought up by her kidnappers, and it's taken her this long to work out who she really is.

I nudge Cam, and whisper, "Do you know anything that could put them out of their misery?"

"Nope," he whispers back. "Wish I did. Debra didn't tell me any background details."

As we pull into the hospice car park, Shelby finally lowers her phone and falls silent. Nate switches off the engine and reaches out to take her hand.

"There's no way this isn't going to be strange and sad," he says to her. "So, it's completely okay to feel both those things. But we're here for you, Shel. And we love you."

Shelby throws her arms around his neck, and I'm bracing for floods of tears. But all she does is squeeze her eyes shut hard, and then sit up again, ramrod straight, shoulders back and chest out.

"Okay, team," she says, in the bracing voice of a coach in the locker room. "Let's do this."

She points at Nate. "Tissues?"

"Check," he replies.

"Smelling salts?"

"How about M&Ms from the vending machine?"

"Done." Shelby makes a circling gesture with her hand. "Let's roll."

Nate leads the way and we're happy to follow. The hospice is surrounded by gardens with paths wide enough for wheelchairs. In warmer months, I can imagine how nice it would be to sit outside, feel the sun on your face. Before I realize I'm doing it, I take Cam's hand, and he looks at me in surprise.

"I'm so grateful for you," I tell him. "So grateful for everything."

His warm, slow smile is exactly what I need to see, and his words exactly what I need to hear.

"Love you, Ava Durant."

"Love you, too, Cam Hollander." I squeeze his hand. "Don't let go now."

Nate's found the front desk and is talking to the receptionist, who looks a million times nicer than Doc Wilson's. The whole hospice has an air of serenity and kindness about it. No one wants to die, but I can see the benefit of ending your days in a place like this. Peacefully, painlessly, surrounded by people who genuinely care.

Cam's hand in mine reminds me that while the hospice isn't a hospital, he might be finding it tough. But when I glance up at him to check, there's no sign of tension. In fact, he's smiling, watching an old couple shuffling up the corridor, arm in arm. It's impossible to tell which of them might be resident here, maybe both? I've heard plenty of stories about couples who've died within hours of each other, not wanting to live another day without their beloved.

Dammit, I'm getting super emotional. But Nate's coming back. No time to cry.

"Down the corridor, second room on the left," he says. And to Shelby, adds, "There's no snack vending machine. But I could bring you a cup of bad coffee with a lot of sugar in it?"

Shelby kisses his cheek. "You're all the sugar I need," she says, making Nate blush. "No, I'm ready. Ready to meet my aunt."

Even though Debra is no relation of mine or Cam's, I feel a surge of nerves. This is a big deal for everyone, and I really hope it's going to go okay. Well, as okay as it can in these sad circumstances.

We find the room, and I'm surprised to see it's big enough to hold four beds. I'd expected that everyone here would have their own room. Maybe some of them do, but here, the curtains are pulled around two of the beds while the two nearest the window are open to view. There's a woman in one, with a whole group around her. They're laughing and joking, and I can see empty champagne glasses on the bedside table. Mimosas for breakfast, perhaps? And why not? Who says dying has to be somber?

The bed we're headed for is opposite. I see Lee, seated right up by the pillow end, with Jackson next to her. The woman in the bed is wearing a wool hat, even though the temperature in here must be seventy-five at least. Lee looks up as we approach. An odd expression flits across her face. I almost feel like she'd rather we weren't here, but then she smiles warmly, and stands to greet us.

She hugs Shelby first, mainly because Shelby throws herself at her mother. Then she hugs Nate, me, and Cam, in that order. I admit I count how long her embrace with Cam lasts, but it's quick. Jackson hugs Shelby but he settles for "Hi" to the rest of us. And now the welcome is over, and the only person left to meet is—

"Hello," says the woman in the bed. "I'm Debra."

Her voice is soft and slow, as if she's trying to conserve energy. Under the hat, I glimpse reddish-gray hair. She's lying sunken in the bed, her arms flat on top of the blankets, her whole posture one of intense weariness. Her skin, however, is luminous, like she's lit from within. And she does look amazingly like Lee.

Shelby sits in the chair her mother just vacated. "I'm Shelby. I'm your niece."

The faintest of smiles. "I can tell."

Debra's head turns toward the rest of us. If her body is failing, her mind certainly isn't. Her gaze is sharp and assessing. And, if I'm not wrong, a little amused.

"Friend Cam," she acknowledges. "And you two must be Nate and Ava."

When all we do is stand there, Debra makes a "tchah" sound.

"You can't catch what I have," she says. "So don't hover. Pull up a chair."

The group across the way seems to have commandeered

all the spares, so Nate and Cam go searching, then come back with a stack and do their best to slot them evenly around the bed. Lee takes the chair next to Shelby, but the rest of us hesitate … is there a seating protocol? Debra makes the "tchah" sound again, and we grab the nearest chair and sit our butts down.

There's a strained silence. None of us knows what to say. We all look to Lee, but she lowers her eyes with a quick shake of her head. Embarrassed, maybe? Or like us, at a loss for the right words. When you're in the company of someone who has only a short time left on this Earth, every subject seems trivial. But equally, you can't wait too long to say the things that need to be said.

Shelby is staring fixedly at Debra, like she's trying to absorb and memorize every detail. I think Debra's about to object, but she lifts her hand a fraction off the blanket, an offer for Shelby to take it. Which Shelby does, like it's a precious gift.

"I imagine you have questions," Debra says to her.

"So many," replies Shelby. "But we should wait for Tyler and Frankie. If that's okay?"

"No guarantees," says Debra with a small smile. Then she winces.

"What can I do?" says Shelby.

"Nothing." Debra's eyes are closing. "Let me rest. Wake me when the others come."

We sit there in silence until Nate says, "I could get us coffee?"

Jackson jumps up. "I'll help you. I've got to know that machine so well, I suspect it thinks I'm about to propose."

Nate takes the coffee orders, and the two men head out. I start watching the group across the way, wondering if they celebrate like this every morning or if this was a special occasion.

"Speaking of proposals," says Lee, quietly, nodding in that direction. "They renewed their vows first thing this morning."

The woman in the bed doesn't look that old, maybe early sixties. The big guy with the mustache must be her husband, sitting close by, attentive. My first instinct is to be sad for him, but although I know he must be grieving, this time with her must feel like a blessing. Not everyone gets a proper chance to say goodbye, to say how much you love them…

Damn it, now I'm definitely going to cry. And Nate's walked off with the tissues.

In front of my face appears a handkerchief.

"Found it when I was grabbing a pair of socks," Cam explains. "Thought it might come in useful."

I wipe my eyes. Blow my nose. Lean my head on Cam's shoulder.

"I know this is a weird time and I'm ridiculously emotional," I murmur, "but could we be together forever?"

He wraps his arm around me, pulls me close, kisses my hair.

"Forever," he murmurs back. "How d'you feel about bees?"

Before I can answer, Nate and Jackson are back with coffee and the remaining two Armstrong siblings: middle brother Tyler, slim and strawberry blond like Shelby, and youngest sister Frankie, pale blonde like Jackson and robustly curvy. Time for hugs and tears, mainly Shelby's. The kerfuffle rouses Debra, and suddenly everyone is silent. Those standing take a seat, those in chairs sit up straighter. Everyone's holding on to their coffee cups, no one is drinking. It's like we're an audience waiting for a play to begin.

"Well, well," says Debra. "Who's brave enough to go first?"

Chapter Thirty-Four

CAM

I know this is a sad occasion. I know Debra is leaving us way too early, with so much left to do in her life, and that her nieces and nephews are missing out on time they should have had with their only aunt. But my heart is soaring. I feel like I did way back in my teen years, driving flat out in my rusty truck, window down, music on, like I was king of the world, invincible.

And it's not just because I'm in love with Ava and she with me. Okay, this might sound stupid, but for the first time since I left home, I feel like I'm surrounded by family. Ten years ago, the Armstrongs welcomed me in, gave me a home, made me feel like I was worth something. It's only now that everyone bar Billy is here that I realize exactly how much I owe them. They never judged, not one of them. They accepted me with all my faults, and there were a lot. They helped me reclaim my life and my sense of who I was. I'm not even sure they understand what a huge deal that is, how much it means to me. I hope I can find the words to let them know while they're all here.

But right now, it's my job to sit and listen. Debra's just thrown down the gauntlet and to my surprise, it's Jackson who picks it up.

"This question could be for Mom, too, but I'll ask you first if that's okay?" He swallows but overcomes his nerves and presses on. "When did you find out you had a sister?"

"Last October," Debra replies. "I was in Sacramento for a teachers' conference. Saw an article on your mom and her art…"

She pauses to regather her energy. No one prompts her. This will take as long as it takes.

"The old cliché—like looking in a mirror. I knew it couldn't be coincidence."

Debra smiles at Lee, whose eyes are welling with tears. It hits me like a train that this is the second time in as many years that she's had someone she loves die. Lee's a strong woman, but this must be hurting like all get out. Maybe that's why she kept it secret? Too painful to share?

"I was adopted out as a baby," Debra tells us. "I had a great childhood, adored my parents. Never felt the need to trace my birth family. Until I saw that photo. In that moment, I became obsessed."

A short, husky laugh turns into a cough. Shelby picks up the water. It's in a lidded plastic beaker with a straw. Shelby carefully helps Debra drink. We wait, all of us barely breathing, until she's okay to continue.

"I didn't want to upset my parents," she says. "So, I

searched for my adoption records without telling them. Found my adoption was closed. My birth mother was likely single and young, maybe even underage. Likely her own parents wanted her to be able to start a new life without the shame hanging over her."

"Very likely," says Frankie. I remember that she's just started practising as a family lawyer. "You were born in the 1960s, when there was still a huge stigma around being an unwed mother. They called it the Baby Scoop Era; closed newborn adoption was at its highest ever. Wasn't until the mid-1970s that they figured this wasn't healthy for anyone." She adds in a mutter, "Just another example of how hard the patriarchy sucks."

Debra smiles at her, and then at Lee. "Smart women in our family."

Tyler and Jackson exchange a look. That Frankie catches.

"Feeling a little shrinkage in your manhood region?" she asks with a grin. "Don't worry, boys. We're coming for the system, not the individuals."

I hear Ava chuckle and know if my sister were here, she'd be applauding. If Ava and I have daughters, they're going to rule the world.

"And now, back to Debra," says Jackson pointedly.

"I don't know whether you want to hear this next bit," she says, raising an eyebrow. "Doesn't paint me in a good light."

"We're all weirdos here," says Shelby. "So don't you worry about that."

"Speak for yourself!" protests Nate.

"Sweetness, you're as weird as they come," says Shelby affectionately. "That's why I love you."

Nate seems about to object, but then he blinks, shuts up and sits back.

"Weirdos of the world unite," murmurs Ava, and I try not to laugh.

"All right, here goes," says Debra. "I stalked your mother. At first online, and then in person. From her Instagram, I knew your mom had moved to the coast, but I also knew she spent a lot of time back in Flora Valley, in Verity and at the vineyard. There was a job going at Martinburg High, so I applied for it. When I got it, I quit my job in San Francisco, sold my apartment, and bought a property just out of Verity. Moved here over the summer…"

She pauses and, for the first time, looks uncertain.

"I went a little crazy. Dyed my hair and wore dark glasses so no one would spot the resemblance. Worked out what your mom's schedule was, followed her whenever I could. Started asking about her around town in Verity. I wanted to know what kind of person she was…"

Her eyes cut to Lee. "I never did ask who tipped you off?"

"Iris at the Cracker Café," replies Lee, with an apologetic half-smile. "She thought you might be from the IRS. Iris has a deep distrust of all forms of governmental authority."

Nate scowls. "She distrusts the whole of humanity. I still have to double-check whether she's slipped ground glass in my key lime pie."

"Iris is a pistol, all right," says Debra. "If I weren't an English teacher, I'd add 'literally'."

Tyler speaks for the first time. "I'm a teacher, too. Elementary."

He was always the quiet kid in the family. Guess when you have Jackson for an older brother, there's no point in competing for attention.

"Enjoy it?" Debra asks.

"Love it," is Tyler's reply. "Though I'm still trying to come to grips with TikTok."

"I refused all forms of social media on principle," says Debra. "Until I started to stalk your mother. Then I was all over everything like a rash."

"Mom, what did you think when Iris said there was someone asking about you?" asks Frankie.

"I didn't know what to think," says Lee. "I had no idea who it could be."

"Why don't you take the story from here?" Debra suggests.

Lee looks reluctant, but it's obvious Debra's running low on energy. With a nod and a deep breath, Lee begins.

"Iris gave me a description, so I started looking around when I went out. I wasn't concerned, just puzzled. I spotted a woman who seemed to fit when I was in the garden center in Martinburg. I approached her."

"And I panicked," admits Debra. "But there was nowhere to run. I was trapped between the custom terrariums and the fiddle leaf figs."

"We talked," says Lee, editing down to two short words

what must have been a seriously tricky conversation. "Then we went for coffee."

"I had coffee," says Debra. "Your mom had compost in a pot."

Everyone smiles. Lee's taste for pungent herbal teas is a long-running family joke. Now Debra's in on it.

"Though I'm hardly one to carp," Debra sighs. "If I'd drunk more compost, I might not be lying here today."

"Cancer doesn't play favorites," says Lee firmly. "Billy was healthy through and through and it still got him."

There's a group intake of breath, as the thought that hit me a few minutes ago now hits everyone. Lee's losing another loved one to cancer.

"Shit," says Jackson. "I'm so sorry this is happening. This is beyond unfair."

"Yes, it's a bitch," says Debra, "but I stopped being angry some time back. No point."

"Did… Did you know you were sick when you met Mom?" says Shelby.

"Nope." Debra shakes her head. "The symptoms seemed minor, and I put them down to the fact that I'd just completely upended my life."

She looks around at us. "It's pancreatic cancer in case you were wondering. And your mom was the one who picked it up."

"I didn't know it was cancer," says Lee. "You were looking a little jaundiced, and I was concerned."

"Mom knew that Nate was anemic before anyone else did," says Shelby. "She's a sorceress."

"Okay, sorceress-Mom, I have a question for you." Frankie has her hand up. "Sorry if it seems a bit confronting—I don't mean it to be—but why didn't you tell us all earlier?"

The question with a capital Q.

"That's my fault," says Debra. "I wanted Lee and I to get to know each other first. If it turned out we fought like cats, we could go our separate ways, and no one would be the wiser. No one would be hurt. And then I was diagnosed. Stage four. Nothing to be done." She nods at Shelby. "This was a week before your wedding. Lee begged me to come and meet you all, but I didn't want to cast a shadow over your happy day. In hindsight, I regret that."

"Oh, so do I!" Shelby picks up Debra's hand and kisses it, her tears falling unabated.

"Don't cry," says Debra.

Her voice has more than a hint of high school teacher in it. Shelby sits up instantly and wipes her eyes. Across the bed, Nate hands her the pack of tissues.

"The organized one," Debra says to Nate, amused.

"Every day, I wake up and intend to be," he says. "And then life happens, and…" He mimes an explosion.

"The best-laid plans gang aft agley," says Jackson, and in response to our looks adds, "Yes, I've read Robbie Burns. I'm not a complete philistine."

Tyler, the quiet one, brings us back to the next important question. "Debra, is there anything you need us to do?"

"There is," she says. Her voice is suddenly strong, like she's had a new burst of energy. "I've made a will and I'm going to tell you what's in it. And if it's going to cause any discord, I need you to speak up. Otherwise, I will haunt you."

Startled glances are ping-ponging around the Armstrong family group, Nate included. Ava and I can relax because we're outside that loop. Which is good. I have enough ghosts to contend with.

"I've been on a teacher's salary all my working life," says Debra. "But I've also been single and frugal, and I've managed to amass a reasonable nest egg. I'm leaving the four of you fifty-thousand dollars each—"

A chorus of gasps drown her out. Jackson hangs his head in his hands. This is a lifesaver for him, and I know he'll use it wisely.

"And I'm leaving you the house and land outside of Verity," Debra continues. "Ten acres plus some outbuildings. No animals yet. I didn't have time…"

Her energy is fading. But she rallies.

"Sell it and split the proceeds between you. Or keep it and rent it out, I don't care which."

"Debra, that's … impossibly generous," says Frankie. "But what about your parents? What about Mom? They're your family, too. Personally, I don't feel comfortable taking what should more rightly be theirs."

"My parents are flying in this afternoon," says Debra. "They are well set up, and they're happy with my decision. As is your mom."

"I have more than I'll ever need," Lee assures her

children. "I was paid a generous amount for my share of the winery. You all know that."

"That's settled, then," says Debra. "But I meant what I said about speaking up. Will the house be an issue for you? Will you be able to agree on what to do with it?"

More glances between the Armstrong siblings. Jackson gets to his feet.

"I have a suggestion," he says. "Feel free to debate me, but I think it's a good one."

He grins at Shelby. "I think you'll like it in particular."

"Tell us," Shelby demands.

Jackson studies his hands for a moment, then lifts his head. And looks right at me. "Rent it to Cam."

Fuck. *That* I did not expect. From the way Ava's hand tightens on mine, neither did she. But it's not my decision. It's Shelby, Tyler, and Frankie's.

"Shel, let the others decide," cautions Nate. "You're too close."

Tyler and Frankie look at each other.

"I'm good with it," Frankie says with a shrug. "I don't want to move back here. No offense, fam. Ty?"

"Considering the usual standard of Jackson's ideas—"

"Cruising for a noogie, little bro," says Jackson.

"—I'd say this one's a winner." Tyler turns to me. "But what do you think, Cam?"

My brain has shut up shop. I can't process any of this. I look to Ava, whose eyes are probably as wide as mine, then to Lee, who smiles and shakes her head. Over to me, is her message.

Lastly, in desperation, I look to Debra. She's not smiling and for a second, my heart stops. She's not in favor.

Then she says, "The answer is simple, friend Cam. Yes or no. Which is it? My time is limited."

"It's yes," I say. "Thank you. Everyone, I don't know how—"

Debra raises her hand to shut me up.

"That's enough for today. I love you all, but I need to rest. Come and see me tomorrow." She sinks back onto her pillow and closes her eyes.

One by one, we quietly get up and take turns to kiss her cheek. And then we file out of the room and make our way to the foyer. Where we stand staring at each other, lost for words.

"Okay," says Nate. "How about we all go to lunch? All I've had today are two coffees. One came out of a hospice machine, and the other was made by Shelby."

Sharp intake of breath from the rest of the Armstrongs.

"Hey!" protests Shelby, but she takes Nate's arm, smiling, and leads the group out the door.

I feel Ava beside me, and realize her hand is still holding mine tight. I lift it and place a kiss on her palm.

"Quite the morning, huh?" she says.

There are dark circles under her eyes, and I'm worried she's overdone it.

"We could skip lunch," I suggest. "Take a bus back to Verity?"

"No, I'd like to hang with the weirdos," she smiles. "It was just ... a lot. I feel wrung out."

"I don't know whether to feel good or bad," I confess. "This is only happening because Debra is dying."

Ava hugs me. "Both," she says. "Because life is beautiful and strange and complicated."

I kiss the top of her head. "Want to share a house in the country?"

She lifts her face to mine, and all the tiredness is gone. She's radiant. "Can I have a horse?"

"Sounds like there's room for more than one."

"I could train them to work at the therapy riding center." Her blue eyes are sparkling. "Make sure they're gentle enough for the kids."

"Long as I only have to hold reins and not ride," I say, "you can train them to do synchronized swimming."

Wrapped up in each other, we walk outside, where we find everyone waiting, Nate tapping his foot impatiently.

"Hold your horses, bro," Ava says to him. And just for me, adds, "I certainly can't wait to see the love of my life holding mine."

Epilogue

AVA

Debra left a couple more instructions in her will, which her lawyer confirmed after she passed away. We are not to hold a funeral. There's a sum of money allocated and we're to throw a party, a celebratory send-off. Any funds left over are to go to a charity of our choice.

The universe kindly arranges to make the best date for the party on Thanksgiving. We decide to hold a midday feast in the barn at Flora Valley Wines and invite everyone who came to Shelby and Nate's wedding, plus their families. Therese from the Therapeutic Riding Society is also invited. The Society is the unanimous winner of our chosen charity, and we make sure to set aside a decent sum for them. Danny, Izzy, and Max will come home and stay with Mom and Dad. Tyler and Frankie will also fly back in, and along with Jackson will bunk up with Shelby and Nate in the Armstrong family home. Debra's parents have stayed on with Lee.

Epilogue

An invitation also goes out to Lee's mom—Debra's birth mother—but she declines, saying it doesn't seem right. Debra's parents shouldn't feel they have to share their daughter with a stranger. Lee tells us that though her mom might regret not coming, it's her decision. Grief and guilt are a potent mix, and her mom has to process them in her own time. Cam and I volunteer to sort out Debra's house and her possessions, as per her instructions, of course. We promise to make up a box for Lee's mom, so she'll have some sense of who her daughter had grown up to be.

The weekend before Thanksgiving, Cam and I drive to Debra's house. The transfer of ownership to the Armstrong siblings is almost complete. As soon as it's official, Cam and I can move in. Clearing out Debra's things feels like such an insignificant gesture when our appreciation for what she's done for us is so immense. But it isn't nothing, and we can do it well, making sure everything ends up where it's supposed to.

This is the first time we've seen the property, and I have to admit, my heart is in my mouth. Debra bought it in a hurry, so it could be a total dump. Then again, I'll be living with the perfect guy to un-dump it.

"This is it," I tell Cam. "If Google maps isn't lying."

We turn off a rural road about four miles out of Verity. The driveway is gravel but neatly kept with no potholes. On either side, there's long meadow grass and trees, almost like it's wild but you can see the design in the way the trees are located. As it's leafless November and I'm no gardener, I can't tell what they are. Guess I'll find out come spring.

Epilogue

"Mostly fruit trees," says Cam. "Plum and apricot. Think I spotted peach, too."

Or I'll find out right now.

"We grew them on the farm," Cam explains.

I'm about to tell him I have zero experience with growing anything except mold on protein bars that I've left in a pocket and forgotten about. But then we round a bend and—

"I've come home to Tara," I say. "If Tara is a super cute bungalow with a sun porch."

The house is adorable! Freshly painted, cobalt blue with white trim. Terracotta tile steps leading up to the porch and the front door. It's surrounded by all kinds of trees and plants I have no clue about. And one of those wooden structures you grow stuff up and over. Loggia? Pergola? Something like that.

Cam switches off the ignition and sets the brake. We've brought the Flora Valley Wines Dodge because it's big enough to carry a whole house. Yesterday, Nate casually mentioned that he's thinking of getting a new pick-up for the winery. Shelby would never let him sell her dad's truck, so if we wanted to look after it…?

It can pull a horse float, so I said yes before Cam could say no.

Right now, Cam's staring out at the house, and I can't read his expression. Maybe he hates it? Maybe it's too pretty and neat, and he was hoping for a manly rough-hewn log cabin?

Epilogue

"Looks just like Blair's place," he says. "Only hers is gray with a red front door."

He doesn't hate the house.

"Ready to check it out?" I ask. "Or do you want to explore the grounds first?"

"What I want is for you to pinch me," is his reply.

He's not joking. His jaw muscles are tight and his eyes wide, almost like he's afraid.

I get it. This does seem too good to be true.

"How about I kiss you?" I suggest. "Less painful."

"Nope. Could be one of my fantasies." He holds out his hand. "Pinch me."

When you grow up with four siblings, you learn how to inflict pain in devious ways. I grab the skin on the top of his hand and give it a sharp twist.

"Ouch!"

He rubs his hand, his expression accusing. "That hurt!"

"Should have taken the kiss," I say with a grin. "Offer's still open, by the way."

This time, he accepts. Good decision.

When we finally stop, Cam gently touches his forehead to mine.

"Are you up for this?" he asks. "I don't want you to push yourself too hard."

"I'm actually feeling good," I say. "Every day, more energy comes back. But..." I add before he can say it, "I promise to take breaks, and I promise to quit as soon as I start to feel tired. Okay?"

"Okay..."

Epilogue

He still sounds hesitant. I wonder what else is on his mind.

"You know, in the hospice?" he begins. "You asked if we could be together forever."

"I did."

"Was that just in the heat of the moment? Or…?"

"I meant it then and I mean it now," I say and kiss him hard. "So come on. Let's go and take a look at our forever home."

Acknowledgments

Huge thanks to my Hawke's Bay romance writing crew, Bronwen, Jackie, Kate, Mariana, Andrene, Kendra, Ruth, Ginny, Pauline, Alana, Donna and Tina. I learn new skills every time we get together. And huge thanks to Steff, who mentored me when I started out, and helped me make sense of the wide and wild world of romance.

The author and One More Chapter would like to thank everyone who contributed to the publication of this story…

Analytics
Abigail Fryer
Maria Osa

Audio
Fionnuala Barrett
Ciara Briggs

Contracts
Sasha Duszynska Lewis

Design
Lucy Bennett
Fiona Greenway
Liane Payne
Dean Russell

Digital Sales
Hannah Lismore
Emily Scorer

Editorial
Laura Burge
Kate Elton
Arsalan Isa
Charlotte Ledger
Federica Leonardis
Bonnie Macleod
Jennie Rothwell

Harper360
Emily Gerbner
Jean Marie Kelly
Emma Sullivan
Sophia Walker

International Sales
Bethan Moore

Marketing & Publicity
Chloe Cummings
Emma Petfield

Operations
Melissa Okusanya
Hannah Stamp

Production
Emily Chan
Denis Manson
Simon Moore
Francesca Tuzzeo

Rights
Rachel McCarron
Hany Sheikh Mohamed
Zoe Shine

The HarperCollins Distribution Team

The HarperCollins Finance & Royalties Team

The HarperCollins Legal Team

The HarperCollins Technology Team

Trade Marketing
Ben Hurd

UK Sales
Laura Carpenter
Isabel Coburn
Jay Cochrane
Sabina Lewis
Holly Martin
Erin White
Harriet Williams
Leah Woods

And every other essential link in the chain from delivery drivers to booksellers to librarians and beyond!

Could the guy she loves to hate turn out to be her perfect pairing?

If Shelby Armstrong wants to keep her late father's beloved Flora Valley Wines in business, she'll have to listen to Nathan Durant's advice. But given the fact that Shelby is all heart and Nate is nothing but tough love, bringing the winery back to life quickly becomes a battle of wills.

Available in paperback and ebook!

ONE MORE CHAPTER

YOUR NUMBER ONE STOP FOR PAGETURNING BOOKS

One More Chapter is an award-winning global division of HarperCollins.

Sign up to our newsletter to get our latest eBook deals and stay up to date with our weekly Book Club!
Subscribe here.

Meet the team at
www.onemorechapter.com

Follow us!
 @OneMoreChapter_
 @OneMoreChapter
 @onemorechapterhc

Do you write unputdownable fiction?
We love to hear from new voices.
Find out how to submit your novel at
www.onemorechapter.com/submissions